A Second Chance for Christmas

"Rob is here?"

Trudy's smile turned into a wide grin. "Aha! I knew there was something between the two of you! Are you two close friends?"

Once, they were. Once, they were so much more than that. "I don't know."

Some of the excitement that had been shining in Trudy's eyes dimmed. "Well, he came to see you. Do you wish to see him? You don't have to, you know."

Nine months ago, she'd broken his heart. Nine months ago, she'd told him they didn't have a future. And after he'd turned around and walked away, she'd realized she'd made the biggest mistake of her life.

"Jah, I do," she said softly, looking at the door. "Please, send Rob on in."

An
AMISH SECOND CHRISTMAS

SHELLEY SHEPARD GRAY

PATRICIA JOHNS

VIRGINIA WISE

KENSINGTON BOOKS
www.kensingtonbooks.com

KENSINGTON BOOKS are published by

Kensington Publishing Corp.
119 West 40th Street
New York, NY 10018

All Kensington titles, imprints, and distributed lines are available at special quantity discounts for bulk purchases for sales promotion, premiums, fund-raising, educational, or institutional use.

Special book excerpts or customized printings can also be created to fit specific needs. For details, write or phone the office of the Kensington Sales Manager: Kensington Publishing Corp., 119 West 40th Street, New York, NY 10018. Attn. Sales Department. Phone: 1-800-221-2647.

Kensington and the K logo Reg. U.S. Pat. & TM Off.

BOUQUET Reg. U.S. Pat. & TM Off.

ISBN-13: 978-1-4967-1784-9 (ebook)
ISBN-10: 1-4967-1784-8 (ebook)
Kensington Electronic Edition: October 2019

ISBN-13: 978-1-4967-1783-2
ISBN-10: 1-4967-1783-X
First Kensington Trade Paperback Edition: October 2019

10 9 8 7 6 5 4 3

Printed in the United States of America

Contents

Their Second Chance

SHELLEY SHEPARD GRAY

Look up to the skies. Who created all these stars?
He leads out the army of heaven one by one and
calls all the stars by name. Because He is strong and
powerful, not one of them is missing.

—Isaiah 40:26

God adds to the beauty of His
world by creating true friends.

—Amish proverb

Chapter 1

The brush of a very wet, very cold nose against her throat woke her up.

"*Nee,* Daisy," Hannah groaned as she pushed away her overgrown boxer. "Go back to sleep. It's not Christmas morning yet."

But instead of listening, Daisy whimpered and nudged her again. Then, for good measure, pawed her arm.

Though she'd recently trimmed Daisy's nails, they still scratched against her cotton nightgown, snagging the delicate fabric. And that nose! Ack, it might as well have been a cold sponge dabbing her skin. "Daisy . . . *halt,* wouldja?" she grumbled as she attempted to flip over on her side.

Daisy responded by barking, pawing at her again, and then licking her cheek for good measure.

Those three things were enough to wake Hannah up completely. Her sweet rescue dog had never woken her up in the middle of the night before. She was also a *gut hund.* Rarely did Daisy not mind her new mistress's directives. Propping herself on her elbows, she reached out and rubbed Daisy's side. "What's wrong, girl?"

Daisy barked again.

Persuading Hannah to at last come to her senses, and thank the good Lord, too. So much was very wrong. The air was thick with smoke and she could hear a suspicious, strange crackling sound. A noise that sounded an awful lot like fire.

Bolting into a sitting position, she cried out. The small kitchen alcove of her one-room apartment was on fire. Flames were climbing the walls. She and Daisy needed to get out. That minute.

But for some reason, her body couldn't seem to move.

Daisy whimpered again.

"I . . . I know," she murmured. Though it was doubtful that the dog could even hear her, the buzzing in the room was so loud. But maybe that was really the buzzing in her ears?

Feeling as if her head were occupying someone else's body, Hannah continued to stare in wonder at the flames licking the set of cookbooks on one of her makeshift shelves. Noticed that a new line of fire was inching its way toward her. Was this what Paul had seen in the moments before he died?

All at once, it seemed as if every nightmare she'd ever had about her fiancé's last moments in the explosion and fire at the Kinsinger lumber mill had come to life. All she could seem to do was stare at the fire and feel the pressure of all the fear and debilitating sadness that had overpowered her in those first few months after his death.

She'd thought her state of mind was so much better. Obviously, she'd only been fooling herself.

Daisy whined, grabbed hold of the fabric of her gown, and pulled. It ripped.

That small thing at last jolted her out of her daze. It was time to stop dwelling on the past and get them both to safety.

As she crawled out of bed, Hannah feared she'd waited far too long. The room had grown hot and that smoke was so thick she could hardly see. Only a thin foot of clear air lingered near the floor.

Grabbing the dog's collar, she started running to the back door. Intent on negotiating the path, she tripped over a piece of singed wood that had fallen from the corner of the ceiling. Awkwardly attempting to right herself, she reached out a hand. . . .

Before she fell, a sharp pain searing through her temple made her cry out. And inhale a thick band of smoke. Her eyes watered; whether from pain, frustration, or the very fact that she was hurting and running out of air she didn't know.

All she did know was that the door now seemed so very far away.

Daisy barked and nipped at her. Pulling herself to her knees, Hannah forced herself to crawl toward the door. She couldn't think of anything beyond getting Daisy to safety.

At that moment, nothing else—not even her own fate—seemed to matter.

The dog's shrill barking confirmed their worst fears. The house was occupied. The four men and one woman surrounding the ladder truck tensed and listened intently for instructions.

"Rob, you with me. Now," Brendan, his captain, ordered into his microphone, his usual staccato speech ringing loud and clear in Rob Prince's ear.

Rob didn't bother to reply, just checked his equipment one last time and followed close behind his captain. Around them, there was a cacophony of sounds and lights. Two fire trucks, an ambulance, and a number of sheriff vehicles had arrived. Each person was moving in sync with the others, illustrating the benefits of their many hours of training.

It was almost as if his body knew what to do before his mind did.

Ahead of the captain, Jerry used the ax to break down the door. They stood back, cautiously making sure the fresh addition of oxygen didn't create an explosion.

Luckily, though, only a thick band of smoke filtered out, followed by the loud, spooked bark of a dog.

Cap cursed under his breath. "I hate dealing with dogs."

Rob knew why. Dogs panicked, and the men entering their home in bulky uniforms looked both foreign and threatening. No, their turnout gear didn't usually create a sense of calm for any of the people or animals they attempted to rescue. Then, too, their captain had shared once that he had a terrible allergy to dogs. He had no experience with them.

But Rob did. He knew dogs, thanks to Rose, his Rottweiler.

When he saw that it was a white boxer and she was both whimpering and growling at both Jerry and Brendan, he pushed his way through.

"Let me help." As the other men stepped aside, he reached out a glove to the dog's neck, murmuring nonsense words as he did so. Immediately the dog's stance softened and she looked up at him with big, brown eyes.

Causing his gaze to lower and see the woman on the ground.

His heart almost stopped. Was that . . .

No, surely it couldn't be Hannah Eicher . . . could it?

While he continued to stare at her prone form, Jerry moved around his side. "I've got her. You get the dog."

Hardly able to take his eyes off the body in Jerry's arms, Rob bent down, murmured, "*Gut hund,*" something his almost girlfriend used to say to Rob's dog, Rose.

Still in a daze, he picked up the boxer and rushed her out to safety. He was vaguely aware of his captain and two other firemen searching the house for more people or bodies.

But Rob could have told him that they wouldn't find any-one else. As far as he knew, Hannah Eicher lived alone. By her choice, not his.

As he walked back outside, holding an eighty-pound boxer in his arms, he knew that if he'd had his way nine months ago Hannah wouldn't have been living alone at all.

She would have been sleeping in his house, in their bed, as his wife.

But that had been his dream. Not hers.

Chapter 2

"You are being *dikk-keppich,* Hannah," Daed said as he gazed down at her from the side of her hospital bed. "*Jah,* mighty stubborn. You need care and family right now. You need to come home."

She loved her parents, but Hannah knew most certainly that of all the things she needed, she did not need to "come home." Things between them hadn't been good for a while and she knew their relationship would only get more strained if she moved back into her old bedroom. "I'm sure I am being stubborn, but it canna be helped. I'm stubborn by nature. You've told me that time and again. Ain't so?" She smiled to take the sting out of her words.

But her father's expression didn't lighten one bit. Instead, he continued to silently study her. Then, as if he couldn't look at her another second, he turned to her mother. "Claire, do something."

"I would if you'd but move, Samuel."

Hannah closed her eyes and counted to seven while her parents switched places. As if her *mamm* weren't about to start saying the exact same thing.

This was a familiar dance, and one she'd once thought rather amusing. But as she'd gotten older, her patience with their attempts to lovingly manipulate her ebbed. Now, on her best days? She was mildly exasperated. On her worst, such as today? More than a little irritated by their performance.

Though she loved them, she no longer wanted much to do with their bossy, interfering ways. She especially did not want to be bullied while sitting in a hospital bed.

"Hannah," Mamm began in a sweet, lilting voice, "you must realize that you ain't thinking straight. No doubt the smoke you inhaled has made you addled."

"I am not addled." She was in pain, had a fierce headache, and was worried about her dog and how many—if any—of her belongings had survived the fire. But she was most definitely not addled. "I do not want to go to your *haus.*"

"It's not *our haus;* it's your home, Daughter."

"Nee, *my* home burned down last night."

Mamm's eyes filled with heavy tears. Ever so slowly, she raised a hand and wiped one away.

The motion was filled with no small bit of drama, and when Hannah was a young teenager it had worked like a charm. All it took were two or three tears and she'd be besieged by guilt.

But now? Now Hannah knew that the tears were all for show.

She sighed.

Mamm blinked. Two seconds later, her bottom lip trembled. "I canna believe you are acting so cold and uncaring. It's like we hardly know you anymore."

Her father stepped closer. Wearing a heavy frown, he loomed over her mother's shoulder. After a pause, he folded his arms over his chest. With his graying hair and long beard, he looked much like an irritated barn owl. "You should be more respectful of your mother's needs, child."

Oh! Oh, for heaven's sake! She was in the hospital recovering from a fire! Yet, once again, her parents had neatly turned the tables so they could focus on their own pain and suffering.

At least Hannah knew now that it did no good to ask them to concentrate on her needs instead of their own wants. They'd simply stare at her in confusion, protesting that they actually were thinking only of her.

If she tried to explain her point of view, they'd accuse her of being disrespectful and things would become even more strained among the three of them.

It was far better to simply send them on their way. "*Danke* for visiting, but I am *verra* tired. I think I need to rest."

"Don't be like this, Hannah," Mamm chided.

"I'm afraid I canna be 'like' any other way. You are leaving me no choice. Please, can't we talk later?" She hated to sound so difficult and rude, but experience had taught her that giving in to them meant losing so much more than just a minor disagreement.

Her mother's tears multiplied. "Oh, Hannah. How could you?"

It was self-preservation, through and through. Her mother had perfected the art of crying a long time ago and had used it to her benefit often. And like a trigger, it forced the same reaction that it usually did. Shame and regret.

But then Hannah remembered what those tears had encouraged her to do. Nine months ago, not ten minutes after Rob Prince had driven away from their home, her parents had gone on the attack. For weeks, they'd pressured her to stop seeing him. They'd used every tactic in their arsenal, too. Threats about how they would disown her. Tales of the dangers that beset Amish folks who lived among the English. When neither of those things worked?

Her mother softly insinuated that a wealthy, successful man like Rob would never be happy with a sheltered Amish girl.

Oh, that had hurt.

Then, when she began to doubt herself, they'd added a healthy dose of guilt.

As she recalled that time, her resentment sprouted—at both the things they'd done and the way she'd allowed herself to believe them. She wished she'd been braver and not let her fears overrule her heart.

"I really need to sleep, Mamm. I'm exhausted and I think the nurse is going to come in soon to change my bandages."

"Let's go, Claire," Daed said. "We can return tonight."

Her mother took one step back before turning to Hannah again. "Are you sure you don't want us to stay? The hospital is a lonely, scary place," Mamm said.

"I'm sure. I'll try to handle being here for a few hours by myself."

"We'll be back soon," he replied, not catching a bit of the sarcasm in her comment, which was really a good thing.

After they turned and walked out, she closed her eyes and leaned back against her hard pillow. Wishing for the peace she used to take for granted.

Before Paul had died in the Kinsinger Mill disaster. Before she'd met Rob and felt something new and fierce. An attraction that had made what she'd felt for Paul seem bland in comparison.

The door opened again. Trudy, her nurse—and her onetime classmate—entered. All smiles.

"You, my dear, have two choices."

"Let me guess—I get to have either my blood pressure taken or my bandages checked?"

"You make me sound so evil!" One of Trudy's dimples appeared. "I actually have two much better options for you."

"And they are?"

"You get to either rest until it's time to check your vitals again . . . or let the person who's been sitting outside your room for the last hour come inside to visit."

"Someone's been waiting out in the hall for me?" It didn't make any sense. Her parents would have told her about Dr. and Mrs. Ross. She'd been their children's nanny for years. Or perhaps it was Joanne, another longtime friend.

Actually, they would have ushered any of her friends in the door.

Unless . . .

With both a sense of foreboding and excitement, she whispered, "Trudy, who has been sitting out there?"

"A very handsome firefighter named Rob."

"Rob is here?"

Trudy's smile turned into a wide grin. "Aha! I knew there was something between the two of you! Are you two close friends?"

Once, they were. Once, they were so much more than that. "I don't know."

Some of the excitement that had been shining in Trudy's eyes dimmed. "Well, he came to see you. Do you wish to see him? You don't have to, you know."

Nine months ago, she'd broken his heart. Nine months ago, she'd told him they didn't have a future. And after he'd turned around and walked away, she'd realized she'd made the biggest mistake of her life.

"Jah, I do," she said softly, looking at the door. "Please, send Rob on in."

Chapter 3

The petite firecracker who was Hannah's nurse ushered Rob into the room with a far more subdued air than five minutes before. "If you'll come this way?" she said very properly.

Walking behind her, Rob wondered what Hannah had told the nurse about him. Obviously, it wasn't anything good. Was she still determined never to speak to him again? But if that was the case, why had she agreed to let him visit?

Maybe it was so she could tell him to leave her alone.

Just the idea of listening to those words brought forth a fresh wave of confusion and pain. Just as it usually did. No, just as it had from the time she'd broken up with him.

Unfortunately, he feared that had become their new normal. Around Hannah Eicher, he never knew the right way to act. It was crazy, really. Most people considered him to be an okay guy. Maybe even a catch. He was well-off, made a pretty good living writing mysteries, and now spent thirty hours a week as a fireman. That job had transformed his body. Made him stronger, bigger. The job had also changed his whole perspective on life.

Risks were always involved, but even in the worst circumstances, it was possible to see blessings.

Yep, for pretty much everyone else, he was someone to be respected or at least to be friends with.

With Hannah? He was reduced to being completely unsuitable. He'd tried to avoid her at all costs because of that—up until last night, he hadn't even known where she lived.

The moment he caught sight of her, he simply stopped and stared. How could a woman who'd just survived a fire still look so beautiful?

"You may stay ten minutes," Trudy announced in a stern tone before casting a meaningful look in Hannah's direction. Then, with her chin held high, she left, leaving the door open about six inches.

Presumably so Hannah could call for help.

Looking back at Hannah, he smiled tentatively. Her eyes were as wide and innocent looking as he remembered. And, just like always, he found himself marveling at how very blue they were. "Hey."

"Hello, Rob." She seemed to focus on him for a few more long moments before looking down at her bandaged hands.

Okay, then. She felt that awkwardness, too. But at least she wasn't yelling at him. Walking to her side, he pointed to the chair. "May I sit down?"

"Of course." Sounding shy, she continued. "You don't have to ask something like that."

"I didn't want to impose."

To his surprise, she didn't look all that pleased about his hesitancy. No, she looked almost pained. What was going on?

"You . . . you aren't imposing." She waved a hand. "Sit down now."

He finally did, leaning forward and resting his hands on the metal bars on the side of the bed. "How are you feeling?"

"I don't know. Stunned? Frightened?" More faintly, she murmured, "Pained."

"I imagine all of those things are normal." He'd seen many survivors of devastating fires who were so shaken up, they were hardly coherent.

She pursed her lips.

He placed two fingers on his temple. "How is your head doing?"

"They told me I received ten stitches."

"Ouch."

A faint light of humor entered her eyes. "I'm thankful that it's nothing worse."

"Your wound looked bad. I asked the staff when I arrived if you had a concussion. They said no."

She blinked. "What do you mean it looked bad?"

Did she not realize he'd been on the scene? "Well, I . . . " He swallowed. "I was one of the firefighters who was called to your apartment."

"You were there, Rob? At my apartment? Truly?"

It was becoming impossible to figure out how she was feeling. He'd come to visit even though he'd realized there was a real good chance that she'd refuse to see him. He'd entered the room prepared to be either ignored or firmly put in his place.

But neither of those things had happened. In contrast, it seemed as if she was feeling uncomfortable around him. As if she was the one who was harboring regrets.

How could that be?

"Well, yes," he finally replied. "I was on shift when the alarm came through. Then, when we got there, your dog was barking like crazy. My captain is a little skittish around dogs, so I volunteered to go in first." Already hating to recall the scene that he was sure would stay with him the rest of his days, he continued. "When we broke down the door, your dog was standing guard over you, looking scared but determined to protect you no matter what."

The first hint of a smile appeared on her lips. "Jah. That sounds like Daisy."

"She seemed like a good dog, Hannah. Daisy is very loyal."

"Is she all right? I assumed my parents had her." Pressing a hand to her forehead, she grimaced. "Oh my word. I was so irritated with my parents, I forgot to ask. I didn't even think." Her bottom lip trembled; then she tried to catch herself. "Rob, did my Daisy die in the fire?"

"What? No. Oh no." He leaned forward. Reached out a hand before he remembered that she wasn't his to touch anymore. "I took her home."

"Why would you do that?"

"Well, she had to go somewhere, and Rose is old now. I figured she wouldn't mind the company." Hoping to alleviate her stress, he decided to give Hannah a sunnier version of what had really happened. "After we doctored Daisy up and wiped her down with a warm rag, we gave her some food and water at the firehouse." He smiled. "She ate everything without a problem. Then, when I got off shift, I took her home and introduced her to Rose. They did a little bit of circling and sniffing but seemed to get along well enough."

"Daisy is a friendly sort. I'm glad she isn't in a kennel or shelter."

"I wouldn't have done that."

"Danke."

"You're welcome, but I was glad to do it. It . . . well, it was the least I could do for an old friend." He almost bit his tongue for saying something so . . . so meaningless. Hannah Eicher wasn't simply an old friend to him.

She would always be something more. From the first time

he'd met her on the street and escorted her to the Rosses' house, he'd been smitten.

And "smitten" had been the operative word. She'd been adorable and so fresh. He'd been sure she was naïve and innocent and guileless—but she'd set him straight about that in short order.

He'd soon realized that she was as strong as any woman working in the center of New York City. Only far more attractive than any other woman he'd met in a long, long time.

She sighed. "I don't know what we are anymore."

"We don't have to talk about that now. You need to get better." He sat down again. Gripped the edge of the wooden chair so he wouldn't do anything stupid, like reaching for her hand or smoothing a lock of hair from her face.

"Rob?"

"Hmm?"

"May I ask you something?"

"Of course. You may ask me anything you want."

"Would you please take care of Daisy for a few days? I know it's an imposition, but the doctors seem to think I might be here one more day."

"Of course I will, and it's not an imposition. She'll be fine." Wondering why Hannah didn't want her parents to watch the dog, he said carefully, "When you're ready for her, you can send word to the firehouse and I'll bring her to your parents' house."

"Nee."

"Okay." So, she didn't want him anywhere near her family. Hurt coursed through him again before he firmly pushed it aside. "How about this, then? You can pick Daisy up from my house as soon as you are ready. Maybe the Rosses can let you know when I'm around?"

"Jah. I can do that. Would you be able to leave me your

phone number? I'll call you when I know what I'm doing. I
need to find a place to live . . ."

As each word registered, a dozen questions filled his head.
Why? Why wasn't she going home to her parents? Why was
she all alone? Why did she want to have him watch Daisy? . . .
Did she really not have anyone else in her life she could trust?

But instead of badgering Hannah, he stood up and crossed
the room to the little desk by the window. Picking up the pen,
he scribbled his cell phone number and the number of the firehouse, in case she changed her mind. Knowing that his neighbors were going to be concerned about her, too, he wrote down
their numbers, just in case she didn't have Melissa's and York's
numbers memorized.

Then he carried the notepad to her and placed it on her bedside table.

"I'm going to let you rest. Do you need anything before I go?
Water, food? Are you in pain? Is it time for more painkillers?"
He gestured to the door. "I can go get the nurse again. . . . "

"I don't need anything more, Rob." Her eyes looked tired
now. The lids were almost at half-mast. "Thank you for coming
here to see me."

Unable to stop himself any longer, he gave in to temptation
and brushed away a lock of her fine, silky blond hair. His fingers brushed her cheeks. Felt her soft skin.

He bit back the wave of longing he suddenly felt.

"Good-bye, Hannah."

She stiffened before nodding slowly. "Good-bye."

He turned before he said anything else. Before he did another thing that would make her never want to see him again.

When she didn't say anything as he closed her door, he
counted that silence as a sign of success.

After all, he already knew what it was like to be told that she
didn't want to see him again. To be informed that everything
he'd thought they'd been was mostly one-sided.

Yep, he knew exactly how it felt to be rejected. It hurt and sliced and made him feel ashamed for even imagining that he'd found love.

It wasn't something that he ever wanted to experience again. And he wouldn't, not if he could help it.

Chapter 4

"And this, obviously, is a new robe and slipper set," Melissa Ross announced as she pulled a pale pink quilted robe out of a shopping bag.

Hannah reached out to touch the slick, cool satin and almost gasped, it felt so wonderful. No doubt, it would feel deliciously sinful against her skin.

On the heels of that reaction was a burst of embarrassment. Where in the world had such a thought come from? She hastily folded her hands on her lap.

Mrs. Ross noticed. "Hannah, do you not care for it?" Placing the robe on her own lap, she eyed it in concern. "Is it too worldly looking? If so, I'll get you something different. Maybe a sturdy robe in white or navy terry cloth?"

"Nee!"

Melissa's eyes widened. "Oh. All right."

"I'm sorry, Mrs. Ross. I know I'm not making sense." She cleared her throat. "I think the robe is beautiful and soft. I will enjoy it very much and can't think of another one that I would like better."

"Are you sure? Because I don't mind going back to the store. . . . "

"Please don't." She not only loved the robe—perhaps too much—but also knew the Rosses didn't have a bit of extra time. Melissa Ross was a bank manager and her husband was a doctor. They both worked a lot and now, with her gone, Hannah could only imagine the chaos that was ensuing at their usually well-organized home. Christopher, their son, was almost three and Dot, their baby, was nine months old.

"Okay then. I won't." She smiled, but her expression was tight. "Hannah, are you sure you're okay? I mean, besides your injuries?"

She was tempted to fib and assure Melissa that she was but ended up shaking her head. "I'm really not. Practically everything in my apartment is gone. It's going to be hard to start over."

Of course, what she really meant was that it was going to be hard to go back home with her family. She worried that her well-meaning parents were going to do everything they possibly could to persuade her to fit back into the mold they'd tried so hard to shape her into. The mold where she was a *gut* Amish woman who still mourned for Paul.

She would be cautioned against working for any more *Englischers* and be told that perhaps the Lord hadn't liked her living on her own.

Melissa crossed her legs and put the other gift bag she'd been holding on the floor. "Hannah, about that . . . "

"Yes?"

"Well, um, I've been thinking. I mean, York and I have."

"Oh?" It took effort, but Hannah attempted to look interested instead of scared to death. What was she going to do if they fired her?

She really couldn't lose her job now, too.

"Well, York and I came up with an idea, though now that

I'm sitting here, talking to you? I must confess to being a little worried."

Hannah bit the inside of her lip so she wouldn't interrupt.

Melissa breathed in deep. "I mean, I don't want you to feel obligated or feel that we'd want you to work all the time. . . . " Her voice drifted off again.

Work? "Maybe you could simply tell me what is on your mind?" *Maybe even as soon as possible?*

Melissa pressed a palm to the center of her chest. "Of course. I'm rambling, aren't I?" She laughed softly. "I don't know what it is about you, Hannah. At work, I never hesitate. But with you? Well, there's something about you that makes me want to weigh my words extra carefully." Looking a little embarrassed, she shook her head. "Goodness. I mean, what I'm trying to say is that I have a real soft spot for you and I never want you to think that we aren't putting your needs first."

"Mrs. Ross, what have you and Dr. Ross been discussing?"

"Oh! I guess I haven't told you, have I? Um, what I'm trying to say is that we want you to move in with us, Hannah."

"Truly?"

"Yes. You know that storage room in the basement?" Before Hannah could do more than nod, she continued. "Now, I know you are probably thinking that you don't want to live in a storage room, but there's a window and it's been built to code."

"Code?"

"Yes. I mean, it's safe in emergencies. It's also carpeted and is completely finished. We'd make it nice for you, too. Put in a bed and a chair and a light." She waved a hand. "You know, all the sorts of things that one would expect in a room."

It sounded wonderful. *Wunderbaar.* "Are you sure you wouldn't mind me being there?"

"We want you there." Melissa stood up, fussing with the tote bags she'd brought. "We'd give you privacy, too. I'd tell the kids that we have to leave you alone on your off times so you can be free to come and go as you see fit." She snapped her fingers. "Oh! I almost forgot. I know there is only a half bathroom downstairs, so you can use the shower off the laundry room. It's not the most convenient, I know, but at least your sink and a toilet is downstairs—"

"Danke," she said quickly. "I accept."

Just as Melissa looked about ready to dive into another long speech, she sputtered to a stop. "Thank you? Does that mean you'll do it?"

"You are making it sound like I am doing you a favor instead of the other way around. But yes, thank you for the offer. Yes, I would love to live at your house for a while."

"You are welcome as long as you want. Oh, I can't wait to tell York. He's going to be so excited! We'll get to work on your room tonight. When will you be released?"

"The *doktah* said I'm free to go tomorrow."

"Okay." Looking much more like her usual confident self, Melissa sat back down. "York and I will look at our schedules and figure things out. Don't you fret, though—one of us will be here to pick you up when you're released."

"Perhaps I could call for a driver?"

"No, don't do that. I think Rob said he could watch the babies for us," she mused, then looked at Hannah in shock. "Oh. My. Word. Rob. You're going to have to see him even more. I didn't even think about the Rob Factor."

"The Rob Factor?"

"Yes. Well, um, York and I really like Rob. He's a good neighbor, and York and he get along great."

"Of course you do. Rob is a good man. So is York."

Melissa smiled quickly before her pleased expression disappeared. "Thank you, dear. But what I'm trying to say is that with Rob, we've set some perimeters."

"I don't know what that means."

"Boundaries. For example, we told him we wouldn't discuss what happened between the two of you. Well, I mean, I wouldn't. I have a feeling he and York have had some discussions. Rob was pretty hurt."

Which made her feel even worse. "I imagine."

"Oh dear. We also asked him not to bother you when you come to our house. We didn't want you to have to worry about him talking to you whenever you were there."

"I didn't know you did that." Guilt hit her hard again. They'd gone to so much trouble because she hadn't stood up to her parents.

"To be honest, I think the Lord had a helping hand in our plans, too. At first, I don't think Rob wanted to see you. Then, he decided to become a firefighter and he wasn't around anyway." She smiled, as if this explanation settled everything.

But all it did was make Hannah feel even more confused. "You did all that for me?"

"Of course, dear. We wanted you to be happy."

She was humbled that her employers would do so much for her. "That's so kind of you."

"No, that's what friends do. Don't you agree?"

"Yes, of course." She smiled weakly. She had never actually thought about how breaking off things with Rob would affect the Rosses. Her only focus had been to do it to Rob as quickly as possible and regain some semblance of normalcy.

And, of course, ensure that her parents would stop being so upset with her.

That had happened, of course. But almost immediately she'd discovered that being a good and dutiful daughter wasn't much of a consolation for having a broken heart.

"Melissa, speaking of Rob . . . He came to see me yesterday."

"He did? What did he say?"

"He came to see how I was doing. He rescued me, you see."

"Yes, York learned that this morning. One of the nurses in

his office was working in the emergency room last night. She told me that her husband had fought the fire with Rob."

"Did he? Hmm. Now isn't it such a small world?"

"It certainly is." Melissa smiled softly. "Or maybe it's just Charm, Ohio, that's so very small."

"Anyway, I have been thinking lately that I made a mistake with him."

Melissa leaned forward. "You really think so?"

"I do. I let my fears about moving forward overrule my heart. It was wrong." She exhaled. "Rob might never forgive me, but I'm going to tell him that."

"Hmm. Does this mean you might not need to be shielded from Rob Prince after all?"

Melissa's voice had turned lighter. It matched the new gleam in her eyes. Which was starting to make Hannah a little worried.

"I think so," Hannah replied softly. "I'm not sure what is going to happen, but I do know that it's time to stop worrying so much about guarding my heart. It will be better when everything is out in the open."

"Honesty really is the best policy—at least I've always thought so."

"Jah."

Melissa picked up the pink robe again and ran a hand over the soft fabric. "Just think, now, why, anything could happen."

"Anything?" It was as if her boss were speaking in code.

"Yes. I mean, it is Christmas. That's a time for miracles, don't you think?"

"I do." After all, hadn't God just saved her and Daisy from a terrible fire?

"But don't you worry," Melissa continued. "I'm sure everything will turn out for the best. I mean, I guess we'll soon find out."

Hannah narrowed her eyes. Was almost tempted to question

if Melissa knew something that she wasn't sharing but then decided against asking.

There was a very good chance that Melissa did know something else about Hannah's situation with Rob that she wasn't sharing.

But maybe that was just as well. After all, she'd been keeping plenty of secrets of her own lately.

Maybe they all had.

Chapter 5

"Sorry I didn't call you earlier, Mom," Rob said as he drove home from the firehouse. "Things have been a little crazy around here today. How has your birthday been?"

"So far so good. But then, it is only three o'clock."

He grinned as he waited at the light. Comments like that were *vintage Mom*. His mother was a pretty positive person, but she always acted as if she weren't. She'd say something positive but always pointed out what could go wrong. He and his sister had learned when they were around twelve or so that she'd done it because her father, their grandfather, was a perpetually half-empty guy. He'd always been sure that something was going to go wrong, so she and her sister had amused themselves by repeating some of his most common phrases.

Rob played along. "You know, you're exactly right. Dad could always burn dinner."

"That's true, but we're going out tonight." She chuckled. "'Course, they might be out of chicken parmigiana at Madison's. That would be a real shame."

"Maybe Dad already called to make sure they saved a serving for you."

"I bet he did, dear." Her voice warmed. "You know what? I can't even pretend to look at the bad side of things right now. It's actually been a great day. Your sister, Susan, stopped by this morning on her way to work and brought me a hazelnut latte and some of my girlfriends brought me lunch."

"That was nice of them." When his mom reached forty-seven, she'd developed some reflex problems that hindered her enough to stop her from driving. Rob knew losing that independence had been difficult for his usually independent mother. The best gift anyone could give her was either take her out of the house or bring her some of her favorite things.

"It really was."

Her voice sounded a bit wistful. Guilt hit him hard. He usually didn't regret his decision to move away from home—except for times like this, when he was helpless to make his mother's life easier. "And you're going to Madison's for dinner? You're gonna be eating well today."

"I really am. Now that you've called, I don't think even no chicken parmesan can spoil my forty-ninth birthday."

His phone call sounded pretty lame compared to all the other special things she was receiving. "I'm sorry I'm not there."

"Nothing to be sorry about, Rob. You know I love to hear from you and there's not a thing to be sad about when it comes to my situation. It is what it is." She blew out a breath of air. "Now, tell me about your shift. Did you fight a fire?"

She asked that every time, and as with her *Sad Sack* jokes, she always seemed disappointed when he didn't fight a fire even though she was actually scared when he did. "I did."

"And? Are you okay?"

"Yes, Mom." He'd learned to accept that she was always going to ask about him before the victims.

But maybe that was a mother's prerogative.

"You sure? You wouldn't lie to me about that, would you?"

"No, ma'am."

"Good. Now, what about the victims? Or was it an empty building?"

"It was a small apartment fire, with a girl and her dog inside."

"Oh no! What happened? Are they all right?"

"Yeah." Still not in any hurry to say *whose* apartment it was, he added, "It was a little dicey at first. The dog was scared and growling at the door. Captain, of course, was not happy."

"So?"

"So I went in and calmed the dog down. Jerry got the woman. She had some smoke inhalation and minor burns and a sprained ankle, too, so they kept her overnight in the hospital. But she's going to be all right."

"Thank the Lord for that." After a pause, she said, "What happened to the dog?"

"I took her home."

"Rob! You're turning into a full-service fireman, aren't you?"

He chuckled. "I like that descriptor. I'll share it with the cap."

"Not that I'm not proud of you, but was that the best decision about the dog?"

"I don't know if it was the right choice or not. But I don't regret it. She's a sweet boxer."

"It's a boxer? Goodness. You're lucky it was a nice dog. They can be protective."

He paused, then figured he might as well share the whole story. "It actually wasn't a stranger, Mom. It was Hannah."

"Who?"

"Hannah. Hannah Eicher."

"The Amish girl?" Her voice had risen. And no, she wasn't happy about this news, not even a little bit.

"Yeah."

"Well." She paused again. "Hmm. I bet that was quite a surprise."

He was pretty impressed that his mother didn't finish the other half of what was no doubt forming in her head—that it was Hannah Eicher *the Amish girl who broke your heart.*

"It was."

"What did she say when you arrived? I hope she looked guilty at the very least."

"She was passed out when we got to her, so she didn't even know I was there."

"That's probably for the best."

"Wow, Mom, that's pretty cold."

"Oh, I know. And I'm trying to feel bad about saying such a thing, too," she muttered, signaling that she didn't feel guilty about her judgmental words. Not one bit. "However, Hannah is okay now, right?"

"Yes. She's in the hospital."

"She's recuperating in the hospital? Oh my. Well, now I do feel bad for being so harsh." She paused. "I'll say a prayer for her and ask God to give me the strength to think warm and comforting thoughts."

"I hope you mean that."

"Of course I mean that. I wouldn't fib about the Lord and prayers, Rob."

His mother was a firecracker. Five feet six inches of attitude. "Anyway, that's why I took the dog. I knew her owner."

"I hope Hannah thanks you when she stops by to get it. Then that will be the end of that."

"Maybe, maybe not."

"Maybe not? Oh, Rob. Not to sound mean, but what could the two of you possibly have to say to each other?"

The smart thing to do would be to give a noncommittal reply and move the conversation on. That's what Susan would do.

But it seemed he was a glutton for punishment. "Actually, Mom . . . it turned out that she acted a lot different than I had thought she would this morning."

"Well, don't keep me in suspense. What did she have to say for herself?"

He could practically see her leaning back in her favorite chair in the living room and rubbing her temples in exasperation. "Hannah seemed happy to see me. Almost like she feels bad about what happened." Actually, if he'd been a betting man, he would have said that she was trying to get up the nerve to tell him something more.

"Really? I'm shocked."

"I was, too. I didn't expect her to be so friendly."

"Why would you? She's had almost a year to make things better."

"I would agree with you except that something didn't seem quite right about her explanation when she broke up with me. Mom, you know what? I'm starting to think maybe there was more to that story than her simply trying to end things."

"What could there have possibly been? She was lucky to have you. Not every man like you would be interested in an Amish girl."

"She wasn't just an Amish girl. She was *Hannah*. And you met her, so you know what I'm talking about."

"Fine. She was sweet and pretty."

She was those things. But there was something more, too. It had been the way she cared for the Rosses' baby. The way she never complained about losing her boyfriend or walking a long distance to get home or even being all alone most every day.

It had been the way she'd stood up for herself against that guy who'd been so angry about his father's death—and the way she'd been willing to defy all of her friends' and family's questions and concerns when she'd started spending time with him.

It had been the way she'd made him feel worthy and smart, even though all he did was write books.

"It might surprise you to find out that not everyone thinks I'm a good catch."

"It might surprise you to discover that a lot of women think you are, Son. Me most of all."

Even though he had a feeling he was blushing, he smiled. "Thanks, Mom. Listen, I need to go. Have a good rest of your day."

"I will. Thanks for calling."

"I'm sorry I brought you down."

"You did no such thing, Rob. If you want to know the truth, it might have even been a good thing you told me all this. I was starting to feel a little sorry for myself. Now you've given me something new to think about."

He frowned. If she was feeling sorry for herself, she must have gotten some news from the doctor. That seemed to be the only thing that gave her the blues. "I'm glad I could help. Tell Dad I'll call him soon, and of course I'll call you both on Christmas Day."

"I'll tell Dad. Now, stop worrying about us and get some sleep, Son."

As if on cue, he yawned. "I will. Happy birthday again. Love you."

"Love you back. Good-bye, honey, and thanks for the call."

"Anytime, Mom." After he disconnected, he sat in his vehicle another minute longer, thinking about his mom. Wondering what news she'd gotten. Thinking about Hannah and her injuries and her dog.

He wondered again why God had brought her back into his life. There had to be a reason—he just hoped he would be prepared for what it was.

Chapter 6

"You don't seem very happy about this dress," Hannah's sister, Malinda, chided as she helped Hannah slip on one of her dresses. "It's my best one, too."

"I'll try not to ruin it," she said sarcastically. "I'll give it back as soon as I make some new clothes."

Malinda scowled. "You know I didn't mean it like that. Of course I'm giving it to you."

"And I appreciate this gift. I do."

"Hannah, what I'm trying to say is that most girls would be happy to see their sister after almost dying. I know I'm mighty happy to see you."

"I'm happy to see you. Of course I am."

"Are you sure about that? Because all you've been doing since I got here is looking off in the distance or at the clock."

Her sister had a point. She had been staring at the large silver clock on the wall and silently begging for its hands to move faster. "I'm sorry. I'm just out of sorts." Moving her arm a bit, Hannah added, "I think I'm feeling the effects of the fire today more than yesterday."

Malinda frowned. "I'm sorry. I should have realized that."

"How could you have known?" When she noticed Malinda making a move to adjust her dress, Hannah held up a hand. "Now don't you worry. I'll be fine." And she would, as soon as she got out of the confining hospital room.

She hurt everywhere; she wanted a cool bath to get rid of the last of the smoke smell that seemed to have embedded itself in every pore of her body. And . . . her sister was right. She had nothing except a dog—and Daisy was being kept by her ex-boyfriend.

What in the world was she going to do?

Pulling out a straight pin, she began to carefully fasten the dress together, then unfolded an apron, awkwardly slipped it over her head and attempted to pin it in place as well. It was difficult, though—taking her almost two minutes when it usually only took seconds.

Malinda sighed. "Stop, and let me help you."

"Danke." Glad to have someone negotiate the fabric and the fastening, Hannah carefully turned, bent, and twisted as Malinda directed until she was finally dressed in her sister's best dress—a lovely long-sleeved garment made out of soft forest green fabric.

"When did you get this pretty thing? I don't remember."

"I made it almost a year ago for Jenna's wedding. I was one of her servers."

Try as she might, she couldn't remember a thing about that. "Are you sure? I don't recall that wedding." And since they knew all the same people, Hannah knew she would have remembered going to the wedding, at the very least.

Malinda glanced up at her from the black-soled boots she was unlacing. "You didn't go, Hannah. Jenna's wedding was just a few months after the fire. You were still mourning Paul."

She remembered that now. It had been four or five months after the fire at the Kinsinger mill, where five men died, one of whom was her Paul. For months afterward, she'd gone through the motions of each day, trying to come to grips with the fact that Paul was gone forever . . . and that the life she'd imagined happening was gone, too. They'd planned to get married right around the same time as Jenna had.

"Well, the dress is mighty pretty, and it will be warm, too. Thank you for lending it to me."

"It's a gift, silly." Holding up a pretty floral tote bag, Malinda added, "Mamm put another dress inside. We ran to the store and picked up some warm tights and underthings as well. And Daed bought you the new boots from Red Wing."

The boots were finely crafted and not inexpensive. The boots, combined with the gifts—and the awful way she'd shut out her parents—made her feel small. "All of you went to a lot of expense and trouble for me."

Malinda nodded. "We did, but it was probably a real *gut* activity for us, too."

"How do you figure that?"

"Mamm and Daed needed something to keep them busy."

Because they were worried about her almost dying in the fire. Because she'd very firmly told them that she wasn't ever moving back home. "Are you mad at me, too?"

Malinda raised her eyebrows. "Me? Oh, nee. If you moved back, we would have had to share a room."

"That's what you're thinking about?" Boy, leave it to her sister to focus on how Hannah's housing crisis affected her!

"Calvin is so difficult right now, he needs to have his own room. Maybe even his own floor."

Calvin was seventeen and disagreeable. Hannah smiled at Malinda. "It's Mamm's and Daed's fault, you know. He's spoiled."

"Of course he is. He's the only son and our parents act as if being a boy was something miraculous." She grunted. "Not to hear him, though. If you listen to his complaints, you would think he was living in one of the downstairs closets. He's always moaning about how difficult and hard his life is at home."

Hannah rolled her eyes. "Jah. It is so difficult having every whim catered to."

Malinda smiled. "I can hardly go be ten minutes in his presence before I get annoyed with all of his complaints. Tell me the truth—was I that bad?"

"Of course not." They were only two years apart in age, but Malinda had never been an irritation. Not ever. Instead, she was everything patient and sweet. Oh, she had a bit of sass inside her, but whereas Hannah had always come off as too bossy, Malinda always made those around her feel that they were a part of whatever joke she was holding inside herself.

"Are you worried about living at the Rosses' *haus* full-time?"

"Not at all. I like them. You know that."

"You're not even worried about Rob living next door?"

"He's a fireman now. He's not going to be around all that much," she said quickly. When Malinda still looked doubtful, she added, "We'll be fine." But were those words more for herself or Malinda?

"If you say so." She darted a look at the open door, then murmured, "Hannah, if you do decide you want to come home, I hope you will. I'll even share a room with Calvin so you can have some privacy."

Hannah reached out and curved an arm around Malinda's shoulders. "Danke, but that won't be necessary. I'm not sure what is supposed to happen next, but I don't believe the Lord wants me to go backwards."

"You really think moving back home would be like that?"

"I do. You, Calvin, and our parents might be the same, but I'm different now."

Malinda wrinkled her nose. "What does that even mean?"

That was part of the problem. No matter how much Hannah tried to explain how she'd grown and changed, her sister would never completely understand because she hadn't experienced the same traumatic events.

Deciding to keep things simple, she murmured, "I think I need to figure out who I am now and what I want."

Looking slightly relieved, Malinda sat back down. "Now what do we do?"

"The nurse said I could leave as soon as Dr. or Mrs. Ross arrives to take me home."

Just as she was about to speak, her sister's eyes widened. "I don't think they're coming, Hannah."

"What? Of course—" Her voice cut off as she spied what Malinda was staring at. Or, rather, *who*.

There was Rob. Looking so handsome and so familiar.

"Hannah, I hope you don't mind, but Melissa asked me to help you out today. York was going to pick you up, but he had an emergency at work."

That same tight tension—which she now realized had never actually left—was buzzing inside of her. While Malinda watched the two of them with wide eyes, Hannah forced herself to reply in a calm tone of voice. "Nee. I don't mind at all."

Rob blinked, then seemed to collect himself. "Okay then. Good." He was still staring at her as if he was just as mesmerized by her as she was by him.

Malinda's not-so-subtle cough brought them back down to earth.

And reminded Hannah of her manners. "I'm sorry. Rob, do you remember my sister, Malinda?"

"I do. How are you?" He smiled as he walked over to her. "I'm sorry I didn't greet you first thing. In my defense, you don't look like the teenager I first met years ago."

"No?" Malinda preened.

"Nope. You look all grown-up now."

It was all Hannah could do to keep a straight face as her sister blushed and attempted to look unaffected by the compliment.

After a few seconds, Malinda said quietly, "Danke, Rob."

He waved off her words. "I didn't see your brother or your parents out in the hall. Are you visiting alone?"

Malinda lifted her chin as if she was doing Rob a favor by answering him. "I am. Hannah needed something to wear. I brought her some clothes."

"That was nice of you."

"Nee, it was the least I could do. We are sisters, after all."

Rob raised his eyebrows at Hannah.

She shrugged, just as taken aback by her sister's suddenly sharp tone. She was sounding mighty un-Malinda-like.

"Do you need a ride home? I'll be happy to drop you off."

Hannah forced herself to remain silent though she was silently biting back a groan. The last thing either she or her parents needed was for Rob to show up in front of their house.

"I don't need a ride," her sister replied stiffly.

"Are you sure, Malinda? I don't mind."

Her sister's cheeks brightened as she darted a look Hannah's way. "Jah."

"She's sure," Hannah blurted, hoping that her sister would understand and eventually forgive her for not even asking how she was going to get home.

But honestly, there was only so much she could handle, and at the moment she was feeling she'd more than reached her limit. "I am ready to leave whenever you are, Rob."

His brown eyes, the ones she used to get lost in, flashed. "I'm here for you, Hannah. Whenever you are ready, I am."

Oh, those words! Reaching for the floral tote bag that now held her entire wardrobe, she stepped forward. "Then I am ready now."

Malinda moved to her side. Pointedly ignoring Rob, she leaned close. "What are you doing? You know Mamm and Daed won't be happy about this."

Oh, she knew. "I'm not going to go backwards. Stop worrying so much."

"I can't help it. I fear you are making a mistake."

Hannah wasn't completely certain about how she felt, what would happen in her future, or even how she felt about Rob. But she was certain about this. "I'm not," she said firmly. "Now be careful getting home, Malinda. Danke for the dress and bringing the other clothes. Danke for coming here, too. I am grateful."

Her sister opened her mouth to speak, then seemed to think better of it. Next, she turned to Rob and sighed dramatically. Seconds after that, she finally strode out of the room.

When the door closed behind her with a snap, Rob raised his eyebrows. "What was that about?"

"Whatever do you mean?" She hoped she sounded more convincing than she felt.

He rolled his eyes. "If you don't want to talk about Malinda's attitude, then don't. But don't play dumb."

"I'm not playing at anything, Rob. I don't know why Malinda was acting so rudely." But even she knew that was kind of a lie. She just didn't want to reveal too much. Not right at this moment, anyway.

He cast her another long look before holding out a hand. "Here, let me help you up."

She took his hand. His skin felt rougher than she remembered. She wondered why, then realized that he no doubt had changed in the past year, too.

No matter what happened, they weren't the same people they used to be. Change was inevitable. Didn't Jeremiah say: "For I know the plans I have for you, plans to prosper you and not harm you, plans to give you hope and a future"? Those were words to live by.

The only thing that mattered now was how she was going to handle all these changes.

Chapter 7

Whether it was because the hospital needed her bed for the next patient or because Rob was a firefighter and knew several people on staff, Hannah had been able to leave without a bit of fuss.

Practically before she knew it, she found herself seated in the passenger seat of his dark gray vehicle. It was plush inside, with soft leather seats that heated, a map on a screen in between their two seats, and all kinds of holders for Rob to store his water bottle or plug in his phone.

Looking at the snow outside the glass, yet feeling comfortable and cozy inside, Hannah felt as if she was in a whole other world.

Then again, maybe she was.

Rob hadn't said much. After he'd helped her sit down and made sure she was comfortable, he'd turned on some Christmas music and started driving.

This silence between them was new. Back when they'd first met, Rob would visit with her either on her way to work or walking home. Or he'd sit with her in the sun outside.

During those times, they seemed to talk nonstop. They'd shared everything. They'd talked about their days and their lives. Then, as they'd gotten to know each other better, they began to share even more information. Little by little, they shared memories of their pasts and their hopes for the future.

She'd found herself constantly comparing his interest in her with Paul's responses. Paul had been kind to her, of course, but he had also known her since they'd been small *kinner*. He'd never needed to ask how she felt about things or wonder if she liked or disliked something. He'd known her almost as well as he'd known himself.

In contrast, Rob had asked her questions about everything—how she liked her job as a nanny. What her church was like, if she really liked Trail bologna. His curiosity and interest in her had been amusing and rather flattering, too. Of course, she'd been just as curious about his days as a writer, growing up in Chicago, and going to high school and college.

Now they seemed to have so much awkwardness between them, it felt as if their words had large hurdles to climb in order to be heard.

As the silence pulled the tension that hung between them even tighter and a song played on the stereo about roasting chestnuts, Hannah hastened to fill the space with something, with anything.

"Your car is cozy, Rob."

"Yeah. It's a good one."

She ran a hand along the smooth, soft leather on the door. "What kind is it?"

"It's a Lexus GS."

"Ah. How interesting."

His lips twitched. "Really? Does that mean anything to you?"

She grinned back at him. "Nee. But I do know that it's warmer than a buggy."

He chuckled. "I suppose that's true." After a pause, he said, "Hannah, why didn't you want me to take your sister home?"

"Because I didn't want you to go to my house."

He winced. "Well, that's honest."

"I want to be honest with you." Silently she added, *From now on.*

"Hmm. Well, if I'm going to be honest, I'm feeling a little confused right about now."

"Oh?"

"Absolutely." He paused at a stop sign, then continued. "When we spoke last night, I thought things between us were better. Did I just imagine it? Or were you simply tired yesterday and I took our conversation the wrong way?"

"You weren't wrong. I do want to move forward." Steeling her spine, she added, "Rob, I regret how I treated you."

"You do?"

Unable to look him in the eye, she nodded. "Nine months ago, when I broke up with you, I guess I was feeling confused. I think I was still mourning Paul and I was afraid about leaving my life."

"About being English?"

She nodded. "I never was baptized, and I know deciding not to be Amish is the right choice for me, but I was still worried."

"And now?"

It was time to face the truth. Taking a deep breath, she said, "Now I realize that I've been more comfortable living in the English world for some time. I am ready to speak to the bishop." She rushed on. "However, my parents want me to turn back time. They want me to move back home. When I refused, they asked Malinda to visit me. At first I thought it was just because she was worried about me, but then I realized that they were using her to encourage me to go home."

"Are you sure about that?"

"Pretty sure. I love my sister and I'm glad for her help, but she came to the hospital with an agenda." The thought made her sad.

"Anyway, I didn't want her pushing her point of view on you while you were doing her a favor and driving her home."

"I could have taken anything she had to dish out, Hannah."

"I know you could have, but you shouldn't have to listen to such things." Hannah knew she also wouldn't have been able to stop herself from saying something to Malinda if she did spout off her opinions. That wouldn't have been good at all!

"Hannah." It was obvious that he was trying not to tease her about trying to protect him.

"Rob, I know you would've been fine, but I'm no longer going to even pretend to listen when people try to make me do things I don't want to do."

"And you think your sister would have done that in the car?" His voice was filled with incredulity.

"Nee. She would have done that to you. Maybe hurt your feelings. Rob, I know you can handle most anything, but that wasn't the point." Determined to show how mature she was now, she added, "You have already done so much."

"Not really. I just picked you up from the hospital."

"Nee, you saved my life."

He groaned. "Hannah, don't ever feel indebted to me for that. I was just doing my job."

Though her head knew exactly what he meant, hearing it explained that way still stung. "Just because it was your job doesn't mean I can't feel grateful."

"I didn't mean you shouldn't feel whatever way you want. I'm just trying to tell you that it isn't necessary."

"All right. Fine." Frustrated with their interplay, she changed topics. "So, how is Daisy?"

His expression lightened. "She's good. Driving Rose crazy, I'm afraid."

"Oh no. Is she acting up?"

"Of course not, she's just been trying to get Rose to play a little more."

"Uh-oh."

"No, it's a good thing. I think Rose secretly likes having another dog to pal around with. Daisy minds well, too. She's a good dog, Hannah. You've done a good job with her."

"Danke, but she was easy to train. I got her from the shelter. She'd been there for two weeks and was pretty miserable. When one of the workers told me about her when we ran into each other at Josephine's Café, I knew I had to see her."

"And?"

"And right away we seemed to form a bond. Even though I only lived in that small one-room apartment, I took her home an hour later. I couldn't think about her spending another day in the shelter." Thinking back to those first few days, she smiled. "We had our challenges, of course. I wasn't used to a dog's schedules and she wasn't used to being home alone all day. But, before long, we developed our own routine."

"And then everything was good."

"Yes." Recalling the first time Daisy ran to her side when she walked in the door, her tail wagging, Hannah smiled. "The two of us seemed to need each other. She's brightened my days and has given me so much companionship and love."

He glanced at her as he turned onto Plum Street. "I bet if Daisy could talk, she'd say the same thing about you."

He did understand! "That's so sweet. I'd like to think of Daisy and me like that, too. I guess we were meant to be."

Still reliving the memory, she smiled at him but immediately regretted doing so. Rob's expression had tightened. Though she was pretty sure she knew what was bothering him, she still pressed. Maybe she was a glutton for punishment. "What did I say?"

"Nothing. My mind just drifted to something it shouldn't have. Do you ever do that?"

Did she ever think about things that hurt? Think about things that she shouldn't because she was filled with regret and the overwhelming knowledge that she couldn't go back in time and change the past?

"Jah," she said quietly. "I do. All the time."

Pulling into the Rosses' driveway, he placed his vehicle in park and sighed. "I wonder when we'll ever stop."

"Stop?"

"Yeah." Turning her way, he gazed at her intently. His dark eyes were full of doubt—and maybe, perhaps, more than a bit of recrimination? "You know what I mean, don't you, Hannah? When will we stop doubting ourselves and our choices? When will we stop regretting things that we can't change? Do you think we ever will?"

"I hope so. Nee, I pray so." She needed the Lord's help right now. More than anything, she wanted to move forward and be happy and make the people she loved happy, too.

But of course, she'd also learned that while the Lord was so very good, He didn't grant wishes and promises. Only that He'd walked through fire by her side.

Yes, she'd definitely learned that over and over again.

Chapter 8

She had her own pretty bedroom in the basement.

Four days ago, the room had been a dark, stark storage area for Christopher's old toys and baby equipment. Now it was painted a soft gray and had a twin-size bed against the wall, a floral rocker in another corner, and a small dresser that had been painted a sparkling white.

Soft flannel sheets in shades of pink covered the bed, along with a really beautiful Daisy Chain quilt and three fluffy pillows. On the white wicker table next to the bed sat a reading light, a vanilla-scented candle, and a stack of books. A vase of pink roses rested on the dresser. Almost like a page from one of Melissa's *Better Homes & Gardens* magazines.

It was surely the prettiest room Hannah had ever seen. She was touched that her employers had gone to so much trouble for her—especially now, when it was so close to Christmas.

"This room is *wunderbaar*," she whispered. And it really was. It was silly, but a part of her feared if she blinked it would vanish.

Melissa still looked doubtful. "Do you think so? I mean, I

know it's just a converted storage room." She bit her bottom lip. "I told York last night that we've taken you for granted. Here you've taken care of my children, cleaned my kitchen, even helped with all the laundry—but I don't know what an Amish girl needs in a bedroom."

An Amish girl? Comments like that always made Hannah want to giggle. "We Amish girls usually like to sleep on beds in our rooms."

The lines of worry around Melissa's eyes eased. "Oh, you. I was serious!"

"I'm being serious, too. A bed is enough for me." Waving a hand, she murmured, "And all of this? Well, it's more than enough. It's a lovely room. So pretty and so cozy, too."

"I'm glad you like it. I told York that you'd probably like a quilt instead of a regular bedspread. When I saw these flannel sheets displayed so prettily on a shelf, I thought they would be a nice touch."

York and Melissa had a toddler, a baby, and two demanding jobs. Yet they'd still gone out of their way to make a special place for her. "Have you gotten any sleep in the last twenty-four hours?" she teased.

"Not much, but it wasn't because of this project," she replied with a chuckle. "Little Miss Dorothy didn't feel like sleeping last night. Or the night before that."

"It's *gut* I'm here then. As soon as I get settled, I'll help you with our tiny night owl."

Melissa shook her head. "Absolutely not! You are going to lie down and let York and me fuss over you."

"*Nee!* I mean, I couldn't let you do that." It was one thing to accept the room, but there was no way she was going to shirk her duties, too.

"I'm afraid we're not giving you a choice. You have stitches, a hurt foot, and a slight concussion. Besides, remember what I told you over a year ago? We're family."

"*Jah*, but—"

"And not to sound mean, but you really do look exhausted, Hannah. You're covered in bruises, and the doctors said you have minor burns and abrasions on your arms. You need rest."

"You are making me sound much worse than I am. They wouldn't have let me leave the hospital if I was in such bad shape."

"Hannah, the doctors and nurses let you leave the hospital. They did not say you could go back to work, however. They expected you to rest and heal." Melissa drew herself up and said firmly, "No, the most I'm going to let you do is pet your dog."

And just like that, the reminder of her sweet, brave boxer brought tears to her eyes. "Daisy is here?"

"Oh, I'm sorry. She's not, but I did see her in the yard this morning. Rob said he was going to bring her by later." She paused. "I know we talked . . . but are you up for that?"

Hannah wasn't sure if Melissa was referring to Hannah playing with her boxer or seeing Rob again so soon. She supposed it didn't matter, though. She really was ready to move forward in her life, and that meant continuing to repair the rift between her and Rob and settling into the Rosses' home.

And, of course, she wanted to see Daisy. That dog had been her lifeline this past year.

"I'm up for everything," she said at last.

Melissa still looked skeptical. "All right. I'll let Rob know." She shook a finger at her. "But that means you need to lie down for at least an hour."

"*Jah, Mamm*," she said with more than a touch of sarcasm.

"That's more like it," Melissa said with a grin. "Now I'd better go rescue York. Christopher has been wanting to play blocks and watch *Dora the Explorer*."

She strode out of the room without another word. Hannah listened to her footsteps on the stairs, then the faint click of her loafers on the wood floor overhead.

Taking advantage of the quiet, Hannah walked into the bathroom and turned on the light. The lights were so bright at the hospital, one look in the mirror had scared her. Now, in the softer glow of the small bathroom, Hannah studied her face.

She had a fierce bruise on her temple and another on her cheek. She had a bandage covering her stitches from the gash she'd gotten when she'd passed out and faint smudges under her eyes. So, she looked like she'd been in an accident.

Or, perhaps, in a fire that had destroyed everything she owned.

Padding back into her new bedroom, Hannah knelt down beside the bed and tried to be grateful. Resting her weight on her knees, she gave thanks for the firemen and the Rosses and her family, who, while demanding, loved her. She gave thanks for Daisy, who was responsible for her waking up, and the doctors and nurses who had taken care of her in the ambulance and the hospital.

Then, when she stopped to take a breath, she finally allowed herself time to mourn her losses. Her grandmother's quilt. The pretty, scallop-edged dishes that she'd paid too much money for and were difficult to clean but she loved so much.

Her dresses, the coat her father had given her when she'd first started working. The keepsake box from Paul. Less important but still heartbreaking to lose was her basket of needlework projects, some of which she'd been working on for years. Her pots and pans, the blankets and bedding, the glider rocking chair she'd just purchased.

Slowly getting to her feet, she reached for a tissue and blew her nose, then climbed into the comfortable bed and wrapped her arms around herself. And right then and there, she began to cry. Real, sharp, painful tears that she hadn't wanted to feel. But experience told her they were as necessary as prayer and laughter.

It was okay to be sad. It was okay to mourn items. It was okay to feel the loss and wish things were different. In an hour or so, when she walked out of the room, she would do her best to smile and concentrate on the future. But for now?

She would allow herself just a little bit more time to cry. Surely the Lord would understand.

Four hours later, Hannah was feeling far more refreshed. She'd taken a two-hour nap, showered, and gone to the kitchen for a warm bowl of soup.

Melissa had served it to her on the couch and little Christopher had snuggled next to her after promising his mommy that he would let Hannah eat.

Sitting in the beautifully decorated living room, with its tall, nine-foot, Christmas tree beribboned and twinkling to their right, Hannah had at last felt like herself again.

After she finished her light meal, she'd read Christopher a story and then fed Dot a bottle while Melissa did the dishes.

Shortly after York took their kids to his parents' house for a visit, Rob and Daisy arrived.

"Daisy!" Hannah called out the moment she spied them.

Daisy wriggled out of Rob's hold and bounded toward her. Seconds later, Hannah was wiping off wet doggy kisses.

"Hey now, Daisy," Rob said as he grabbed hold of the boxer's collar. "You've got to go easy on Hannah here. She's not a hundred percent yet."

When Daisy whined, then attempted to squirm out of his grip, Hannah intervened. "It's all right, Rob. Let her go. I think I need this."

"All right, but be careful."

Daisy pawed at Hannah's knee, then snuggled closer. So happy to see her sweet pup, Hannah wrapped her arms around the excited dog and pressed her head against Daisy's body. "It's all right. Before you know it, we'll be back together." Where, she didn't know. She just hoped she could find someplace within her price range that took dogs sooner rather than later.

Daisy responded with a lick to Hannah's cheek.

Hannah chuckled again as she leaned back on the couch. "Thank you, Rob. She is the best medicine."

"Anytime, sweetheart."

Sweetheart. Unable to help it, Hannah felt warmth spread through her again. It was becoming obvious that Daisy wasn't the only thing that was going to help her recover.

Chapter 9

Hannah was blushing, just the way she used to. The sight was so familiar yet unexpected, it made him pause. Just so he could revel in the memories. For a few seconds Rob felt as if everything between them were good again.

That wasn't true, of course. Not much between them was good. However, her reaction did allow him to hold on to the idea that it could be.

While Daisy continued to enjoy her mistress's attention, craning her neck so Hannah could scratch under her ears, Rob sat down next to Hannah on the couch.

"Rob?"

"Just taking a seat. That's all."

Hannah darted him a confused look but didn't move away, and for that he was glad. The fact was, he wanted to be near her. Maybe almost as much as that boxer did. Hannah made him feel better, just by being herself.

Hearing her laughter, her light, almost musical voice, was like medicine for him—medicine that he was not going to take for granted.

He had really missed her.

After cooing at the dog a little bit longer, Hannah curled one leg on the couch and turned toward him. "I hope Daisy hasn't been too much trouble. She can sometimes be a lot of work, especially at night." Looking hesitant, she asked, "Did she wake you up last night?"

"Only for a couple of minutes." *Or an hour or two.*

"I'm sorry. I don't know why she always wants to go out at two or three in the morning."

Rob shrugged. "I have another shift tomorrow. I've got someone coming over to play with her and Rose for a few hours in the afternoon and then I'll put her in her crate. She'll be fine."

"Hopefully you won't have to watch her too much longer."

He was privately hoping that he would. He was willing to do whatever it took to be firmly back in Hannah's life. "Don't worry about it." He reached out and rubbed the dog's head. Daisy was now sprawled on the floor next to the couch. "She's a good dog, Hannah."

"She is." Glancing down at her, Hannah murmured, "She's such a happy *hund.*"

"That's because she's with you."

Her blue eyes darted to his before they warmed. "Thank you for saying that."

He watched her closely, ready to tease her again. But then the puffiness around her eyes registered. It wasn't from lack of sleep or the residual effects of the fire.

She'd been crying.

Why? Just from everything? She had lost her home and most of her belongings—of course she'd be sad because of that. Or was she in pain?

"Rob, is everything all right?"

"Hmm? Oh. Yeah." He shook his head and tried to sound like the author he was. Surely he had some decent words inside his head somewhere. "I mean, there's no need to thank me for telling you the truth."

She shifted again. "Enough about me. Tell me about firefighting."

"All right. Well, you know why I moved here."

"To get over your girlfriend's death."

"Yeah. I did move here from Chicago so I wasn't reminded of Julia so much. But that wasn't the only reason."

"No?"

"It was a lot of things. I needed a change. I needed to do something new for myself." Thinking back to that time, when he'd been so tired and weighed down by too many responsibilities and city living, he continued. "I think I needed to be a little bit uncomfortable."

Her eyebrows rose. "You wanted to make yourself uncomfortable?"

"Yeah. I decided I needed to shake myself up." Thinking about the person he'd been back then, he shook his head. "No, it was more like I needed to wake myself up."

"Hmm." A faint wrinkle appeared on her brow.

"Sorry, I guess that sounds crazy."

"Nee. I was just thinking that it sounded familiar."

He scanned her face. A year ago, he would have asked what she meant, prodded her to tell him more about herself. But now he was too afraid to push her away, so he held his tongue. He cleared his throat. "Well. Anyway, last year, after we broke up, I was kind of at a loss as to what I wanted to do. And after a few weeks of moping and trying to write but only coming up with dreck that I continually deleted, I realized that I needed to do something more with my life. Soon after, I heard that the fire department was about to start a new training class." He shrugged. "I signed up."

"Just like that?"

Thinking back to that time, he grinned. "Yeah. Get this, two days after I signed up, I went to my first class. It was as if God had decided that He wasn't going to let me change my mind."

She leaned closer, her eyes bright again. "Well, what happened?"

Hannah smelled faintly of gardenias. After pushing that thought away, he spoke. "I realized that I had made the right decision." He paused, letting himself appreciate her scent for a few seconds longer before moving a few inches away. "I'm not going to lie—it was hard. The training, the sense of responsibility. Shoot, even the grunt work. I'd gotten kind of spoiled and soft."

"But you didn't give up."

"No, I didn't. And now I love it almost as much as writing."

"I suppose the Lord led you to it then."

He'd never thought that. He'd used Hannah as his excuse. Julia's death, too—since she'd been killed in a car accident. He even told himself that he had too much time on his hands, so he needed to be busier.

But he had a feeling she was right. The Lord didn't make mistakes and He'd certainly guided him through quite a few situations lately.

And maybe the Lord was guiding him back to Hannah again. Maybe they were both ready, since they were now older and a little wiser.

Seeing how vulnerable she looked, how her emotion seemed to match the vulnerability he was feeling, he shifted again. Allowed himself to move closer.

He took her hand and clasped it in between his.

"Rob?"

"I can't help myself, Hannah. Even though neither of us knows what will happen next, I need you to know that I'm glad I'm sitting here with you."

She looked down at their hands and seemed to come to a decision. "I'm glad, too," she whispered as she met his gaze.

Then she smiled.

It was a real smile, wide, unguarded. A little wonky looking. And because of that, it was beautiful. Just as familiar and missed as her blushes.

Unable to help himself, he raised one of her hands and brought it to his lips. When she didn't pull away, he kissed her knuckles.

She inhaled sharply.

After pressing his lips to her hand once again, he smiled back at her. And decided to keep her hand nestled firmly in his own. If only for a few minutes longer.

Chapter 10

"Christopher, you are a mighty good helper today," Hannah said as she took Dorothy's pacifier from his outstretched palm.

Christopher, still a toddler but looking like a mighty responsible man, nodded. "Dot is tired."

"Is she?"

"Uh-huh. It's her nap time."

"What about you? Are you tired?"

He shook his head. "I'm not a baby."

She stood up and carefully put a sleeping Dot in the pack and play in the corner of the room. Then gazed at her favorite little boy in the world—who was now acting mighty grown-up. "I know you are almost three, but I know that even three-year-olds take naps in the afternoon."

"But I'm not tired. Daddy didn't make me sleep yesterday."

No, York had not.

And they'd all paid the price for that!

Boy, had they. By five o'clock, Christopher had been a pouty, whiney mess. He didn't want to pick up his toys, wash his face, eat his supper, or listen to anyone. He'd even dissolved into a full-blown temper tantrum when Hannah had told him to leave poor Daisy and Rose alone.

The dogs were good-natured, but it had been obvious that they'd needed a break from tiny hands fussing with them nonstop.

After four or five minutes of tears and foot stomping, he'd thrown himself on the floor, kicked his legs, and bellowed his irritation for a good eight minutes.

Hannah had stood over him and watched the little boy wear himself out. When York had attempted to pick Christopher up, Hannah had even dared to tell him to go sit down.

To her amazement, York had done exactly that.

Christopher had not been happy to be ignored but had soon fallen asleep. Figuring a nap on soft carpet wouldn't hurt him one bit, Hannah had covered him up with a warm blanket.

When Hannah overheard Melissa tell her husband that he was a very good doctor but had a thing to learn about being firm with his son, she'd privately agreed.

Today, she'd sent both Melissa and York to work. There was no way Hannah was going to allow these children's schedules to run amuck if she could help it.

"Christopher, it is nap time now." When his brow furrowed, she added, "That means you are going to lie on your bed with a book. We're having quiet time."

"For how long?"

"Thirty minutes." She smiled, hoping to soften his pout. "That's a half an hour, Chris." She also knew from experience that his thirty-minute break would likely turn into an hour's nap.

"Like always?"

"Jah, just like always."

"Okay."

"*Gut* boy." She allowed him to pick out a book and helped him take off his socks. Then she tucked him in his bed and handed him the book.

"You could read to me, Hannah."

"I could, but then it wouldn't be quiet time, now would it?"

She walked out and closed the door behind her. Just as she'd done a week ago, before she'd had her accident, when her employers had taken the children's schedules into their own hands.

Experience told her that he would be sound asleep within ten minutes and would sleep at least an hour. That meant she now had a whole hour to relax, as well. Even better, no one was around to watch her limp, wince, or lie down on the couch.

Because of that, she allowed herself a little moan as she gingerly shifted to her side and closed her eyes. She was exhausted.

She hadn't been sleeping well. Every time she closed her eyes, she dreamed of Daisy trying to tug her awake. But unfortunately, half the time in her dreams Daisy wasn't successful. Hannah would jolt awake, sure that flames were biting at her toes or that Daisy was stuck and hurting.

Or that neither of them could breathe because of the thick cloud of smoke.

Then there were all the dreams involving Paul dying or her being responsible for Rob getting hurt. Yes, every bit of these nightmares was awful. Worse, she didn't have any idea how to make them go away. All she seemed capable of doing was praying and hoping that they would end soon.

She needed that.

Now, though, with Daisy over at Rob's, Christopher upstairs in his room, and Dot asleep across the room, Hannah allowed herself to relax a little more. She let herself close her eyes and look at the twinkling lights of the Rosses' Christmas tree and imagine how things might one day be different.

If she ever found a way to move forward.

Chapter 11

Rob knew he really ought to say something to York and Melissa about installing better locks on their doors. Or, better yet, he should encourage Hannah to make sure she locked all the doors before deciding to take a nap.

But not right now. At the moment, the unlocked back door was helping him out. He'd walked over to bring Hannah some soup from Josephine's and caught sight of her through the window. She was sound asleep on the couch in York's den.

She'd looked so sweet. Hannah was curled on her side with her arms folded tightly in front of her, much the way Dot slept in her port-a-crib whenever Melissa put her down in the kitchen.

After staring at her for a few moments, Rob had planned to simply set the bag on the back porch and go home. Maybe even call the Rosses' house in an hour to tell Hannah about the soup so it wouldn't sit out all night, forgotten.

But then she cried out in her sleep.

Unable to help himself, he turned the knob on the door, found it unlocked, and let himself in.

Rob knew he shouldn't go inside uninvited. No doubt, she was fine. He was seriously taking advantage of their friendship and the Rosses' trust.

Moreover, he knew he shouldn't approach Hannah when she was in the middle of a bad dream. But caution wasn't in his vocabulary when it came to her. His need to make sure she was safe and happy overrode everything else.

Besides, he was only going to stay for a moment. Just make sure she was okay and then dart back outside.

As he walked closer, he realized that even asleep Hannah Eicher had a calming effect on him.

It had always been that way.

With Hannah, he didn't need to watch himself or try too hard. He didn't need to try to impress her with expensive gifts or attempt to entertain her with amusing stories about his writing career. All he needed was to be in the same room with her.

Stepping closer, he smiled. She'd just shifted. Now she was flat on her back, her arms flung up above her head like a child. Then she frowned and uttered a soft cry.

She really was in the throes of a nightmare. It was a bad one, too, based on the way she was shaking.

He was unable to stay away. Kneeling next to her, he gently shook her. "Hannah. Hannah, wake up."

She shuddered and shook her head. "*Nee.*"

He ran a hand along her cheek, along her temple, right to the edge of her white *kaap*. "Come on, Hannah, wake up now," he whispered. Then gave in to temptation and pressed his lips on her cheek.

She started.

Eyes open, she stared at him in alarm. Sucked in a breath.

"Don't be scared. It's just me."

"Rob?"

He sat back on his haunches. "Yeah. You okay?"

She blinked again, then slowly looked around. "The *boppli!* Is Dorothy all right?"

He got to his feet and looked over at the pack and play. Thank the good Lord, little Dot was still sound asleep. She had a tiny thumb in her mouth and was lying on her side. Boy, he hadn't even realized she was there. "She's just fine," he whispered as he walked back to Hannah's side. "Sleeping like an angel."

"I canna believe I fell asleep."

"I can. Your body is still healing. You need your rest." Actually, he was starting to worry that she needed more rest than she was getting. Should York and Melissa have really just thrown her into watching two babies full-time? It seemed like a bit much to him.

She was sitting up now. Her *kapp* was slightly askew and her dress was more wrinkled than he'd ever seen it. He thought she looked adorable. "How are you feeling? Are you all right?"

Rubbing her face, she shook her head. "I don't rightly know. At the moment, I'm feeling mighty confused."

"How come?"

"I don't remember you coming in." Her voice hardened. "How did you get in here?"

There was nothing to do but tell her the truth. "I was about to knock on the door when I saw you sleeping on the couch through the window next to the front door."

"Rob, you just brought yourself inside?"

Yep, she sounded horrified, and he didn't blame her. "Not exactly. I was going to leave, but you cried out in your sleep. I was worried that you were having a nightmare." So, that was the truth. And, yes, his excuse almost sounded reasonable. But that didn't mean he wasn't embarrassed about his actions.

"I still don't understand."

He sat down. "Isn't it kind of obvious? I still care about

you. I hate the idea of you hurting. Even when you're asleep, I worry about you."

For a moment her gaze softened and he thought she understood what he was saying. That even though they'd broken up and she'd broken his heart, he still cared about her. Enough that he wouldn't let their past get in the way. Maybe not even a closed door and her need for privacy. "Rob, what you are saying is sweet, and I am grateful for your help. But this . . . you coming into the Rosses' house uninvited and while I was sleeping? You canna do that again."

Everything she said made sense. "All right." He got to his feet. "But can you tell me one thing?"

"What?"

"What were you dreaming about? Was it the fire?"

She got to her feet as well. She fussed with her dress, straightening out the fabric, and checked the pins while she talked. "Jah. I keep dreaming that I canna get out and that Daisy gets hurt." Her blue eyes filled with tears and she quickly blinked them away as her hands fell by her sides. "Sometimes I dream about you getting hurt, too."

"But I'm fine."

"Jah. But sometimes I can't help thinking that something could happen to you, Rob. Just like—" She shook her head, cutting off her next words.

But he knew what she was trying not to say. "Just like Paul?"

"Jah. Just like Paul." She shuddered. "I hate these nightmares. I don't know why I'm still having them."

"You've been through some tough times, Hannah. Give yourself time."

"Do you ever get scared of the fires? Are you ever afraid?"

"Of course I am. I would be crazy not to be afraid of some of the fires we've put out. But that's part of the job. I've had so much training and the guys around me are so experienced, I no longer panic. I just get to work."

"But what about your bad dreams?" she asked faintly. "What do you do when they come?"

He wished he could tell her that his bad dreams were about fighting fires, but his all revolved around losing her again. "I know the other guys have nightmares about fighting fires," he said hesitantly. "I'm not sure what's the best way to fight them, though."

"No?"

"All I can do is tell you that getting hurt in a fire isn't my greatest fear anymore." And there he'd gone again. Throwing caution to the wind around her.

"What is?"

He shook his head. "That is a story for another day."

She stepped forward. "Rob—"

"Hannah?" Christopher called out. "Hannah, where are you?"

"I'm here in your daddy's den, Chris," she answered. "If you wait, I'll come get you."

"No, I'm coming down to see you!"

Which startled Dot, too. She cried out.

Hannah rubbed her temple. "I'm sorry, Rob, but I must see to the—"

"You take Chris; I'll get Dot."

"But—are you sure?"

"Yeah. Don't worry. I've held babies before," he said as he reached down to gently pull Dot into his arms.

"Rob, you're here to play!" Christopher cried as he zoomed past Hannah and circled Rob's legs.

Reaching down, he brushed a hand over the little boy's rumpled hair. "Hey, buddy."

"Are you gonna stay for lunch?"

"I'm gonna stay all afternoon," he said, making a decision.

Hannah's gaze widened; then she seemed to come to a conclusion. "I hope you like grilled cheese sandwiches, Rob."

"I love them."

"Gut. Then you may help Christopher with his pull-up while I go change Miss Dorothy. Afterward, we shall have lunch."

Changing a pull-up? That was a new one, but he figured if he could carry grown men out of burning buildings he could handle changing a toddler's diaper. "Sounds like a plan," he said as he handed the baby to Hannah and took hold of Christopher's hand. "Lead the way, buddy. Let's go get you settled so we can have lunch."

Christopher grinned up at him. "Hannah makes good sandwiches."

Unable to help himself, Rob looked over at Hannah and smiled. "I know, buddy. Hannah makes the best sandwiches ever."

Chapter 12

After another two days passed, Hannah allowed herself to believe that things with Rob were going well.

For some reason, knowing that he was willing to walk into the Rosses' home uninvited and even risk offending her because he cared more about her being safe than anything else had erased the last of Hannah's fears. If Rob was willing to risk so much for their relationship, she was willing to let down the last of her guard and be with him wholeheartedly.

Hannah would be lying if she said the beauty of the Christmas season wasn't playing a part in her change of heart as well. There was something about this season of hope that inspired her to have hope, too. And there was no better place to do that with Christopher, Dot, their parents, and Rob.

Melissa and York had not only made her feel welcome in their home, but they'd also made her a part of the family. She'd spent most of Saturday decorating a second Christmas tree in the basement, which Melissa said would be for her. Of course it was her very first time doing such a thing, but it had been great fun, especially with Melissa's penchant for silly Christmas songs and love of Disney ornaments. Such secular items helped Hannah draw the line between the *Englischer* love of "Christmas" and what she'd been brought up to think about Jesus's birth.

It might not have made a lot of sense to other people, but in her mind the dividing line was clear, and because of that she was able to await both Jesus's birthday and Santa's arrival with equal enthusiasm. It was rather fun to have so much to look forward to.

Actually, this morning was the first time in a week that she'd woken up with a sense of foreboding. It was Sunday and she was going to church at Amelia and Simon's house. She wasn't dreading either seeing her friends or partaking in the usual three-hour Amish church service. It was sitting with her sister, Malinda, and her mother and fielding their questions.

She'd also accepted Rob's offer to drive her to the Hochstetlers' house and pick her up afterward. He'd even offered to sit with her during the service, remembering that everyone was welcome to worship. But she'd refused his offer. Men and women sat across from each other, so she would be subjecting him to sitting with strangers. The service would also be in Pennsylvania Dutch, so he wouldn't understand much of it at all.

But his willingness to put himself in that situation meant everything to her. She now knew that she wasn't just falling in love with him; she was already there. All she had left to do was decide what that love meant in her life.

After gathering a ruby red scarf and her thick black cloak, she walked downstairs. It was still early. She planned to grab only a piece of fruit and some coffee before leaving for church. But Melissa, York, and Dot were in the kitchen.

"Hannah, good morning!" York said with a smile. "You look like you're almost back to normal."

"I'm feeling much better," she agreed. "This morning, I didn't even need to wrap my ankle in the bandage you gave me, and the burns on my arms are much better."

"That's good to hear, but don't overdo it."

"*Jah, Doktah.*"

His eyes brightened. "Tease me all you want about looking after you. I'll still do it, though."

"I won't complain about that. I'm grateful for your help."

"We were just about to make some waffles," Melissa said, neatly ushering her to the kitchen table. "Would you like one?"

"No, thank you. Rob will be here soon. I just thought I'd have some coffee and a banana or something."

"You sure? That's it?"

"Jah. They'll serve a big dinner after church, and then Rob said he might even take me out for something, too."

Melissa poured her a cup of coffee and added a large dose of vanilla creamer, just how she liked it.

Hannah grabbed a banana, sat down, and sipped the coffee gratefully. "The first sip always tastes so good."

"I always think the same thing," York said.

"So, how are things going with you and Rob?" Melissa asked.

"Good." She tried to pretend she wasn't really pleased about that, but knew she wasn't fooling any of them. "We seem to have stopped worrying about the past. Now I only worry when he's on duty."

"I think we'll always worry about that," Melissa said. "Fire-fighting is a demanding profession and it does have its dangers. I do know he's well trained, though," she added in a rush. "Rob graduated at the top of his class."

"I didn't know that, but I do know what kind of man he is. I need to trust in Rob's abilities and the Lord's guiding hand." She took a breath. "No, I *am* going to believe that. Anything less would make me feel like I wasn't being fair to him."

Melissa and York exchanged glances.

"You sound really determined, Hannah," Melissa said softly. "Are you serious about Rob now?"

"I am. I think he is serious about me, too."

"Oh, I know Rob is," York said. After taking a sip of coffee, he added, "I don't think he would have started things up again if he wasn't."

She knew he wouldn't. "I don't think so, either."

"What about you?" Melissa murmured. "I know you just said you were serious, but what are you going to do about your future?"

These were hard questions. During another time in her life, she might have even said that they were too personal—far too personal for her bosses to be asking of her.

But lately, she'd realized that she'd been keeping everyone at a safe distance. Ever since Paul had died. Or maybe even Paul, too.

She and Paul had had a lovely relationship. He'd been safe and kind. Those two things had encouraged her to feel much the same way. Everything between them had been sweet and easy. He'd never asked too much of her, and because of that, she'd never given him more than she was comfortable giving.

In addition—and it didn't make her feel very good to admit this—she had liked how her relationship with Paul had been accepted so easily by her family. They'd been happy with her, which meant that she hadn't had to worry too much about causing waves.

She would have coasted right along into an engagement and marriage. Never expecting too much of herself. Never expecting too much of their relationship or of her life. She would have put blinders on and firmly looked straight ahead, never wanting to be tempted by any other options in her life.

Maybe that was why when he died she'd felt both devastated by his loss and curiously abandoned. She'd not only lost

Paul but also the easy, agreeable life she'd planned to have with him.

When she'd started working at the Rosses' house and met Rob next door, she'd been jarred awake. She'd suddenly started thinking about how different her life could be. It had been as exciting as it was terrifying—which was why when her parents had pushed and pushed for her to stop seeing Rob Prince she had given in.

It wasn't because her parents were bad people or that Rob wasn't the man for her. It was because she'd been afraid to completely disrupt her whole life.

But it had taken a fire for her to realize that Rob hadn't changed her—she'd already changed. She wasn't the same woman she used to be and she no longer wanted things to be easy and agreeable. She wanted challenges and emotion.

Maybe Rob had been doing the same thing, only for him those challenges meant putting his life in danger and fighting fires.

Melissa cleared her throat. "Hannah, are you okay? Did my questions upset you?"

Realizing that she'd been staring off into space, Hannah shook her head. "Not at all. Actually, I think they did the complete opposite. You made me realize that I've made my share of mistakes."

"Oh?"

"Jah. I think I need to see my parents soon."

Melissa and York exchanged worried glances again. But this time it was York who nodded agreeably. "I don't mind picking them up and bringing them over, Hannah. If you arrange a time to see them, just let me know."

"Thank you, York."

"Nothing to thank me for," he said easily as he stood up. "Family is important. Both family by birth and family by choice. As far as I'm concerned, you're the little sister I never had."

"Truly?" His words made her feel so soft and good inside.

"Absolutely! Although I have a feeling you're far less annoying now than you would have been if we'd grown up together."

That made Hannah chuckle. "Don't worry, York. My siblings would be happy to share with you all sorts of stories about how annoying their older sister was."

He grinned. "Remind me to have a chat with them sometime soon, then."

Chapter 13

"You tired yet, Hollywood?" Jerry asked from across the table where they were eating a late lunch.

Or maybe it was dinner? Rob wondered. He could never figure out what to call the middle of the shift meals. He'd come on shift at seven that morning and it was now four in the afternoon. After this meal, he would try to take a nap so he would be ready in case they got called out later that night.

Or, for that matter, why he even dwelled on such things.

But maybe thinking about that kind of stuff was easier than thinking about how his latest mystery series was going to get picked up for a miniseries next fall.

Which was why all the guys at the station house were now calling him Hollywood.

"Yep." He grinned at Trenton. "But I've been tired since Thanksgiving, so it's nothing new."

"I hear you." Their engineer leaned back and propped a foot on the seat of the empty chair next to him. "It's been a crazy Christmas season. How many space heaters have caught on fire? Five? Six?"

"Too many," Jill said as she walked into the small kitchenette and joined them. "I wish we could go into every house in the area and inspect them."

Rob pushed his empty plate away. "That's probably a good idea. I bet a lot of people would be happy for us to do that."

Jill shrugged. "Yeah. Maybe. But of course there's going to be just that many people who tell us to stay out of their house and their business."

Trent whistled softly. "Boy, somebody's grumpy today."

Sitting down with a large serving of lasagna that the captain's wife had brought by a few hours ago, Jill grimaced. "You're right. I'm sorry. It's my daughter's birthday today and I've been feeling pretty guilty about not being with her."

Often, things at the firehouse were so busy, all they talked about was work. Because of that, sometimes Rob forgot just how much the other members of his squad gave up for their jobs. "How old is your daughter?"

"Lacey is seven." She smiled tiredly. "I don't know why I'm feeling so guilty. Her daddy is taking her out to a special dinner and then I'm taking her out for ice cream and cake tomorrow. Lace keeps telling me that she's lucky because she gets to have a two-day birthday."

"It's still hard not being there, though," Rob said.

"It is." After taking another bite of the lasagna, she said, "I know you don't have any kids. Who are you missing?"

Hannah. "A woman I've been seeing."

"The Amish girl?"

"Yeah. Her name's Hannah."

"Wait," Trent interrupted. "Is that the girl you rescued?"

"Yep."

"Wow, you work fast."

"It's not like that. I've known her for a while. She's my neighbors' nanny."

"Are you dating?"

"Yes. I mean, we're seeing each other."

"But how is that possible? I mean, I'm surprised that she'd even give you the time of day, what with her being Amish and you not."

"That's usually how it would be, I guess. But there's something there, you know?"

Jill smiled. "I like that idea. That love can't be stopped, no matter what the obstacles."

Trent groaned. "Don't get mushy on us, Greer. I was just starting to think of you as one of the guys."

"Sorry. I may be able to carry a hundred pounds up a ladder, but I'm still a softie at heart." Looking just beyond their door, her eyes lit up. "Speaking of which . . . "

Rob turned around, wondering what she was pointing out. And then jumped to his feet. "Hannah?"

Hannah, looking very festive and sweet in a cranberry red dress with an open black wool cloak over it, smiled. "Hi, Rob. And, um, everyone."

While the other members of his team called out greetings, he walked to her side. "What brings you here?"

She held out the plate of cookies in her hands. "York is driving me over to see my family today. When Melissa mentioned that they sometimes bring the crew on duty snacks, I decided to make you some cookies." She looked worriedly at the others. "I hope that is okay?"

"It's better than okay," Jill said. "Thank you so much."

"Yeah, thanks a lot," Trent said as he took the cookies and set them on the table. Eyeing them appreciatively, he said, "What kind are they?"

"They're cranberry oatmeal with some white chocolate chips added. And you're welcome," she said with a smile.

"Why don't you go take five, Rob?" Trent suggested.

"Thanks." He hesitated, then went ahead and took Hannah's arm as he led her to a corner of the firehouse. "It's good to see you. Really good."

"I debated whether to stop by, but York said your captain doesn't mind your getting visitors if they don't stay long."

"I would never mind you visiting me, Hannah," he murmured. "Now, tell me how you decided to see your parents."

"I've been thinking about a lot of things. Mainly that I don't want to be so angry with them."

"I'm glad." He hated how he was already thinking of the worst, but he said, "I'll be home in the morning. After I sleep for a bit, how about Daisy and I stop by?"

"I'd like that." Her face shined up into his. Easing his worries.

He wanted nothing more than to kiss her. But this wasn't the place and it certainly wasn't the time. "Let me walk you out."

"There's no need. York is right outside."

Just as he was about to tell her that he didn't mind, the alarm rang through the house. "I've got to go."

"Rob?" Worry filled her expression.

Unable to help himself, he leaned down and gently kissed her lips. "I'll be all right. Bye."

He turned away to put on his turnout gear, firmly putting all thoughts of Hannah to one side. There was no way he could start thinking about her while he was working.

That would be a recipe for disaster.

Chapter 14

Hannah had been a little worried about how she would be received when she went home. But from the moment her little brother met her with a big grin, she realized she shouldn't have worried so much.

Yes, things were different, but her siblings were still her siblings. That hadn't changed one bit.

"Hey, Hannah!" Calvin called out from the porch. "I didn't think you were supposed to be out in the cold."

"I'm recovering from an accident, not the flu." Noticing that he wasn't wearing a coat and there were five or six inches of snow on the ground, she said, "Besides, one of us isn't dressed for the weather at all. Why don't you have a coat on?"

"I've been chopping wood." Picking up three logs from the neat pile on the side, he said, "Come on in, Sister. We'll sit in front of the fire and get warm together."

After getting the door for him, she followed Calvin into the house and was immediately greeted by the scent of peppermint and cranberry. "Mamm's been busy."

"Jah. She's been making candles for all our neighbors." He

pointed to a neat row of twenty jelly jars filled with red wax. In the middle of each was a long string that still needed to be trimmed. Also on the counter was a spool of burlap ribbon.

"These are going to be such pretty gifts." Their mother really had a way with arts and crafts.

"You know Mamm—she loves Christmas."

Hannah smiled as she sat down in one of the cushy chairs situated in front of the fireplace. "I think we all do."

Calvin added a log to the fire, neatly stacked the other logs, and then sat down next to her in his chair. "We can't help it, I guess. Christmas in this house is a good time of year."

It really was. And back before Paul had died, she'd been much like their mother, eager for the holiday and determined to fill everyone's life with merriment and joy. For the last two years, she'd been adrift, but of late she seemed to have come into her own again. Maybe she'd needed to lose everything in order to find herself once more.

"You seem different," Calvin murmured, still looking at her closely. "Better."

"I think I am."

"How come? Is it because you're back with Rob?"

"I don't know if that's the whole reason, but he does have something to do with my mood, I guess. I feel better."

He relaxed. "I'm glad."

"Me, too."

"Hannah?" her mother called out as she entered the room, an armful of neatly folded laundry in her arms. "I didn't know you were here."

"I stopped by the firehouse to see Rob and decided to come over to see everyone."

"I'm glad you did." Looking tentative, she added, "Would you like some *kaffi* or tea?"

"Hot tea sounds *gut*."

"Malinda, come help!" Mamm called out. "Hannah's here!"

"Hannah, hiya," Malinda said with a smile as she went to put on the kettle—just as their father joined the group.

Ten minutes later, the five of them were all sipping hot tea in the house's great room, just like old times. There was a fire crackling in the fireplace, and the scent of cookies and candles in the air. Malinda was telling a story about two of her girl-friends and their mother was keeping her hands busy by tying bows on the jars and trimming wicks.

It felt just like it used to. They were a family again. Sharing stories and making plans. Hannah almost forgot just how much she had loved these moments.

When there was a break in the conversation, Daed said, "You know, I never thought I'd say this, but I wish Daisy was here."

"If you never thought you'd say it, I never thought I'd hear it!" Hannah teased. "You always complained about all of her fur."

"Even though she never shed that much," Calvin inter-jected.

"Well, she did save your life," Daed remarked. "I decided that more than made up for her fur." Sharing a look with Han-nah's mamm, he added, "Your almost dying made us rethink a lot of things."

"Like what?"

"Like the way we might have pushed you in the wrong di-rection nine months ago," he said quietly.

She was shocked. Treading carefully, she murmured, "I love you all, but I need to follow my own path, I think."

Looking serious, her mother nodded. "Jah. I agree."

Taking the plunge, she looked around the table. "Mamm, Daed, I am not going to be baptized in our church." She held her breath, ready to hear whatever recriminations they dished out.

But though they looked worried, both of her parents simply nodded. Calvin and Malinda didn't look surprised at all. In fact, Calvin even smiled.

"I figured as much," Daed said.

"I'm sorry for telling this to you."

He shook his head. "Don't apologize for speaking the truth."

"So . . . things with Rob are still *gut?*" Mamm asked.

"Jah." She took a deep breath. "I used to think I was falling in love with him, but now I know I have."

"Have you told him this?" Malinda asked.

"Not in so many words. But I will."

"What's been holding you back?"

"I wanted to talk to you about my decision . . . and fear, I guess."

Her father eyed her closely. "What have you been afraid of?"

"Of changing. And of disappointing all of you."

"Why would we be disappointed in you?" Calvin asked.

"Because I would be different."

Malinda tilted her head to one side. "Hannah, if you weren't Amish anymore, would you still believe in God?"

"Of course I would. I'm just saying that I wouldn't be baptized."

"Oh, Hannah," Malinda chided. "You didn't really think we believed you were going to eventually marry one of our Amish neighbors, did you?"

"Wait, you weren't hoping for that?"

"Nee. I hoped for you to be happy," Mamm said. "That's what we all want."

"I know Rob is going to make me happy."

"Then you need to embrace that," Daed said. "Nee, we all need to follow that advice. For too long, all of us have been wishing things were different instead of being grateful for how things are. If you have found love again, you need to embrace it."

"You make it sound so easy."

"That's because it is. After all, not everyone can get a second chance at love."

He was right. She had been given a second chance. Now all

she had to do was move forward. Smiling brightly, she said, "Danke. I don't think I realized how much I needed to hear that."

"We all need each other, dear," Mamm said. "Don't forget that. Not for one minute."

Just as she stood up to give her mother a hug, there was a loud knock at the door.

They all turned to watch Daed open it.

Hannah felt dizzy when she realized who had arrived. "York?"

After the briefest of pauses, he stepped forward. "Hannah, I'm sorry to tell you this, but one of Rob's coworkers just called. There was a fire in downtown Sugarcreek and Rob got hurt."

Dr. Ross looked so worried, so hesitant, she immediately thought the worst. "Is . . . is Rob dead?" she whispered.

York gasped. "No. No! Not at all. I think he broke his leg, but otherwise he's fine. He's been asking for you, though. Do you want to see him?"

"Of course." Turning to her family, she started to say her good-byes but then realized that they were all standing right beside her.

"We're going to the hospital, too," Mamm said.

"But that isn't necessary."

"I'm thinking it definitely is," Daed said. "If Rob is yours, then he is going to be ours one day, too. That means he needs his family around him."

"I can't fit everyone, but I have room for three more people," York said.

"You two go ahead," Daed told Calvin and Malinda. "Mamm and I will get the house put to rights and then call for a driver."

Still, Hannah hesitated. She felt frozen. A handful of questions kept repeating themselves in her head, each one hurting her heart because she didn't have any answers.

She couldn't bear the thought of being without Rob Prince.

"Danke, Daed. I'll take care of Hannah," Calvin said. When she merely stared at him, he pulled her cloak from the set of hooks by the door. "Come on, Sissy. Put on your cloak."

"What?"

He thrust the garment into her hands before reaching for his own coat and hat. "Put it on. Now. We need to go."

"Jah. All right."

With fumbling fingers, she fastened her cloak around her shoulders. Then, after her mother gave her an encouraging nod, Hannah pulled herself together and followed Calvin, York, and Malinda out the door.

She wasn't alone. Her family was supporting her and helping her.

Even though she was worried about Rob, her spirits began to lift.

Here was what she'd been needing all along. Support and love and hope.

At last she had all three in abundance.

Chapter 15

The first thing Rob learned when he woke up was that Hannah had cried when she'd first seen him. Then, right before everyone's eyes, she pulled herself together and positioned herself by his side and refused to leave him. Later, it had taken his mother, Melissa Ross, and her mother to cajole her to get some rest.

Every time he thought about that scene, Rob felt like shaking his head in amazement. That must have been a sight to see—three such different women all working together to try to convince one petite Amish girl to do their bidding.

If he'd been awake, he would have told them all that it was a mistake to underestimate Hannah Eicher. She was far tougher than most people realized.

Though he would have said such a thing, he also knew that he would have apologized to Hannah the moment he could. She'd already buried one fiancé; she didn't need to be frightened about the second.

Just as he smiled, he realized that he hadn't actually proposed yet. He'd wanted to. He'd been meaning to—he just hadn't found the right moment.

Boy, he needed to stop being frightened, too.

He was saved from more self-recriminations when his hospital room door opened and his parents walked in.

"Oh good," his dad said. "You're awake."

"Hi, Dad. Hey, Mom."

His mother walked over to his side and kissed his brow. "How are you feeling?"

He shrugged. "Kind of like I fell about fifteen feet last night."

She visibly winced. "That isn't funny."

"But it's true. I'm okay, though."

His father approached his other side and placed a hand on the side of his neck. "The doctor said that you are a lucky man. All you have is a broken leg and a couple of cuts and bruises."

"And burns, Ted." His mom pointed to his bandaged forearms. "Don't forget the burns."

"Right." Looking even more worried, his father gazed at Rob's bandages. "Our boy has got his fair share of burns."

"No, Dad was right in the first place, Mom. It could have been a lot worse. I'm lucky. I guess the Lord was looking out for me."

Her expression softened. "I know He was, in more ways than one. He gave you Hannah."

He couldn't resist smiling, even though he probably looked like a besotted fool. "A nurse this morning told me that you met Hannah last night."

"We sure did," his father said. "She is really something, isn't she?" he asked with a grin. "She looks so meek and mild, but she's tough as nails. She didn't want to leave your side, not even for a few minutes."

"That sounds like Hannah."

"She's really lovely, Rob," his mother added.

Rob peered at the open door. "Where is she now? Did she go home to sleep?"

"I think so. Your neighbors took her home."

"Melissa and York?" he asked, just to be sure.

"Yep," his dad answered. "She didn't want to go, but your mom, Hannah's mother, and Melissa ganged up against her." He visibly shuddered. "I tell ya what, I don't know of anyone who would've won that fight."

"I like her, Rob," his mother said softly. "She's everything you said she was and then some."

Though he didn't need his parents' approval, it was great to have. "I told you she was special."

"I know. But it was still a surprise. I certainly didn't want to like her after she broke your heart."

His body was hurting and his mind was still a little fuzzy, but he was clearheaded enough to defend Hannah. "Everything about us was new and different for her. I don't think we can blame her for being cautious. Now I realize that it just wasn't the right time."

"What are you going to do now?"

"Ask her to marry me."

His parents gaped at him.

His dad recovered first. "And when are you going to do this?"

"As soon as I can get a ring." He knew, because she'd grown up Amish, that she wouldn't expect one, but he wanted them to spend the rest of their lives together. And because of that, he wanted her to wear his ring.

"Do you want some help?"

"I can buy my own ring, Dad."

"I know, Son. I meant, do you want us to do your shopping? We can go to the store and send you pictures."

"Then you can pay us back," Mom said, just as if ring shopping was exactly the project they needed.

Though everything inside of him was shouting that he wanted to be the one to do the groundwork, he also realized that he wasn't going to be able to do that anytime soon with a cast on his leg. "Thanks."

"So that's a yes?"

"Yeah."

In her typical way, his mother got out a little notepad from her purse. "Tell me what you have in mind and we'll go from there. I mean, if you know."

"I know." He started describing the white gold diamond engagement ring that he'd been imagining on Hannah's finger.

Mom wrote everything down, and to her credit, she didn't say a word, but his father looked doubtful. "You sure about this? It sounds pretty plain."

"She might not be Amish anymore, but she isn't fancy, Dad. I'm sure."

Dad pulled on his jacket. "Expect a call from us in a couple of hours."

"Wait, you're going right this minute?"

"Christmas is in two days, Rob," his father replied. "Of course we're going right now."

His mom patted his arm. "Keep your phone handy."

"I'll do my best," he murmured as they walked out the door, just as Trudy was walking in.

"Here you are!" she said, looking like a Christmas elf, dressed in red and green scrubs. "You look much better."

"Thanks. I feel better."

"Sleep always does a world of good, doesn't it?" she asked

as she held his wrist and took his pulse. "Now, Hannah's outside again. Are you ready to see her?"

"Of course."

After taking his blood pressure and examining his arm, she winked. "That's what I thought. I'll bring you something to eat in an hour or so."

He was just about to ask why he had to wait so long when Hannah came in.

And then he forgot all his words.

"Look at you." She was dressed in loose jeans, a long-sleeved button-down, and a forest green cardigan over it. She had socks and loafers on.

All in all, she looked rather like a college girl. Fresh and excited. Shy. Her head wasn't covered by a *kapp*. Instead, she'd pulled her hair into a ponytail. It hung down her back.

"I know." Looking both excited yet embarrassed, she bit her lip. "After my parents took me to talk to the bishop, I asked Melissa to take me shopping. What do you think?"

"I think you look beautiful." Worried that she was trying to change too quickly, he said, "Hannah, you don't have to wear jeans right now. I mean, you could still wear a dress if you would be more comfortable. . . . "

She shook her head. "I've been thinking about this for some time." Lowering her voice, she whispered, "And I actually did wear jeans a time or two during my run-around time. I like them."

Only Hannah! "Well, I meant what I said then. You look beautiful. Gorgeous, even."

"Truly?"

He nodded. "But you've always been beautiful to me."

"Is it prideful to admit that I've known that?" Before he could shake his head, she looked down at her feet. "I mean, I'm not saying that I thought I was beautiful, just that I knew you thought so."

"I guess I should be embarrassed that I was so obvious, but I'm too glad to see you."

Her eyes filled with worry again. "I wish you hadn't gotten so hurt."

"The doctor said I'm going to be fine. I'll probably be released in the morning."

"And then?"

"And then, I hope we'll get to spend some time together. Maybe even Christmas?"

"I'd like that, Rob."

Gazing at her, he took in the way her hair looked in a ponytail, how she looked so fresh and English but still very much like the same Hannah he'd first met.

They were different now but essentially still the same. Everything inside of him breathed a sigh of relief. He didn't want to wait any longer for her. Didn't want to wait any longer to plan a future together. "Good."

She carefully sat down next to him and clasped his hand in between hers. "At first, when I heard you'd gotten hurt . . . I was so afraid."

"I know. I'm sorry you had to worry."

"I had to keep reminding myself that you weren't Paul, and that firefighting is your job."

"That's right. I've gone through a lot of training. In addition, I'm still the low guy on the totem pole. That means the other guys stay by my side and help me. We don't do anything when we're fighting a fire that hasn't been carefully mapped out first. As much as that can be done."

"That's what your parents told me."

"Really?" When she nodded, he grinned. "That's a change, isn't it? They weren't real happy about this new job of mine."

"They were nice to me and they got along with my parents." She raised her eyebrows. "I hardly knew what to think about that."

He held out his hand to her. "I'm thinking we should simply count our blessings."

Perching on the chair next to him, she covered his hand with both of hers. "Indeed. We have so many things to be thankful for right now. I feel very blessed."

Epilogue

One year later

"You make a lovely Christmas bride, Hannah," her daed whispered as they stood in front of the closed doors leading into the church's sanctuary.

"Danke, Daed," Hannah whispered, feeling tears in her eyes. It was a year after Rob's accident and the Christmas when they all made so many changes.

She had finally started living again, her parents had started accepting the present instead of longing for the past, and Rob had found balance in his life.

He now only worked at the firehouse twenty-five hours a week and devoted the rest of his time to writing and being with her.

She'd also made some changes. She still worked for Melissa and York but now wasn't their full-time nanny; instead, she just worked three days a week. She'd begun to realize that she needed to spend some time learning how to fit into an English world while still remaining connected to her Amish roots.

All of their friends and family helped her and Rob, too. It was as if they had suddenly realized they needed to stop worrying about what was "right" and "wrong" and concentrate instead on looking for blessings.

All that was why Hannah was now wearing a beautiful white satin wedding gown and standing at the entrance to the church. Rob had told her that they could have any kind of wedding she wanted—from a simple, very small ceremony with just their family, to a quick wedding on a beach, to whatever she wanted.

But she wanted this—to make a grand entrance, symbolizing her fresh start in life with her husband.

Slowly the doors opened. "Are you ready, Hannah?" the volunteer whispered, just as the first strands of the "Wedding March" sounded.

Peeking out, Hannah saw almost every pew in the sanctuary was filled. By their request, there wasn't designated seating for the bride and the groom. Because of that, there were *kapps* interspersed with fancy English updos. Plain black jackets and well-tailored navy suits.

But there were also lots of white roses and red poinsettias and greenery. It looked joyful and happy and Christmassy.

This was going to be her favorite day ever.

"I'm very ready, Joan," she said with a smile.

"Let's go then," Daed said. And then, just as if he'd done it a hundred times, he began a slow step forward, her hand on his arm, moving in time with the music.

And as they walked, Hannah took a moment to smile at the many faces smiling back at her.

And then she had eyes for one man only.

Rob Prince, who was standing at the front of the church. He was dressed in a black tuxedo and had a white rose in his lapel. And he was staring at her in wonder.

"Your man is smitten," Daed almost whispered, laughter in his voice as he stopped and pressed a gentle kiss on her temple. "He only has eyes for you."

As she beamed, he added, "That's how it should be. You did *gut*, Daughter. I am happy for you."

The words made her tear up just as Rob stepped forward and reached for her hand. "Hannah," he said in a low voice. "Look at you. You are beautiful."

"Thank you."

"So, are you ready to get married?"

"More than ready," she said with a laugh.

When Rob chuckled, too, the pastor shook his head in mock irritation.

But she didn't care that they weren't doing everything exactly like they were supposed to. Actually, as far as she was concerned, there wasn't anything more to say.

After all this time, God had given them a second chance. That was a blessing in itself. Yes, it was more than enough.

His Amish Angel

PATRICIA JOHNS

To my husband, my very own Happily Ever After

Chapter 1

Magdalena Lapp, or Maggie as her family called her, stood at the kitchen counter peeling apples from the cellar for Christmas strudel. The windowsill was decorated with sprigs of evergreen and candles that stood unlit at this time of day. It should have been a pleasant morning of Christmas baking and chatting with her mother, if it weren't for the trouble Maggie had gotten herself into. The bishop had come last night, and it wasn't to help her daet with the repairs after the fire in the barn or to wish them a Happy Christmas. He'd come to tell her that he and the elders knew what she'd been up to—and she'd better stop.

Outside the kitchen window, past the evergreen cover on the windowsill, December snow swirled, the wind whistling past the house. She leaned closer to the cold glass, trying to get a view of the barn. She couldn't see the part that was blackened by smoke, but Daet had gotten the fire out before it caused too much damage and this morning the men from the surrounding farms had come to help Daet with the repairs.

"You should have been thinking about your future, Maggie,"

her mamm said, her tone tight. "You're twenty-five years old, and you do something like this?"

Maggie looked back toward her mother. Levinia Lapp was a petite woman, slender through the waist and with large, dewy eyes that made her look younger than her sixty years. The *something* that Mamm referred to was adding to Maggie's already heavy reputation of being too forward, too opinionated, too brassy, to be marriageable. And at twenty-five, she was playing with a different kind of fire. She'd stopped attending the youth group two years ago when her younger sister got married. Maggie had been the oldest one there, and it was just getting embarrassing. She wouldn't meet a man there, anyway. They were all too young for her.

"I needed something that was mine—my contribution. Did you think my quilts sold for so much?" Maggie asked, putting down her knife with a click. "That was how I was making the extra money, Mamm. And it was welcome this last year, was it not? With the lost calves and last spring's drought—"

"I believed what you told me," Mamm snapped back, and she closed her eyes and sucked in a breath through her nose. She remained motionless for a moment, seeming to gather her self-restraint, then opened her eyes again. "If I'd known where that money was coming from . . . Do you think the Lord needs you to sacrifice your future for a few extra dollars? We would have managed. *What will people think?*"

What people thought—that was the most important part. Maggie had been writing a column in Morinville, Indiana's local Englisher newspaper—"Amish Advice for English Problems"—and it had been a hit. People from all over were writing in, looking for her advice on how to deal with their personal issues, and Maggie didn't hold her tongue. It was a relief to be able to say it like she saw it. She called a sow a sow and gave some solid Amish advice and a few old proverbs thrown in. She didn't use her own name, of course. They called her Miss Amish and there was no reason why anyone should have found out who Maggie was. After the bishop's lengthy lecture about the proper meekness of Mary in the Christmas story, he'd let slip that Atley Troyer was the one who had clued them in to her column . . . Atley—the bishop's nephew who'd broken her heart and moved away. How had *he* known? Was breaking her heart not enough?

"Mamm, I didn't say anything that went against the church, or that would embarrass anyone," Maggie replied. "In my column, I answered their questions honestly, and I said what we believe. That's it. I have nothing to be ashamed of."

"It's not the words you used, but the pride!" her mother said. "Maggie, you put yourself before the eyes of countless Englishers! You made yourself into a . . . a—"

"I used a fake name," Maggie cut in. "And no one knew who I was, so I wasn't before anyone's eyes."

"And lying about who you were." Her mother threw up her hands. "That doesn't improve it. You're a baptized member of the church. . . . Oh, no—"

"What?" Maggie picked up the knife and apple again and continued to peel.

"Are you thinking of leaving?" Mamm's face visibly paled.

"No." Maggie sighed. "Mamm, I'm an Amish woman, and I love our life. Why else would I write about our ways?"

But she'd written about their Amish ways without church approval, and Maggie knew she'd been wrong there. If she hadn't been baptized yet, then it would have been different. But she'd made her choice and joined the church—the rules applied to her most strictly.

The writing had been a blessed relief. She'd sat out in the barn, her pen and a pad of paper balanced on her lap as she pored over the letters that were sent to her and wrote out her answer in longhand, her thoughts flowing onto paper. When she wrote, there was no one to answer to, no one to shoot her warning glances. No one to remind her that a man didn't want a wife who had no control over her own tongue. Maggie's problem had never been a lack of control over her own words, just a lack of proper Amish meekness that would keep those words inside of her. And at twenty-five with no offers of marriage in the offing, it would seem that the warnings had been right.

"You're too much like your aunt Ruth," Mamm said miserably. "You must try harder, Maggie. If you don't, you'll end up an old maid, just like her. Alone. Lonely."

"She's also smart as a whip and rather funny," Maggie said, shooting her mother a conciliatory smile.

"Without children," her mother retorted. "Without a family. Are you really going to argue that she's better off single?"

No. Maggie wasn't going to do that, because she knew that her aunt hadn't wanted to end up this way. It had just happened. There was always someone left over, and when enough harvests went by with the available men marrying other girls . . . Maggie understood it all too well. She was living it.

Boots thunked against the outside steps. The men would come back for lunch soon enough, and they'd have a kitchen filled with hungry stomachs to feed. A man's work was worth at least the food it took to fuel him, and their neighbors had come out this frigid December morning mere days before Christmas to help them in their time of need. Maggie put down her knife once more and headed over through the mudroom just as there was a knock at the door. She pulled open the door, and when she saw the man on the stoop her heart stuttered to a stop in her chest. He was clean shaven, with wind-reddened cheeks, broad shoulders, and that familiar little half-smile she knew so well.

"Atley," she breathed.

"Maggie," he replied. "I'm sorry to just appear on your step like this, but—"

He stopped, not finishing whatever he was going to say. Icy wind whipped into the house, and Maggie stepped back to allow him to enter, shutting the door after him. She crossed her arms under her breasts, eyeing him. He'd left town with his family five years ago, managed to reveal her Miss Amish writing from Bountiful, Pennsylvania, and now was back?

"What are you doing here?" she demanded, then felt the heat hit her cheeks. That was rude. "I mean . . . No, that is what I meant. Atley, why are you here?"

"I came to spend Christmas with my uncle," he replied. "And when I arrived, my aunt told me that everyone was here. The fire—"

"Yes, the fire. They're fixing things up now. It wasn't too bad, which is a blessing." She swallowed, looking up at him as her mind spun to catch up. "I see you're not married," she added. The clean shave made that plain enough, but it mattered. When he'd written her that letter telling her it was over, he'd mentioned another girl in Bountiful—someone more appropriate.

"Not yet." He licked his lips. "You?"

"No." Her single status was a sharper jab than his. A man could put off marriage all he wanted—there would be girls enough willing to marry him if he was financially stable. But a woman? No, she hadn't had another offer of marriage after his. "And I think you know more about me than you pretend, Atley Troyer."

He dropped his gaze. "You mean the newspaper. I'm sorry about that. If I caused you any trouble—"

"You declared your love, moved away, broke up with me, and then have the nerve to tell your uncle, the bishop, that I have one pleasure left in life. Did it ever occur to you, Atley, that you could have simply kept quiet?"

Atley was silent for a moment; then he sighed. "I'm sorry."

"Not as sorry as I am," she retorted.

"I saw the paper, and I thought it was interesting that an Amish woman would write for Englishers. We were all following it. You're more famous than you think. I finally realized it was you, and I mentioned it to my father. He told my uncle"— he caught her eye and smiled wryly—"and the chain of gossip wasn't your point."

"How did you know?" she asked, lowering her voice. "I used a false name, I never breathed a word about it to anyone in our community—"

"It was some advice you gave a girl whose boyfriend wanted more from her than she felt comfortable giving. And you said that she should be careful because a boy from next door could sweep you off your feet, promise to marry you at the celery harvest, and tell you that your fingertips tasted like strawberries"—he stopped, lifted his shoulders—"and it was still possible for that boy to leave you behind, move on to another girl."

Maggie's throat tightened. "It was good advice. She needed to hear it."

"That was *me*," he said. "I said that about your fingertips. By the stream. When we'd sit there—" He cleared his throat. "And that's when I knew that Miss Amish was you. I spoke to my father before I'd thought it through," he said. "And for that I apologize. You're right—I should have kept quiet. I came back to celebrate Christmas with my uncle and aunt, but also to see you—"

"Maggie, who is it?" Mamm came into the mudroom and stopped short, her eyes widening. "Atley Troyer."

Mamm's voice didn't sound fully welcoming at first, but after she swallowed and pasted a smile on her face she adjusted her tone. "Atley," she repeated. "*Freulich Kristag.* Happy Christmas. Come inside—"

"No, I only came by to say hello," Atley said quickly. "I thank you, though. I meant to head on over to the barn and lend a hand."

"It's kind of you, Atley," Mamm said, her smile relaxing. "We had no idea you were even here—"

"Maggie can explain," he said, putting a hand on the doorknob. His dark gaze swung back over to Maggie again, and she noted that he'd changed over the last five years. He was broader, stronger, definitely older. But those eyes were the same, and they still managed to pin her to the spot, whether she liked it or not.

And she didn't like it. She'd rather resent him than forgive him. She'd rather remember his betrayal than see those dark eyes meeting hers again, bringing up old feelings that she'd buried long ago, stamping dirt over top of them and letting the weeds take root.

Atley opened the door and stepped back outside, the wind whisking past him and making the gooseflesh stand up on her arms.

"We'll see you at lunch, then," Mamm said, and she put a hand on Maggie's elbow, giving her a firm squeeze.

"We'll see you at lunch," Maggie echoed, and she watched Atley as he tramped through the spinning snow, back out to his horse and buggy. Another gust of wind took her breath away, and she swung the door shut.

"Maggie?" Mamm said quietly.

"He didn't have to tell his father anything, or Bishop Graber." She brushed past her mother and went back to the counter where the apples waited. Atley had known it was her, and he could have simply kept the secret in honor of whatever it was he'd felt for her all those years ago, even if whatever he'd felt hadn't been enough to keep him.

Atley had betrayed her once five years ago when he broke her heart, and he'd done it again when he exposed her secret and took away the last place she could speak her mind. A good Amish woman might be meek like Mary in the Christmas story, but Maggie hadn't been doing any harm. And that vent for her thoughts and ideas had been slammed shut on her, and she could already feel the pressure inside of her mounting.

He could have kept quiet!

Atley dumped the last shovelful of wet ash into the wheelbarrow, knocking against metal with a satisfying clang. The fire had broken out when a kerosene lantern had fallen into a box of feed and several stalls had been burned, and the northwest corner of the barn had been burned black before they managed to put it out. Looking around at the damage, Atley could only think that the Lapps would be grateful it hadn't been worse.

He'd worked in this barn before . . . years ago, when he had been taking Maggie home from singing every week. He used to help her daet on the farm from time to time—an excuse to see her, mostly. And looking around at the familiar space made sadness well up inside of him. He'd had hopes back then that included Magdalena, even though his parents had been against the match from the beginning.

The other men had gone into the house for lunch, and since Atley's aunt had fed him a quick meal before he'd headed on over to the Lapp farm this morning, he said he wasn't hungry and wanted to keep working.

The other men had exchanged a look and didn't argue it—they knew his history with Maggie Lapp, and perhaps they understood. He'd rather be hungry than face her with an audience. There was too much unsaid between them.

Atley scooped up another shovelful of ash and dumped it into the wheelbarrow. He worked methodically, pausing to sweep up the smaller cinders into a pile before he slid the shovel underneath it. There was a burned hole in the wall, and snow blew inside, melting on the floor as he worked.

His mind wasn't on the work, though. He was still thinking of Maggie and the fact that she'd been the writer behind that column. He'd been reading it for the better part of a year before he'd realized who was writing it, and in that time he'd grown to appreciate that compassionate yet direct voice from the newspaper. And he wasn't the only one. The young people from his community liked reading that column, too, and they'd gone so far as to have a new copy of the *Morinville Chronicle* mailed to them in Bountiful, Pennsylvania, regularly, and it was passed around from house to house as the teens read "Amish Advice for English Problems."

The writer was sensitive, funny, insightful. She was most definitely Amish—they'd all recognized that right away—but she was compassionate to the Englisher problems, too. She genuinely seemed to care, and reading the column, one couldn't help but feel that she'd care about any of her readers' problems. A couple of the Amish teens had even written to her, asking her advice, and she'd answered one of them. It had been a question from a young man about whether or not a girl was interested in him and whether he should ask to drive her home from singing.

Is she kind? Miss Amish had asked. *Does she care about your feelings, or does she just wait for you to do things for her? Will she be there for you when you need love and support, or will she expect you to always be perfect to earn her affection? Kindness matters. Only ask to drive her if you are certain about that quality in her character.*

It had been a good answer, and her simplicity in breaking down the problem made fans of all of them.

So when he finally made the connection that Maggie Lapp was Miss Amish, he'd been stunned, and the words had just fallen out of him around the dinner table that night. He hadn't meant to get her into any trouble, but it would seem that he had. But maybe he should have made the connection earlier. Whoever was writing for an Englisher paper had to be a brave woman—a woman unafraid of declaring her opinion to anyone at large—and that didn't describe very many Amish women.

The barn door opened behind him, and Atley turned. Maggie came inside, a basket over her arm. She shook the snow from her shawl that she'd draped over her head and dropped it down around her shoulders. He stood there watching her, uncertain of what to say, when she met his gaze and gave him a curt nod.

"I told my mother you wouldn't want to see me, but she insisted that I bring you your lunch."

Atley smiled wanly at her dry humor. "I didn't mean to put you to extra work."

"Sometimes we succeed where we don't even mean to," she replied with a small smile.

Atley leaned the shovel against the wall and pulled off his work gloves. She always did have a teasing remark on the tip of her tongue. The barn was cold with the wind whipping in through that charred hole, and he angled around the half-burned stall and met her by the hay bales—thankfully safe from the fire.

"It was nice of you to bring it," he said, accepting the basket and peeking under the towel. There were some dinner rolls visible and two bowls covered by plates. He could smell the fried chicken, though, and his stomach growled.

"You could have come in," she said as he sat down on a bale and pulled the plates off the bowls. There was fried chicken, as he'd smelled, and a bowl of Waldorf salad.

"I thought I'd just get more work done." He didn't meet her gaze. Instead, he pulled out a fork and cloth napkin, then bowed his head for a silent prayer.

"You're helping us out," she said once he'd raised his head. "And that's worth a meal, at least, Atley."

"I . . ." He paused, met her gaze. "I did want to see you."

Was he wrong to admit to that? He'd willingly come to his uncle's farm, right next to the Lapp land. He'd known he'd see her, and he'd even been hoping to. He'd been unfair to her five years ago, and he hadn't been able to let go of the nagging guilt. He hadn't been able to commit to another woman, and he had to wonder if his reluctance was rooted in his guilt. Maybe God wanted him to make amends with Maggie first.

"Why?" she asked, then shook her head. "You made your choice, and it wasn't me."

"I was wrong in how I broke it off," he said. "I should have talked to you—face-to-face."

"You were in Bountiful," she replied. "I didn't expect it."

Hadn't she? She'd written him back, and her letter had torn his heart to shreds. She'd said how she loved him, how she hated him for what he'd done to her, how she'd never love another man like she'd loved him. . . . He'd kept it and read it, reread it. Finally, he'd had to burn it, hoping to put her behind him. It hadn't worked.

"I'm sorry, Maggie," he said. "I never meant to become your cautionary tale of men who break the hearts of good girls. I hate that."

"You *are* my cautionary tale," she said curtly. "Not that I need to repeat the story to the girls here. It's common knowledge."

"The column, though—" He winced. "You're a good writer. I didn't know that about you."

"Well, now the bishop has ordered me to stop writing for the *Chronicle*. It's over."

"He ordered you—" Atley heaved a sigh. Of course he would. It was untraditional, and Uncle Ben was nothing if not a guardian of the Ordnung. "You are a good writer, though."

"I'm a woman," she said, and her voice sounded hollow. "My role is not to write. My role is cook, care for the men, and teach the next generation how to do the same. Your uncle was very clear on that, as were my parents and several of the elders. Maybe I'll follow in my aunt Ruth's footsteps and teach school."

"Will you keep writing?" he asked.

"For who?" She lifted her shoulders weakly. "Not for the *Chronicle*. That has been forbidden. Not for the Amish—who would listen to me? For my children?"

"You'll marry," he said. Look at her—she was beautiful! She always had been, with the fire in her eyes. She'd always been able to make him catch his breath.

"Will I?" She dropped her gaze. "I always thought so, but I'm not meek or gentle. Not enough, at least. I think too much and I talk too much. I've tried to be better, but it doesn't work. If I was to be married, it would have happened by now."

Wasn't that what his own father had said about Maggie? Magdalena wasn't the kind of woman who could find sweet comfort in motherhood and in following her husband's leadership. She was stubborn by nature, and she was vocal. Marriage was for life with the Amish, for better or for worse. And the choice in wife was one that would follow a man for the rest of his days. Or hers. Maggie would be trouble, Atley's father assured him. And Atley had grudgingly seen his father's point. His heart could only take him so far. A marriage without prudence was doomed.

As for Maggie's marital future, all he knew was that finding her still single had been a wild, irrational relief. And he felt guilty for that, too, because he couldn't be the one to marry her.

"Your daet asked me to help him a little over Christmas," he said. "I didn't answer him yet. I wasn't sure if you'd want me to."

"If my daet needs help—"

"Maggie, I'm asking *you!*" He reached over and caught her hand. It had been by instinct, and as his fingers closed around hers he realized his mistake. It was too personal—they weren't what they used to be the last time he'd sat in this barn with her. He released her hand and pushed himself to his feet. "I've done you wrong, Maggie. I don't want to make it worse. If you want me to leave your family's farm alone, I will. I'm sure my uncle will understand. As will your daet."

"Your uncle has his own farm to run," she replied. "And we have a barn to repair before Christmas, if possible. Daet needs you."

That sounded like permission to him, and he eyed her for a moment. "I am sorry, Maggie."

"For what?" she asked. "For breaking my heart, or stealing my voice?"

For both. He just looked at her.

She gestured to the plates. "Leave the dishes when you're done eating. I'll collect them later."

"Maggie—"

"Atley, you've done enough. Help my daet to fix the barn. Then you can go back to your life in Bountiful with a clear conscience."

She rose to her feet and moved toward the door. She moved briskly, and she didn't look back.

She'd stifle here in Morinville without her letters and her column. It would be like sucking the breath right from her lungs—he could see that clear as day. And maybe that was proof that she wasn't the kind of woman for an Amish man to tie himself to. He needed a woman who was stable and sweet, honest and kind, who was satisfied with raising children and keeping a home. He needed the kind of girl she'd described in that letter, who would be the foundation he needed when times were hard.

Maggie disappeared out the barn door, and it clattered shut behind her.

She'd stifle here in Morinville, and that was his fault. Because she wasn't like the other Amish women and he'd betrayed her secret.

Chapter 2

The next afternoon, Maggie took the buggy to town to bring her newly finished quilt to Morinville Quilts and Crafts. She parked the buggy in an Amish parking area on Morinville's Main Street and attached a feed bag to her mare's muzzle, then threw a saddle blanket over her back to keep her warm in the gently drifting snow.

Maggie pulled the heavy quilt down from the buggy seat. She'd wrapped it in plastic to protect it from the weather. The Englishers would pay a fair amount for an "authentic Amish" piece of work. That meant if Amish fingers had done the stitching, women sitting in a quilting circle or hunched over a pattern in the evening, their work lit by kerosene lanterns and fingers warmed by the potbellied stove. It mattered to the English, somehow, and gave the quilt a higher price than if a skilled Englisher had made it by hand. There had been a time when that had been mildly offensive to her, but that Englisher curiosity was also why she'd been able to write her column, and Maggie couldn't resent that. Her life, her thoughts, her opinions—they were marketable, too. Not just her stitching. The Amish repre-

sented something to the Englishers that she didn't fully understand, but whatever it was had given her a voice.

That opportunity was over now, of course, and the realization slowly closed around her heart. The thrill of seeing her
words in a newspaper, seeming more important, somehow, because of the black ink and the tiny type . . . She used to love
thinking over her answers as she went about her regular work
at home, her secret time in the barn where she wrote out her
answers to the letters in careful, double-spaced handwriting.
Other women her age might be married with kinner of their
own, but she had *this*. Until Atley told on her.

Main Street was decorated for Christmas, and while the Lapp
home was only moderately decorated with a few spruce boughs
tied with red ribbons, she did enjoy the glitter of Christmas
lights in town. The shops glowed merrily, their windowpanes
lined with settling snow and shining ornaments hanging for
passersby to admire. Maggie walked down the sidewalk, her
plastic-wrapped quilt clutched in front of her, slipping past her
gloved hands so that she had to keep stopping to hoist it back
up again.

The *Morinville Chronicle* office was the first building she
passed, and she looked in the main window as she hurried on
by. It wasn't as decked out as the surrounding stores were.
There was a wreath on the door and a wood-crafted sign that
said "Freulich Kristag" with a picture of an Amish buggy beside it.

Through the window, Maggie could see the receptionist,
Karen, at her desk, but Maggie hurried on, pushing down the rising ache of sadness inside of her. She didn't want to explain yet.

Karen looked up, and Maggie ducked her head and plunged
on. Later. The last thing she wanted was to cry when she said
she had to quit, and right now that was a very real possibility.

Morinville Quilts and Crafts was two shops down the street.
She paused at the door while an Englisher woman pushed it

open, then held it for Maggie so she could go inside. That lump was still thick in her throat, and Maggie nodded her thanks, and let out a breath of relief as the warm air from the store hit her cold hands.

"Magdalena," the shopkeeper, Cherie, said with a smile. "Have you finished the quilt?"

"It's done," Maggie said.

"Just in time. I've had a few requests for Amish quilts for Christmas gifts, and I'm sure yours will sell fast." Cherie peeled back the plastic and fingered the stitching. "Beautiful as always, Magdalena. Was this a group effort, or—"

"I made it," Maggie said simply. "Alone."

Again, the Englishers liked a story with their purchase. *This quilt was made by four Amish ladies working together. They're sisters, and as they work, they sing. . . .*

But this quilt had no such story. Maggie made it alone, and as she worked she thought of answers for the questions her readers sent to her. This was the work of an Amish rebel.

Cherie wrote out a receipt and handed it over. "Well, thank you for bringing it by. I'm sure I'll get a good price for it."

"Okay." This part of the interaction was always awkward.

"Come by on Boxing Day and check to see if it's sold. I'm sure it will be. This is gorgeous."

"That's Second Christmas," Maggie said. The day after Christmas Day was spent visiting family and friends. Christmas didn't end quite so quickly for the Amish.

"Oh—right. I'm sorry, I'd forgotten about that. So the twenty-seventh, then. Or whenever you manage to make it by. I'll have your money set aside for you."

Maggie tucked the receipt up her sleeve, then wrapped her woolen shawl closer.

"Okay. Thank you."

"You're very welcome."

Maggie went back to the door and pushed back out onto the

street. Another customer was entering the shop, and Maggie glanced back. Would that be the Englisher to buy her quilt? It was hard to imagine where her handiwork ended up after it was sold, but she had a strange affection for the Englishers now after being a secret part of their lives, answering their questions, reading their letters. . . . They weren't so frightening anymore.

Cold air wrapped around Maggie's legs as she stepped back out into the street, and she tugged her shawl closer. She ducked her head against a blast of snow and headed farther down the street to a fabric shop. She wasn't going to buy anything today, but she wanted to see the new shipments all the same. It was time to get her pleasure out of the Amish pastimes again, and she used to love new fabric.

"Maggie?"

Maggie startled at the sound of Atley's voice, and she looked up to find him standing in front of her on the sidewalk. His coat was buttoned all the way up, and his hands were pushed into his pockets. The tips of his ears were red from cold, and for a moment it was like no time at all had passed. A gust of wind lifted his hat, and he pulled a hand out of his pocket to push it back down on his head.

"Atley, it's you." She wasn't sure if she sounded politely pleased to see him or not. She had no more energy to pretend— not with him.

"I didn't expect to run into you here. What are you doing?" he asked.

"I'm going to the fabric shop," she said.

"Ah." He nodded. "I was just picking up a few Christmas gifts."

He held a plastic bag in one hand, but what was inside she couldn't tell.

"Well . . . " She wasn't sure what else to say.

"Are you hungry?" he asked. "I'll buy you lunch."

Maggie hesitated. "Do we really want to do this, Atley? We don't have to pretend that everything is fine between us."

"Maybe it isn't fine, but I still miss you," he said, those dark eyes meeting hers, and she couldn't help but feel a twinge at those words.

"You have no right to miss me," she replied. "You left me. Not the other way around. If an Englisher girl asked my advice about a situation like this, I'd tell her to move on."

He dropped his gaze. "I could at least tell you what happened. I think you deserve to know."

Maggie paused at that—it was the one thing she'd wondered about most over the years. How had he gone from loving her like he had to . . . not? How had a different community changed his feelings for her so completely?

"You said me helping out was worth a meal," he added. "Come eat with me."

Atley was teasing—she could hear it in his voice. But she was also hungry, she had to admit, and Maggie glanced across the street to a restaurant. Perhaps he did owe her something, after all.

"All right," she agreed.

They waited at the curb until a few cars had passed, and then hurried across the slushy street to the other side. The restaurant was called Uncle Tom's, and it had burgers and fries—Englisher food. Atley held open the door for her, then followed her into the fragrant warmth of the restaurant. They stood by the big Englisher sign asking them to wait to be seated, and a few Englisher diners looked over at them in open curiosity. Maggie dropped her gaze, ignoring them.

A waitress came by and led them to a table next to the window. Maggie ordered a burger and fries. Atley ordered a slice of pizza.

When the waitress left them, Maggie looked out at the falling snow.

"I'm sorry that I said anything to my father," Atley began. "It was wrong of me. The thing is, you've become a bit of a celebrity in Bountiful. The young people order in the newspaper to read your column, and they pass it around to all the different homes. They like you—some of the boys are just about in love with you."

"Really." She looked over at Atley, then sighed. "But not you, apparently."

Atley winced. "I read the column, too—"

"You know what I mean. What happened? You'd asked me to marry you. We were going to tell our parents. Then, you moved with your family so your daet could work the carpentry shop with his brother and you were done."

"It wasn't quite like that," Atley said. "It was . . . more complicated."

"You said you'd explain," she prompted.

The bell over the front door dingled, and Maggie glanced up as an Englisher man stepped inside, and when he saw her a smile broke over his face. Maggie's stomach sank. It was Horace Schmidt, her editor. He was a man in his mid-thirties, thin, with one of those little beards that went around the upper lip and chin that the Englishers seemed to like. He wore a pair of thick-rimmed glasses and a cap.

Horace waved off the waitress who approached him and headed over to their table.

"Maggie!" he said, then looked over at Atley, and the men regarded each other uncertainly.

"This is my editor, Horace," Maggie said, then shot Horace a wan smile. "Horace, this is Atley Troyer. It's okay. Atley knows about my column."

"Pleasure." Horace reached over and shook Atley's hand, then pulled a manila envelope out of his coat and put it down on the table, turning his attention to Maggie. "Karen said she saw you come in here, so forgive the intrusion, but I needed to get the newest batch of letters to you."

Maggie looked at the envelope but didn't touch it. Her heart hammered in her throat.

"I can't," she whispered.

"Can't?" Horace leaned closer. "What do you mean?"

"I've been caught," she said with a weak shrug. "And the bishop has ordered me to stop writing for you."

Horace froze for a couple of beats, then nodded twice. He understood the risk here. She'd explained it rather thoroughly before she began writing for them.

"Would it help if I talked to him?" Horace asked. "You're the best columnist we've got, Maggie. If there is some way to keep you—"

"No offense, Horace, but he doesn't care about the opinions of Englishers," Maggie said with a sigh.

"So, this is it, then?" Horace asked.

"I wish I could keep writing this column, Horace. I don't think there's much hope."

Horace regarded her for a moment and tapped the envelope with two fingers. "Take it with you. If you can't write the column, I'll understand. But if you find a way to continue—" He let it hang.

Maggie pulled the envelope into her lap and glanced up at Horace.

"I don't know what to say," she said. "I can't promise anything."

Horace crossed his fingers. "There will be no hard feelings, if you can't. But I'm hoping for the best."

Atley had remained silent, but she could feel his eyes on her. Horace gave her a nod and headed back toward the front door again. The envelope was deliciously thick, and she fiddled with the flap. She'd been forbidden, but she was curious about the newest batch of letters.

Dear Miss Amish . . .

What advice would she give to an Amish woman in her situation? *Follow the rules. Find pleasure in the life you were born to. Weigh the benefits. What life do you want? If you want an Amish life, you know what you have to do.*

Except she'd never anticipated feeling quite like this—the longing to continue writing a column the bishop had already forbidden. Having a voice that people listened to was more intoxicating than she'd realized, and she couldn't go back to not knowing how it felt.

It was like the Tree of Knowledge. She now knew too much.

Atley watched as the Englisher man left the restaurant. He'd been so open and easy with Maggie, and Atley felt a stab of annoyance at that. Maggie and this editor seemed to be particular friends, but Atley liked it better when the Englishers were a little less candid with them. What kind of friendship did she have with this man? He couldn't ask, though. It had long ago stopped being his business.

The waitress returned with their food, putting their plates in front of them. They nodded their thanks to the young woman, and when she retreated, Atley met Maggie's gaze.

"What will you do?" he asked.

"I've been forbidden," she said curtly. "What can I do?"

That envelope lay on the tabletop next to her, and he sighed. Right. Atley bowed his head, saying a silent grace, and Maggie did the same. When they raised their heads, Atley picked up his pizza.

"You said you'd tell me what happened," Maggie said, fixing him with her clear gaze.

He had promised that . . . and in the moment when he'd said it he was anxious to just get a bit of time alone with her. But he had promised, hadn't he? How could he put all this into a simple explanation? Nothing about his feelings for her had been simple.

"I realized—" Atley began, and then he stopped. No, that wasn't the right start, either. "I had no intention of breaking things off when I left," he said instead.

"So what changed?" She picked up a fry and dipped it in ketchup, but she didn't lift it to her mouth. It just hung there over that little dish of ketchup, forgotten.

"I had time to think," Atley said. "My feelings for you were the same, but my daet sat me down and pointed out the reality of things. Feelings can only take us so far."

"And I wasn't appropriate as an Amish wife." Her voice shook.

"You're—" He licked his lips. "Maggie, you're not like anyone I've ever met! You're different. You're not a woman who loves taking care of the home."

"I cook. I clean." She shot him a sharp look.

"But you don't love it," he countered. "You don't take joy in it."

"Do you?" she snapped.

He chuckled. "Like that there—you're not like the Amish girls, Maggie. You're louder. You say more. You don't bite back your words."

She smiled bitterly but didn't answer.

"Like I said, I had some time to think," he said, lowering his voice. "My daet said that he and Mamm could never give their blessing for our marriage, and that would have complicated things for us. It wasn't fair to bring you into that kind of tension. We're very different, you and I. I want an Amish life, with an Amish woman. I want children and grandchildren. I want a carpentry shop of my own, and . . . I need a woman who wants all of that with me."

"You thought I didn't want an Amish life?" She shook her head.

"All I know is that the differences that are so appealing in the flush of young love end up making for an unhappy marriage sometimes."

She finally raised the fry to her mouth and took a bite. "Your brother, you mean."

She knew him too well, and that could be annoying, too. But she was right. They'd all been thinking of his brother who married a girl he fell in love with from a different town. No one warned him.

"Abram married Waneta, and it wasn't that she was a bad woman, exactly—"

"No, not bad," Maggie agreed. Waneta and Abram lived here in Morinville—she knew them both.

"But she wasn't inclined to be happy with him," Atley said. "They started out like we did—you know that. But it's hard to hide unhappiness, on both sides."

"I suppose."

"I talked to my brother, and he said that she wanted a different life. He wanted to farm, and she wanted to run a shop in town. He wanted lots of time with us, and she wanted more space from the family. She was less religious than he was, and . . . They were just different, Maggie."

"And you thought we'd be like them," Maggie said.

He'd feared it—that was true. Before Abram took those vows, he'd been headlong in love with Waneta. After marriage, they'd struggled. A lot. They seemed to be on better terms now, but they'd been married six years, and they were never exactly warm with each other. Mostly, Abram seemed to have just made peace with the fact that this was his wife. The thought of stumbling into his situation scared Atley more than he cared to admit to most people.

"We're different, Maggie," he said at last.

She nodded. "I heard you got engaged."

"I did," he confirmed. "She was a girl from the new community, but it didn't last."

"Why not?"

"This is getting personal," he said.

"It's all personal, Atley." She smiled slightly. "So what went wrong?"

It wasn't anything big that had slipped between him and the other girl. It was a hundred little things—and the fact that Amish didn't divorce. Marriage was for life, and an unhappy marriage was no excuse to be let free. But on top of all of that, he knew what love felt like. . . .

"She wasn't you," he said, his voice low.

Maggie met his gaze, and she didn't look surprised. Tears misted her eyes; then she blinked them back. "I'm glad you didn't get over me that quickly."

"Are you?" he asked with a low laugh.

"Yes. But all the same, I hope you find a good woman," she said. "The one who will take rare pleasure in your laundry."

Still able to get a barb in. He shot her a rueful smile. "And I will take equal pleasure in the running of a farm."

Maggie met his gaze easily. "You thought I'd go Mennonite."

"It did occur to me."

She shook her head. "Didn't you read those columns I wrote? I love our Amish ways. And perhaps there is special virtue in loving the household chores, but there are other virtues, too."

"Yah," he agreed. "There are."

But the other virtues didn't guarantee a happy marriage in the Amish ways, and he cleared his throat. They both ate for the next few minutes, but the pizza, normally a treat, didn't taste as good as he remembered it. He didn't finish the slice and pushed it aside.

"You haven't gotten married to anyone else, yet, either," Maggie said, taking a bite of her hamburger. She seemed to have more of an appetite than he did.

"It's hard to vow the rest of my life to a woman I don't know well enough," he said. "I got spooked. I'm not proud of it."

"At least I wasn't the only one," she said with a wan smile.

"You didn't get married, either," he pointed out.

She tipped her head to the side. "No, I didn't, but I did find something that I liked—something that filled my heart. I never realized it mattered to me so much, but to have things to say, and people who want to hear them. The thing is, this isn't just something to fill the emptiness of not having a husband. If I'd found this after getting married, I'd still want to do it. It's . . . it's like that first warm spring wind after a hard winter, when you can smell warmer days ahead. Words on paper feel like summer."

"Even if you'd married me—" He pressed his lips together.

"Yes," she said with a lift of her shoulders.

"It isn't our way, though," Atley argued. "Women don't do this—put themselves in the public sphere that way."

"I'm technically not," she replied. "I've hidden behind a fake name. No one knew it was me. If you'd have kept your mouth shut—"

"I know, but eventually you would have slipped. Someone would have figured you out. Writing for the Englishers . . . it isn't our way. Women do women's work. Men do men's work. And neither the men nor the women put themselves into the English spotlight. Writing for an Englisher newspaper . . . where does that land?"

"I don't know," she said. "But I was already unmarriageable before anyone knew that I was Miss Amish. I'm not quiet and shy. I'm not afraid to speak my mind. In fact, I have a hard time *not* speaking my mind! The rest of the men have realized what you did—I'm Amish to the core, but I'm not womanly enough in the Amish ways. I'm too . . . brazen."

"Is it worth giving up marriage and a family of your own?" he asked.

She was silent for a beat, and then she shook her head. "If nothing else, I've learned from Waneta. I've gotten to know her, and I've seen how hard she tried to be the wife your brother wanted. He wanted her to be stricter, more serious, more religious. And she tried! But she couldn't change herself. A woman can only pretend for so long."

"What will you do, then?" he asked quietly.

"I'm seriously considering teaching school like Aunt Ruth did," she said quietly. "Perhaps I'll start a business here in town. I have to do something, don't I? Making quilts won't be enough, not if I'm to support myself. I can't go on with my parents forever. I thought I'd found something in writing a column, but . . ."

And somehow, that rebounding spirit didn't surprise him. She'd always been strong and resourceful. Many an unmarried woman had done just as she'd suggested and simply gone about building her life alone. She found a way to be useful and did so.

But Maggie . . . sweet, beautiful Maggie . . .

"I didn't mean to waste your time—" he started.

"I'm not your problem to solve, Atley," she said, putting her hand over his. "I daresay I'm not so easy to fix. Or to match. I'll figure it out myself."

"I'm not trying to fix you," he said. He turned his hand over and ran a thumb over her soft fingers.

"Aren't you?" She pulled her hand back, and he felt a little foolish for the tender gesture. They weren't dating anymore. He had no right to all these personal questions or to hold her hand, no matter how natural it felt.

"I really am sorry that I ruined the column for you," he said.

"I know."

"Do you forgive me for that?" he asked.

"I will," she said with a quirky little smile. "Eventually."

He couldn't help but grin. That was Maggie—never saying the sweetly appropriate thing. She'd been like that as long as he'd known her, and it was why everyone loved reading her words so much. She was honest, heartbreakingly so. Hilariously so. She said it like she saw it, and while it was entertaining for an audience, it was dangerous in a wife.

His daet had been right. Maggie wasn't a traditional woman and she'd never make a traditional wife. She wanted more than the role of Amish wife could fulfill.

"Thank you for eating with me," he said.

"Thank you for lunch." She smiled—her brown eyes warming and that one dimple in her cheek deepening as her gaze met his. He knew she wasn't right for him . . . he had proof of it. So why were those old feelings flooding back in spite of all the logic in the world?

He couldn't make his brother's mistake. His heart couldn't lead him into a lifetime of regret.

Chapter 3

The next afternoon, Maggie flicked the reins and leaned back in the buggy seat. There wasn't a cloud in the sky, and the sun sparkled on all that new-fallen snow. She'd been trying not to think about Atley, but Christmas had always reminded her of him and all the hopes she'd had for the future that first Christmas they were officially courting.

Amish gifts were always small and useful, but that Christmas, Atley's gift for her was special. He'd found her a pincushion shaped like a strawberry, and he'd given it to her so that she'd remember how he liked to kiss the tips of her fingers. She still had it, hidden deep in a drawer where only she knew of its existence.

Funny that those silly words about her fingertips would have meant so much to him, too. Young love was a strange thing. It seeped into the cracks. For better or for worse. Amish girls were warned to be careful in their dating so they'd have no regrets. No one warned them that even if a girl behaved herself perfectly, only letting him kiss the very tips of her fingers, she'd never be able to scrub away the last of her feelings for him.

And now he was back—just for a few days—and she was

trying to push him from her mind. She had bigger problems right now, and the last thing she needed was to be reliving old heartbreak. She was determined to leave those days in the past. What other choice did she have?

The horse's hooves plodded in a comforting rhythm along the road. She hadn't seen a car since she'd started back from her younger sister's home. Naomi was married to a farmer, with two kinner of her own, and Naomi was pregnant again. Three years younger, and already a mamm to a toddler and a bobbily who'd just gotten her first two teeth. Naomi had more experience than Maggie did now. She was the one giving out advice about finding a husband and how to balance two children with the housework. She was the one doing her Christmas baking and putting a hand up to her head and sighing, "It's harder when you're pregnant. I get so tired out." It was Maggie helping her younger sister with housework at this delicate time, keeping her mouth shut because she had nothing to add to the conversation.

The winter wind blew cold and moist. Maggie drew her gloved hands underneath her shawl for extra protection from the elements. Was she fooling herself by thinking that her voice was worthy of being heard out there with the Englishers? Because behind a false name she could wax eloquent. In her sister's kitchen, she was less sure of herself. With her own family, simply being Amish wasn't enough if she wasn't married.

Ahead, along the side of the road, she could see a man working on a fence. His movements were slowed by the deep, wet snow, and he paused in his work, shading his eyes against the bright sunlight to look in her direction. This was the Graber property, wasn't it? The far side of it, at least. The Grabers could afford to hire some help and she was used to seeing their farmhands around, but she recognized something in that man's stance that made her heart stumble in her chest. It was Atley. He didn't seem to recognize her, though.

He turned back to his work again, pulling out a hammer and after some fiddling giving some solid, echoing thwacks. Farther into the field, there was a feeder overflowing with hay, and cattle surrounded it, tails flicking. A curious steer was standing closer to the broken fence. Given a chance, it would make a run for the other side of the road.

As Maggie approached, she reined in her horses and watched for a moment while Atley worked. The steer walked closer, and Atley looked from the steer toward her and shot her a grin.

"I thought that was you," he said. "So you drive yourself around now, do you?"

"I'm twenty-five," she replied. "I might as well."

The steer angled toward the sagging part of the fence.

"Hey! Get back!" Atley barked, and the animal stopped; then Atley turned back to her. "Did you open the envelope?"

"What?" Maggie tied off the reins and tossed the lap blanket off so that she could get down from the buggy.

"The envelope—the one the Englisher fella gave you," he said. "Did you open it?"

Maggie felt some heat in her cheeks. "Yah."

She'd gone out to the barn on her way for gathering eggs and opened it out there.

"And?" he prodded. "Look, if we're not going to get any more columns, at least satisfy my curiosity. What was in the letters?"

Maggie chuckled. "Watch out. The cow—"

Atley turned and waved his hand at the approaching animal. "Get back! Hya!"

The steer was getting braver now, and Maggie looked up and down the road. They were alone. She sighed and pulled up her skirt to her knees as she stepped into the deeper snow.

"Maggie, you don't have to—" he started, and then when she took a long step over the ditch he shot out a hand and caught her, tugging her against him as she landed. She let out a laugh and looked up into his face. His cheeks were red from cold, and their breath mingled in a cloud together between them.

"You need help," she said.

He released her, but his dark gaze followed her as she stepped around him. She bent and picked a reed that hung broken from the ditch, and she thwacked the steer's nose with it. The steer took a step back.

"That does help," Atley said, and he turned back to mending the fence. He put two nails between his lips and started hammering again. He glanced up at her, then said past the nails, "Well?"

"The letters, you mean?" she said, and she waved the stiff reed at the cow again warningly. "Well, one was from a girl who said that she wanted to get married, but her boyfriend wanted to live together first. She wasn't sure what to do."

"Ah." Atley straightened. "What would your advice be?"

"I always tell the readers what we do as Amish," she said. "I'd tell her that we get married if we're serious and break up if we're not. Period. We don't play with anything in between."

"Right." He met her gaze. "So your advice would be . . . "

"To either get married or move on," she said. "Of course."

"And the heartbreak?" he asked. "That's what's stopping her, most likely."

"Heartbreak, like hard work, can't be avoided if you're going to do the right thing."

"Would you say that?" he asked.

"Of course."

Atley took a nail from between his lips and moved down the rail. "Why do the Englishers like your advice, I wonder? It goes against their ways."

"They come to me for a reason," she said. "Maybe they like things a little more defined, after all."

"Maybe she wanted to be told to break it off and it was easier than making the choice herself," Atley replied.

"Maybe."

Atley had broken it off with her . . . and then again with the girl he'd been courting in Bountiful. He seemed willing to take the emotional beating that came with hard choices. But Maggie could sympathize with a girl caught between the boy she loved and the life she wanted. It wasn't an easy position to be in.

Atley hammered another nail firmly into the wood before he straightened. "Any other letters?"

"An older woman who had a misbehaving grandson," she said. "He's ten, and horribly rude. Won't listen to adults, swears, and defies guidance."

Atley raised his eyebrows.

"I can't answer that one," she said with a small smile.

"Because you don't have children?" he asked.

"There is that," she agreed. "Have you seen the men younger than you with kinner of their own?"

"Yah." He looked up at her, and their eyes met. He smiled ruefully. "They're men with families already, and I'm . . . wasting time."

"It isn't so simple, though, is it?" she countered.

"No, not so simple," he agreed.

But it was easier for him—he was a man. He didn't come with an expiry date attached. He could decide to marry at any time, if he were less afraid of marrying wrong.

"I'm better with the teenagers' questions, really," Maggie said. "I've been their age before. With parenting questions— I'm no expert. But it's more than that. Sometimes we can't say what we Amish would do. With that boy, I'd tell her to whip him. I gave that advice once, and Horace said I can't say that. He had me answer a different letter instead."

"You can't say it, even if it's honest Amish advice?" he said.

"Apparently." She shrugged. "If that child were raised Amish, the whipping wouldn't even be necessary. He'd know better at this point."

"Yah," he agreed.

Atley dropped his hammer headfirst into his pocket and took a high step through the deep snow, coming closer to her.

"What other letters?" he asked.

"A boy . . . " She licked her lips. "He didn't have much money but wanted to get his sweetheart a gift."

"Ah." Atley was close enough to her that she could feel the warmth of his breath in the air between them. "That's a problem as old as time."

"Yah," she agreed.

"Well?" His dark gaze moved over her face. "What would you tell him?"

"What would you?" she countered.

"Me?" He laughed softly. "I'm not Miss Amish."

"Still, you were a boy once," she said. He'd been a handsome boy with eyes that made her melt into a puddle.

"I don't know what I'd advise, really," he said. "I remember giving you something sentimental and silly. You probably find it funny now."

"I have it in my dresser drawer," she breathed. "In the back corner. It's safe there."

"I'm embarrassed about it now," he said.

"It was perfect. It reminds me—" She stopped. "It reminded me of sweet days in the barn loft with the hay tickling my legs and you—"

She stopped, not wanting to say exactly what it reminded her of. But she could vividly remember the way he'd hold her fingers and kiss the tips, his hat on the hay beside them, their fingers twined together. . . . His lips had been so soft, and even as she remembered those hazy days her breath caught in her throat.

He dropped his gaze, smiling slightly. "I was laughable."

"You loved me. . . . "

His gaze flickered up to her again, and his dark eyes were filled with tenderness. "Yah, Maggie. I did love you."

Atley reached out and caught her hand. They were both in gloves, so she couldn't feel his skin against hers, but she licked her lips and looked up tentatively.

"If love had been enough, Maggie . . . " he murmured.

But it hadn't been. She tugged her hand free of his. Her feet were cold in her boots, and some snow had drifted in over the tops of them.

"I need to go home," she said.

"Right. Yah." He cleared his throat. "I was going to help out your daet this afternoon. We're going to finally patch that hole in the wall before a storm comes in."

"Do you want a ride back?" she asked.

He smiled that relaxed, boyish grin of his. "Yah, if you're offering."

It was like nothing had changed, and her heart skipped a beat like back in the days when they were sneaking around to see more of each other and parking the buggy under some trees to get a few minutes before he had to drop her off after singing. . . .

Except they weren't young anymore, life had only gotten more complicated, and love hadn't been enough. Whatever this was—memories, torment—it had to stop. Her life might not be what she'd hoped, but she had to move on.

Atley hopped across the ditch and held out a hand. Maggie eyed him, then looked down into the slushy marsh between them. She squinted into the sunlight, her dark hair shining. She was beautiful—more than he remembered. Back then, she'd been a girl, barely a woman, but now she'd matured, he found himself looking at her differently.

She was wrong for him—anyone could tell him that. But

when it came to Maggie, he couldn't look away. Those dark eyes, the lustrous hair that he could only see a glimpse of before it disappeared beneath her white kapp . . . And then there was that one dimple in her cheek that had always made him want to make her smile so he could see it.

"I'll catch you," he said.

She smiled halfway. "You'd better not drop me, Atley Troyer. That ditch is all slush."

He shot her a grin. She wasn't very big compared to him, and the last five years of hard work had hardened him into manhood. He certainly wouldn't drop her.

"Come on. Jump."

"I'm serious," she said.

"So am I. I've caught beams heavier than you. Come on."

Maggie eyed him skeptically for a moment. "Are you ready?"

"Jump already!" He laughed.

She leapt, and he reached out, caught her arm as her foot came down onto solid ground, and pulled her against his chest. Her eyes widened as she landed against him, her chest rising and falling with her quickened breath. Her gaze met his, and he felt a smile tug at his lips.

"See?" he said. She felt good in his arms. Too good . . . "I'm not exactly an old man yet, Maggie."

She didn't answer, and he was about to let her go but couldn't quite make himself do it. She was warm and soft, and she smelled ever so faintly like fresh baking. She'd always smelled good, like sunshine and vanilla.

"Atley—" she began, and his gaze flickered down to her lips.

He'd missed her so much more than he'd realized, and as he stood here with her lips so close to his the only thing he could seem to think about was dipping his head down and catching them. But he'd never kissed those lips before—not even back when they were dating.

The sound of a car's engine floated on the wind, and he shut his eyes, then dropped his arms. A car slowed as it passed the buggy, the occupants looking out the window at them, and he pressed his lips together. The Englishers were always so curious, staring at regular Amish folk like they were animals in a zoo. But maybe that was a veiled blessing. He and Maggie were out in public, and he shouldn't be thinking those kinds of thoughts about her anyway.

"We should get back," he said gruffly.

"Yah." Maggie turned toward the buggy, and he felt like miles had suddenly slipped between them.

He'd upset her. He could feel it, and he inwardly chastised himself. What was he doing? Would he really have kissed her, if that car hadn't interrupted them? It would have been stupid, and she likely wouldn't have forgiven him. He was the one who'd broken her heart all those years ago, after all. And he couldn't offer her anything more now.

The horses shuffled their hooves, and Atley made a point of keeping his hands at his sides as he and Maggie made their way through the snow back to the buggy. She hoisted herself up without any help from him, and he pulled himself up after her, settling next to her in the seat.

"Maggie, back there—" He winced. "I hope you don't think that I . . . That we . . . I hope you don't . . . " He didn't have the words, but he wanted to fix this, somehow.

"We need to be more careful," she said simply.

"I've missed you," he admitted.

Maggie looked over at him, sadness welling in her eyes. "I'm glad you did. It's only right."

She flicked the reins and the horses started onto the road again with a jerk. The wheels crunched over the icy gravel.

"Why did you come for Christmas?" she asked with a sigh. "Of all times, Atley?"

"My uncle asked if I'd—" He stopped. He knew what she was saying. He'd known that he'd see her, and Christmas, of all times of the year, would be difficult.

"Did you think it would be easy seeing each other again?" She fixed him with those glittering dark eyes, and he wasn't sure what answer she wanted.

"No, not easy," he said. "I've been reading your column, after all."

"What does that mean?" She flicked the reins, her movements practiced.

"Maggie, we all fell halfway in love with you reading that column," he said with a low laugh. "I'm no exception."

She didn't answer, but her brow furrowed. He wasn't explaining himself very well, and to any other Amish woman that would sound like a proposal. Who was he fooling? Maybe it sounded that way to her, too. Except she didn't look at him again. She kept her gaze riveted to the road.

"I'm looking for some human foibles in you," he went on. "I'm looking for the real woman, because Miss Amish is just a little too—"

He stopped. Alluringly open. Intoxicatingly honest. An Amish woman with an English boldness about her. She was all wrong for him, always had been. So why couldn't he just let her go, move on with his life, and find that sweet Amish girl he knew he needed?

"But you know that I'm not what you want. You've known that for years," she countered.

"You want the truth?" he asked.

"I see little reason to ask for anything else," she replied. He'd annoyed her, and somehow he liked that. It made this easier. She wasn't like the other girls, breathlessly awaiting some declaration of feeling from him.

"I thought I'd find you with another man standing guard and it would help me to picture you differently. I'd stop remembering you as . . . mine."

"I am different now," she said. "Even without a guard. And I'm most certainly not yours."

"Yah." He chuckled softly. This was what he'd come for—a forthright tongue-lashing. Her gaze flickered over toward him, and he sighed. "Maggie, I thought I could set whatever I felt for you to rest. I haven't moved on. I should have been able to. It's been a long time. The fact that I couldn't marry a very sweet girl just because she wasn't you—"

He stopped. He didn't want to say all of this, expose himself. This was supposed to be a private affair where he got to see Maggie again in her life, as she was, and maybe that would help him to make his peace with it all—see how right his father had been.

And his father *had* been right, but somehow, that didn't fix it.

"And has this helped?" she asked, her voice tight.

"Not a lot," he admitted. As if almost kissing her on the side of the road weren't proof enough.

The horses knew their way home, and without any urging from her, they turned into the Lapps' drive. She drove in silence as the buggy's wheels rattled over the icy gravel drive. Finally, she reined in next to the buggy barn. Another buggy was already parked under the visitors' shelter, and they both looked instinctively toward the house.

"I'll have to help my mother serve the guests," she said.

"I'll unhitch. You go ahead," Atley replied.

"Are you sure?"

He shot her a grin. "Let me do this much."

Maggie turned toward the house, the side door opened. Atley recognized his brother immediately, and he frowned. Abram might live in Morinville, but he wasn't supposed to be here this Christmas. He spotted them and headed in their direction with a cordial smile.

"Hey, little brother!" Abram said, and he clapped an arm around Atley's shoulder, giving him a rough hug.

"Abram," he said, hugging his brother back. "Freulich Kristag! I didn't think I'd be seeing you and Waneta this trip. You decided to stick around?"

"Are Waneta and the kinner inside?" Maggie asked.

"No, they, uh—" Abram cleared his throat and dropped his arm. "They're with Waneta's aunt in Pennsylvania."

"Oh." Maggie nodded, her smile faltering. "Right. Well, Freulich Kristag. To your Waneta and the kids, too."

"I'll let them know. To you, too."

"I'll just head in, then. . . . " Maggie met Atley's gaze.

"I'll unhitch. Go on in," Atley said. "Abram will help me, right?"

"Of course," his brother said.

Maggie headed toward the house, and Abram fell in beside Atley as they unhitched the horses together.

"It's good to see you, Brother," Abram said. "You'll look better with a married man's beard, though."

"Yah, pester me about marriage instead of explaining yourself," Atley retorted now that Maggie was out of earshot.

"I heard about the fire," Abram said, his tone chilling. "I'm here to lend a hand. It's what neighbors do."

"It is. But husbands and wives normally travel together over Christmas."

Abram fell silent; the only sound was the jingle of breeching as Abram pulled it off the horse's back.

"Abe?" Atley turned, looking his brother in the face. "Are you two separated then?"

"No, we're not separated," Abram sighed.

"Then why are you spending Christmas apart?"

"I'm here to help," Abram replied.

"That sounds like a lie."

Abram's face colored and he scowled in Atley's direction.

"Will you press me to speak of personal matters between my wife and me, little brother?" Abram snapped. "We fought. She's taking some space. That's it. Not that it's your business."

And maybe it wasn't, but Atley did care. They carried the saddles and breeching into the stable and put them away. The brothers worked quickly—they both knew their way around the Lapp stable; it was a regular stop for church services.

"Is it that bad, Abe?" Atley asked.

"You're single. You don't get it," Abram said. "Just do your duty and find a wife of your own and leave me to mine."

"I'm glad to see you all the same," Atley said as they went back out to bring the horses in for hay and water.

"Don't tell Mamm and Daet about this when you go back," Abram said. "I'll sort it out."

He'd have to. There was no divorce for the Amish. There were a few couples who separated, but that was only in extreme cases. They weren't permitted to marry again until one of them died.

"What happened?" Atley asked as he closed the last stall door.

"I can't make her happy," Abram replied. "She calls me obstinate and stubborn. She accuses me of not loving her like I used to."

"Do you?"

Abram sighed. "Marriage is about duty, Atley. It's about children and raising them right."

So it was as bad as that. "Is that what she thinks?"

Abram cast him an annoyed look.

"What are you going to do?" Atley asked.

"I'm going to pray that God will speak to her," Abram said.

"You could speak to her yourself," Atley said.

"I've tried. This is where it has gotten me. The Lord will have to soften us both, if we are to go on."

"And the kinner?" Atley prodded. "They are having Christmas without their daet."

"Marriage is complicated, Atley. You have no idea. Don't try to meddle in another man's relationship."

Atley didn't answer. His brother was right—he didn't know about marriage firsthand, nor did he know the details about his brother's. It was this volatile relationship that served as a warning to him and any other young man thinking of blithely following his heart.

"Let's go lend a hand, Brother," Abram said. "Whatever a man's hand finds to do, he must do it with all his might."

It was never a good sign when Abram started quoting scripture, but a marriage was private business and Atley knew better than to press too hard. His brother was in town, and Atley would make the most of the time with him this Christmas.

And they'd do their duty to the community and help the Lapps fix their barn. This was how life went forward when a man's heart was wounded: one duty at a time.

Chapter 4

That evening, Maggie slipped her envelope into the egg bucket and headed out the side door. That moment in the snow by the fence had been haunting her thoughts. She knew Atley well once upon a time, but this was a much older version of that young man. He was stronger, more direct, and that tenderness that had simmered in his eyes as his gaze had settled on her lips made her stomach flip to think about. He was now a hardened man, and he was better looking now, if that were even possible. The strength and certainty of manhood had broadened and deepened him, and he was more tempting this time around. And so much more dangerous.

She wasn't that twenty-year-old girl anymore, either. And she knew better than to play with these emotions. He didn't want an outspoken woman like her, and she didn't want to give up this newfound outlet to her energies. Whatever they had was in the past, and it had to stay there, because the last five years had only made them more of themselves. It didn't matter how she once felt about him . . . it didn't matter how she felt about him now! It would end in heartbreak all over again, and she wasn't sure her heart could survive it.

Her future and her ability to distract herself from Atley's charms lay in the letters that tickled at the back of her mind. The voices in those letters tugged at her. They wanted answers, advice . . . they wanted *her*.

It was a tempting feeling to be wanted for something. So far, she felt more like a disappointment to everyone. It had been her duty to find a husband and carry on the traditions, and she would have done so if it were possible. She'd even gone to another community for a little while, but there were meek, quiet girls there, too. And she hadn't settled in very easily. She'd come home, lonesome and discouraged. Her parents, her uncles and aunts, the members of her church, all looked at her differently after that. They now saw an old maid.

But these letter writers were reaching out to her, and when she sat alone and thought about them she didn't feel like a failure. She had something other than housework in her childhood home to occupy her thoughts, and she liked it so much more than she realized. She might not be married, but she was a grown woman, and she was ready for a home of her own. Her independence would be difficult to achieve just now and it would require finding a way to financially support herself, but she itched for something more. This column had been more than her secret; it had been her chance.

The sun had already set, and as Maggie trudged through the snow past the buggy barn she could hear her daet mucking out the horse stalls, the sound of shovel against wooden floorboards echoing out into the icy stillness. That meant that Daet was done with the cattle. She picked up her pace. She'd told Mamm that she was checking on one sickly late-born calf in the barn, and it wasn't a lie—she was doing just that. But she was also looking for solitude.

The silvery full moon was low in the sky, making the patches of snow that remained untrampled sparkle. When she got to the barn, she looked over her shoulder once with mild guilt at her secrecy, then slipped inside to the warmth and tangy scent of cattle.

Maggie lit a kerosene lamp and looked toward the charred corner of the barn. The hole had been patched over with boards, but the black licks remained on the wall. She stared at it a moment, then headed over to the stall where the calf lay curled up in the straw. It opened large, liquid eyes as she approached.

"Hello, my bobbily," she crooned, and she grabbed an old blanket, then opened the stall and settled it over the calf's body for some extra warmth. Then she pulled the envelope out of the egg bucket, turned the bucket over, and used it as a stool, wrapping her shawl a little closer around herself.

She opened the envelope and pulled out the stack of fluttering pages. People wrote on different stationery—one had scrawled her question on a piece of lined paper. Others were emails that her editor had printed off for her. She paused to look at the strange lettering in that block before the actual letter began.

She'd been answering these English letters for some time now, and she still wasn't used to the look of a printed email. It was complicated, confusing.

Time passed as she reread the letters. Perhaps she could send some personal responses that wouldn't be published in the actual paper. Would that be acceptable to the bishop? It would be more like having many pen pals instead of putting herself into the public eye. Even if she only answered these, she would feel better.

She pulled out some lined paper and scanned the first letter. Then she started to write:

> *Dear Diana,*
> *The young man who isn't ready for marriage now will likely not be ready for marriage in the near future. What he means when he says that he just wants to live with you is that he wants the benefits of a wife without promising her his future or his fidelity. With the Amish, we often tell girls not to do anything that will make for regrets later. And that isn't only about her reputation, which is important to us. This is about her heart. Hearts are not so easily mended as the youth seem to think. Once you have given everything of yourself to this young man, what will it do to you if he decides to move on to another girl and marry her? What will happen to your heart if he decides that you are not what he wants in a wife? These things happen, and while a young man is declaring his love for you, if he isn't willing to commit at the same time, you should be wary. You must think pragmatically, too. . . .*

As Maggie wrote, she felt her muscles start to relax, and the pressures of the day lift. She answered the first letter and then the second. She'd moved on to the third when she heard the barn door open, and she turned, straining to see beyond the stall slats. She hurriedly pushed the papers back into the envelope, her heart pounding.

"Daet?" she called.

"No, it's me." Atley's deep voice echoed through the barn. "Maggie?"

She rose to her feet, bathed in the yellow light of the kerosene lamp. There was no need to hide the envelope from him, but she still held it instinctively behind her.

"What are you doing here?" she asked with a breathy laugh of relief.

"I forgot my work gloves here in the barn, and I'll need them come morning."

"Oh. . . . "

Atley looked around. "I can't see enough. Could you bring your lamp over?"

Maggie adjusted the envelope under her shawl, then picked up the lamp and let herself out of the stall. She made her way over to where he stood. He watched her approach, and she felt self-conscious under that scrutiny. She stopped a couple of feet from him, and he put his broad hand over hers, then lifted the lamp higher. He looked around himself, then released her hand and headed over to the bales of hay and picked up the pair of black gloves.

"Found them," he said, then came back over to where she stood. "What are you doing out here?"

She slowly pulled out the envelope, then shrugged weakly. "Answering letters."

"Answering them?" His eyebrows climbed. "But . . . does that mean you'll continue with the column?"

"No—not exactly." She licked her lips. "I can't go against the bishop's orders, can I? But I wanted to answer these letters individually—not to be published, but to be sent back to them. They wanted answers." She hesitated. "Are you going to tell your uncle this?"

"No. It isn't going against his orders," Atley replied. "And even if it were—"

"You'd keep a wicked secret?" she asked, eyeing him uncertainly.

"Maggie, you aren't wicked."

"Just dangerously opinionated."

"Well, you are that." He smiled teasingly.

Maggie hung the lamp from a nail and rubbed her hands together. Atley put his hands over hers, and the warmth from his palms was a welcome relief. They shouldn't be touching each other or standing this close. It was a whole new scandal if someone saw them. He lifted her hands to his mouth and blew his breath over her hands.

"Atley, you shouldn't. . . . "

"You're cold."

"I could go back to the house."

"You could." He smiled faintly. "Are you going to?"

She shook her head mutely, and he pressed his lips against her knuckles. His lips were warm, and she could feel the scratch of his stubble on his chin against her fingers. He was a grown man now, and his stubble was rough.

"I'm trying very hard not to miss you, Atley," she said quietly.

"I know."

"And this isn't helping. . . . "

He lowered her hands. "Seeing you again—I'd thought I'd feel less for you, prove to myself it had been a youthful infatuation. It didn't work."

"Just because it was real love back when our hearts were easier to fill doesn't mean it's real now," she said.

"Is that Miss Amish talking?"

"It's Magdalena. It's Miss Amish. There is no difference. I only write what I think."

"Can't we be friends again?" he asked quietly. "Before we started courting, we were friends."

"We were kinner, then," she said with a short laugh. "And if I recall, you had a wild crush on Miriam Peachy with her blond hair and perfectly ironed creases."

"All the boys had crushes on her," he replied. "And you hurt my ego. You always won in target practice."

They used to play together, running through the fields. They'd set up cracked canning jars on the fence posts and stand back behind a predetermined line and throw their stones. She hadn't known how to throw properly at first, but when he taught her how to throw overhand, the right moment to release, she'd quickly surpassed him in skill. She could still remember Atley Troyer in dirty bare feet. And she hadn't been any neater, her hair coming free of her kapp and her glittering gaze fixed on her target. He'd hated that she was a better shot, and she didn't care. When her rock hit glass, it was a beautiful, shattering sight.

"You gave Miriam your prize rock," Maggie said. "And I hated you for it. She didn't deserve that rock. I did."

"True, but I gave that rock to her because she smiled at me," he said. "And you wanted it as a reward for beating me."

Maggie laughed softly. "I still say I deserved it."

"Yah, you did," he agreed with a low laugh. "That was before I forgave you for being a better shot than I was. But you see? We *were* friends. We used to walk to the creek together and catch minnows. We used to climb haystacks. Friendship is forged on the top of a haystack."

"We aren't kinner anymore."

"No, we're definitely grown enough to know better. . . . " He stepped closer, then reached out and touched her arm through the shawl, his hand gentle, tentative.

Somehow being grown didn't make this any easier. Back when they were kinner, she'd longed for him to pine for her the way he pined for Miriam. But maybe that was for the best, after all. Miriam Peachy grew up to be an appropriate Amish woman. She kept her apron gleaming white, and she never had a hair come loose from her kapp. She was married by nineteen. Atley could have done worse.

"Be my friend again, Maggie," he murmured.

"I'm a scandalous friend to claim right now," she said, attempting a joke.

"I'll take the risk."

His voice was low and deep, as warm as low-burning coals. She didn't have anything to say to that and she knew she should step back, but she couldn't bring herself to do it. She opened her mouth to say something—a very appropriate excuse to leave—but nothing came out, and when he stepped closer still, his lips hovering a breath away from hers, it was she who closed that distance between them, pressing her lips against his as her heart threatened to explode inside of her chest.

Her touch was all it took for Atley to take over the kiss, and he slipped his hands over her cheeks, his fingers warming the back of her neck. His mouth moved over hers—no longer the fumbling boy finding his way. He was now a man who knew exactly what he wanted, and she could feel the tremble of his self-control.

She pulled back, and he rested his forehead against hers, his eyes shut and his breath coming fast.

"I'm sorry," she whispered. That kiss had been all her fault, and it was wrong on every level. She still didn't know why she'd done it.

His eyes opened, and he smiled faintly. "If we're to be friends, there can't be any more of that."

"No. There can't be—"

And then he moved close again, slowly and confidently, and his warm lips covered hers once more.

Atley slipped his arms around her waist, pulling her in close against his chest, his heart hammering so hard in his ears that he couldn't seem to think. She'd kissed him the first time, but this was his turn. If they were to regret it later, then let him have something worth regretting on his own conscience. He kissed her slowly, deliberately, and with all that longing that was pent up inside of him. He just wanted to hold her close, feel her heart beating fast against him, feel her skin against his starved fingertips.

There were good reasons not to be kissing Magdalena, but right now with his lips on hers, with her hands moving up his biceps toward his shoulders, he had no idea what those reasons were.

He'd missed her so much over the last five years. No woman could match up to her in the way she made his heart speed up. No other girl could catch his eye quite like Maggie had. There was something about her that intoxicated him and didn't let go.

He pulled back and smiled ruefully down at her.

"What were we saying?" he breathed.

"That we shouldn't do that . . . " Her whisper was ragged, and he longed to kiss her some more, let the minutes drag by while he could forget about everything else around them. He'd guiltily dreamed of this over the years, Maggie slipping into his slumbering mind, and he'd wake up feeling as guilty as if he'd really kissed her.

Coming here was supposed to stop the dreams, stop whatever part of his heart was still hooked on her. But instead of being the cure, she was the fever. She only made him worse.

"Right," he said, letting go of her. He sucked in a breath, then took off his hat and ran a hand through his hair.

Maggie blinked up at him, and suddenly tears welled in her eyes. He stared at her in confusion, and he was filled with remorse. What had he just done? Reopening those old feelings was a mistake—they both knew it—but the last thing he'd wanted to do was hurt her. He'd thought she'd been equally in this. . . .

"Maggie—" He put his hat back on his head and reached a hand toward hers.

"Stop it." She stepped away, wiping the tears from under her eyes with the flat of her hand.

"I'm sorry," he said. "I thought . . . I thought you wanted—" He winced. "I was wrong."

"I'm not blaming you," she said. "But we *have* to stop. No more of that."

"I know." He met her gaze, misery worming up within his chest. "It was a mistake. It feels too much like old times—"

"This is *nothing* like old times," she said bitterly. "Back then, I honestly thought we had a future. Back then, you stopped at my fingertips."

He wasn't the kind of man who toyed with a woman in a barn. He was honest, honorable. He'd been doing the right thing for years now, and a few days spent on the farm next to Maggie Lapp and all of his personal resolve seemed to be seep out from under him.

"I meant it when I said I wanted to be friends," he said quietly.

"Do you really think that's possible?" she retorted.

"We could try." He smiled coaxingly. "I'll write you letters. You can write me back as Miss Amish. I like her too much to let her fade away."

"Do you think that can last?" she asked, shaking her head.

"Why not?" he countered.

"You'll get married. Is your wife going to be perfectly satisfied with you writing to me? Is she going to find these games amusing?"

"I'm not being unfaithful to anyone," he said irritably. "There is no wife, Maggie."

"There will be. And in order to be a good husband, you will write me one last letter informing me of the date of your wedding, and then you will go silent. As you should. We aren't kinner anymore. We know how this goes."

The barn door rattled and Atley's gaze whipped over his shoulder. They both took a step back, that manila envelope on a bale of hay between them. The door opened, and Noah Lapp stepped inside, a lantern held high. He paused in the doorway.

"There you are, Magdalena," her father said, caution in his tone. "We started to worry when you didn't come back. What are you doing out here, Atley?"

"I forgot my gloves," Atley said, holding them up as proof. There was a beat of silence.

"Ah." Noah came inside and the door banged shut behind him in a gust of wind. "Well, now you have them, I see. Maggie, your mamm is asking for you."

"Of course," Maggie said quickly. "I'll come right in."

Her father glanced between them once more, and Atley could only guess as to what he was thinking. The older man's gaze moved down to the envelope on the bale of hay, and he stepped forward, picking it up. "What's this, Maggie?"

Maggie's face paled, and she opened her mouth to reply. He couldn't let her be found out . . . not like this. She wasn't doing anything wrong. Before she could say anything, Atley plucked the envelope from Noah's hands with a forced smile. "Thank you. I'll take that."

The lie that the envelope belonged to him was implied and it did tweak Atley's conscience, but the look of relief on Maggie's face was enough to make him feel better. This was hers, and the least he could do was help protect the last of her secret.

"Atley, if it is your intention to court our daughter—" Noah began.

"No, that's not what's happening here," Atley said. "We're old friends. That's all."

The last thing he needed to do was mar her reputation any further.

"I thank you for your help in patching up our barn," Noah said, "but I won't keep you from your family any longer. Give my best to the bishop."

There were volumes between the lines, and Atley nodded. If he wasn't here to make an honest woman of Maggie, he needed to move along. He didn't blame Noah a whit.

"It was my pleasure," Atley said. "I'll pass along your greetings to my uncle."

Maggie stood silent, her glittering gaze following him.

"Happy Christmas, Maggie," he said.

"Happy Christmas." Her voice was wooden.

And he nodded to Noah, then headed for the barn door.

That night, Atley shared a guest bedroom with his brother, who was sleeping in the middle of the double bed they were supposed to share. But Atley wasn't ready to sleep yet. He'd hidden the envelope under his clothes in his suitcase, and now he pulled it out. Moonlight flooded through the window, illuminating the room just enough so that Atley could make out Maggie's rounded handwriting.

Abram moaned in his sleep, and Atley looked back at his brother, watching him until his soft snoring resumed. Then he pulled out the stack of papers, Maggie's pages seemingly interspersed with the letters sent to her.

He scanned the first few letters and her answers—some were common questions about the Amish life like why they wore the clothes they did or why they didn't use cars. There were a couple of questions about parenting, and he smiled to see that her answer to both included a paddling. And then there was a letter from a girl asking about moving in with her boyfriend.

Maggie's answer filled a whole page, but a paragraph in the middle caught his eye:

Hearts are not so easily mended as the youth seem to think. Once you have given everything of yourself to this young man, what will it do to you if he decides to move on to another girl and marry her? What will happen to your heart if he decides that you are not what he wants in a wife? These things happen, and while a young man is declaring his love for you, if he isn't willing to commit at the same time, you should be wary. You must think pragmatically, too.

He could hear her voice in those words, and he could hear her heart in them, too. She'd given him everything she could—within the bounds of decency, of course. She'd given him her heart, her trust, her promise to marry him. And he'd dashed it all. . . .

How deeply had he hurt her? Atley had tried to be fair. He'd written a letter right away so that she could move on to a man who wanted marriage. It wasn't right to waste a woman's time. He'd borne the agony of that choice alone, dreaming of her, thinking of her, unable to see any other girl except as in comparison to Magdalena. He hadn't broken it off because his feelings had changed. He still loved her—he just didn't think it would last in the face of a real marriage.

Abram lay in the center of the bed, and he rolled, flinging an arm out. When it landed on the blanket, Abram roused, sat up halfway, and looked around.

"Waneta?" Abram said groggily. He blinked his eyes open, then sighed and lay back down, rolling over so that his back was to Atley. But he didn't slip back into those soft snores again. Instead, Abram lay still, obviously awake.

Atley had been wrong to kiss Maggie. He'd been wrong to ask her to be his friend, to write him letters. . . . Not only was it cruel to her, but it was cruel to him, too. The wrong marriage was a lifetime of pain.

And Atley wasn't over her, after all.

Chapter 5

Christmas Eve, Maggie stood at the kitchen counter cutting out perfect circles of shortbread cookies and sliding them onto a cookie sheet. Her mind was on that envelope that Atley had taken with him last night. It was kind of him to protect it for her, but she needed it back. Would she have a chance to retrieve it before he left? She could only hope.

The Lapp women had been baking all day, everything from bread and dinner rolls for the following evening to cookies, pies, and tarts. Naomi sat at the table forming little roses out of dough to top the dinner rolls, her two young kinner playing with blocks in the hallway, well out of harm's way. Aunt Ruth stood by the stove, stirring a pot of thickening fruit so that it wouldn't stick at the bottom.

"Amos has a second cousin who was recently widowed," Naomi said, glancing up at Maggie. "He's older than you—about fifty—but he's got a very profitable business in green-house vegetables. We were going to suggest he meet you."

"He's fifty?" Maggie said, her voice tight.

"Not that it matters," Naomi said. "I don't think Amos will do it, now."

"He won't?" Mamm interjected. "This little matter will be swept away quickly enough. I'm sure we can still arrange a meeting—"

"Amos's family is very proper," Naomi said primly.

"Naomi, this is your sister's future we're talking about!" Mamm shot back.

"I know," Naomi replied. "And she should have been more careful. A girl like her should—"

"I'm older than you are," Maggie snapped.

Naomi fell silent, and Maggie exchanged a look with her aunt. Ruth continued to stir. If an unmarried woman was still a "girl," then so was Aunt Ruth, who was nearly sixty. Naomi might enjoy rubbing Maggie's unmarried state in her face, but she wouldn't do the same to their aunt. There were lines.

"I read those columns," Ruth said. "Did you, Naomi?"

"I don't recall," Naomi said primly.

"Don't lie, now," Maggie said. "You either read them, or you didn't."

"I read them when I thought the author was a stranger to us, not my sister making a fool of herself!"

Maggie bit back a retort. She was a fool, now? Apparently, everyone had read her replies to those letters, even her own sister.

"They were well written," Ruth said. "There were other communities reading them, too. I heard that some papers were sent all the way to Pennsylvania."

"As far as that!" Mamm said, then heaved a sigh. "Still, it isn't proper. Whether she's good at it or not."

"Maggie, do you want to meet this new widower?" Ruth asked pointedly.

"No," Maggie replied.

"Now, Maggie—" Mamm started.

"I don't want to!" Maggie replied. "A man in his fifties with children my age, no doubt. And grandchildren. No, I don't want that at all. I'd rather provide for myself."

"How?" Naomi asked, aghast.

"I could teach school like Aunt Ruth," Maggie replied. "Or I could start my own business. I won't make enough off the quilts I make myself, but I could start some quilting classes in town. I'm sure the Englishers would gobble up a chance to sit with an Amish woman in a quilting circle." The idea had only struck her now, but she liked it. "I could serve tea and a few of our baked goods, and I could teach them to stitch by hand. They could come back week after week and continue working on the quilt. . . . Or maybe something small for themselves so they can take it away with them after a few weeks. I could sell it as a package—two evenings a week for three weeks, or something like that. . . . "

"She's the smart one," Ruth said, shooting Mamm a grin.

"And her brain will keep her single," Mamm retorted. "A man doesn't want a woman with smarts. He wants a woman with a heart and an ability to cook."

"Some intelligence doesn't hurt," Ruth countered. "You don't raise children, keep a home, can your own food, keep your own garden, and make some money on the side because you're stupid. It takes a brain to run a home as well as anything else."

Mamm sighed. "Ruth, you're not helping. She needs a man to marry, not a career option!"

"She needs to be happy," Ruth shot back.

That was true—Maggie needed something to fill her heart, to use her skills, to keep her mind busy. But she also longed for a family of her own, and she simply couldn't be a proper Amish woman writing columns for the paper—not without the bishop's permission.

"Are *you* happy, Aunt Ruth?" Naomi voiced the question, and the kitchen fell silent.

Maggie shot her sister a scandalized glare, and for a moment she wasn't sure if her aunt would even answer.

"Yes, I think I am," Ruth replied. "I'm happy enough."

"But wouldn't you rather have gotten married?" Naomi pressed. "Looking back on it."

"I didn't get the proposal," Ruth replied. "And so I built a very satisfying life for myself teaching school. I taught all of you, didn't I?"

"Do you think Maggie should find an older widower?" Naomi pressed. "If you were to act as Miss Amish and give her some advice, what would it be?"

Ruth sighed. "When Christmastime comes and you're baking for your nieces and nephews instead of your own kinner, it isn't easy."

Maggie stole a glance at her aunt, who continued to stir the pot on the stove. Her gaze had turned inward, though, and she pursed her lips. That was all she was going to say, it seemed, and Maggie understood her aunt's intent. Nieces and nephews didn't take the place of her own kinner. A brother's home wasn't home enough come Christmastime. Aunt Ruth had been passed over in her day, and she'd paid for it. Maggie would very likely pay the same dues.

The problem was, Maggie didn't want to be married off to whoever would have her. That was insulting, too. When she thought of wearing a wedding apron and taking those vows, the foggy man who materialized in her imagination had Atley's dark, laughing eyes. It was silly—he didn't want her, and she couldn't have him, either. She didn't need a willing man; she needed the right man, the one who wouldn't be intimidated by her thoughts and ideas. A man who wouldn't give her lectures for saying what she thought. She couldn't muzzle herself, even for a husband.

"Why doesn't Aunt Ruth meet the widower?" Maggie asked.

"Yes, why not?" Mamm turned to Naomi.

There was silence for a moment, and then Ruth said, "It's a little late for that."

"It doesn't have to be," Mamm replied. "You said yourself that this life you have isn't quite enough."

"I'm set in my ways," Ruth replied with a shrug. "I've gotten so used to doing what I want that I'm not sure I could stop. There comes a point of no return, and I'm afraid I've passed it."

Had Maggie passed her own point of no return? She'd tasted a freedom like none other—a whole audience of people who wanted to hear her advice. There was no undoing it.

Naomi looked relieved that Ruth had turned down this newly available gentleman. Perhaps they'd promised him a young woman with tight skin and eager for more babies. That could be a strong lure for some men.

"The Grabers have been helping us a great deal since the barn fire," Mamm said, changing the subject. "We'll send some baked goodies over to them today."

The Graber farm, where Atley was staying. This might be her chance to get her letters back.

"I'll bring a basket over," Maggie said quickly. "It won't take me long."

"Would you?" Mamm said with a relieved smile. "That would really help, Magdalena. Let me put one together. Leave those cookies. I'll finish them."

In the kitchen window, candles nestled in fresh evergreen wreaths were already lit. It was Christmas Eve, and outside the house she could hear the clatter of a wagon and the laughter of the youth group. Naomi got to her feet and her little girls dashed to the window to look outside.

"The carolers are here," Ruth said, a smile breaking over her face. "It doesn't feel like Christmas until the young people come caroling."

Outside, the teenagers broke into song—"It Came Upon a Midnight Clear"—and Maggie felt tears prick her eyes. Ruth was right. The carolers did make it seem like Christmas.

She was too old to be out there singing with them, single or not. Maybe she was more like her aunt Ruth than she'd realized. This very well might be her life from now on—doting on her siblings' kinner and accepting that she had become more than passed over.... She'd become too set in her ways to marry.

"Naomi, get some tarts and cookies together so we can bring them out to the young people," Mamm said with a smile. "And Maggie, grab a jar of strawberry rhubarb jam for the basket for the Grabers, would you?"

Maggie did as her mother requested, then passed it over to her.

"There, done," Mamm said with a smile. She handed the basket to Maggie, then went to the door and opened it wide to better listen as the young people sang. She looked over her shoulder. "Hurry back, Maggie. Daet and Amos will be in soon enough, and we don't want to start Christmas without you."

Maggie put down the basket for a moment and reached for her shawl. The young people started a new carol, and Maggie pushed her feet into her boots and pulled on her gloves. Then she picked up the basket again.

It was cold this Christmas Eve. And there were festive goodies to deliver. The young people sang about the angels, singing over the earth as they told their good news. . . .

Christmas was about more than her broken heart, and that was strangely comforting.

Atley gave the horse one last long stroke with the brush before patting its flank. Uncle Ben knocked the shovel against the wheelbarrow, tapping the last of the dirt off the blade. Outside, the night was dark and stars already twinkled overhead. It felt appropriate to be out in a stable on Christmas Eve, smelling the tang of manure, listening to the nickers of horses.

"Uncle," Atley said, coming out of the stall and closing the gate behind him. "I wanted to talk to you about something alone."

"Oh?" The bishop looked up. "You know that your aunt has pie and treats for us inside, don't you?"

"Yah, I do." Atley shoved his hands into his coat pockets. "It's about Maggie Lapp."

"Ah. And what about her?"

"I was hoping to plead her case," he said.

"So, she's asked you to speak to me?"

"On the contrary. She refused to ask you to change your mind," Atley said. "But I never did tell you all the good that column was doing."

"It's a mockery of our way of life," his uncle retorted. "An Amish woman answering the base and sinful questions of Englishers."

"The questions they post might be peculiar," Atley agreed. "But they are honest. I'm sure of that. And when Maggie answered, she never said anything that would go against church teaching. She simply explained how we Amish live, and the reason why we make the choices we do."

"She's a woman. Her place is in the home," the bishop sighed.

"She's unmarried, and she's likely to stay that way," Atley said, and the truth of it made his voice catch. "She's not neglecting any children or a husband. If she were, it would be different. But she's more like her aunt Ruth, finding a way in our community without a family of her own. If you take this away from her—"

"Atley, it doesn't change that this isn't appropriate," the bishop went on. "A woman, whether she has a husband or not, is to be meek and quiet, listening to the leadership in the community. In this one thing I can commend her. Yes, she made a mistake, but when informed of the leadership's decision she accepted it like a good Amish woman."

She accepted it, even if it crushed her. Atley couldn't just give this up. Maggie deserved someone on her side, a man willing to speak for her.

"Uncle, she's doing good. God didn't send His son that first Christmas for only one group of people. There is neither Jew nor gentile, remember. There is neither slave nor free. Man nor woman. The Savior came to save all of us, and by speaking her faith, Maggie is spreading it! These are people who might never listen to a minister, but they listen to her."

The bishop was silent, pursing his lips in thought. Then he said, "At this time of year, we think of Mary, the mother of Christ, as our example. She was meek and gentle, the perfect example to our young women. When the angel told Joseph they had to flee to Egypt, she followed her husband and allowed him to be her protector—"

"This might be the only time many of these people hear about our faith, Uncle," Atley interrupted. "Would you be the reason that they don't?"

Uncle Ben sighed. "It doesn't change the fact that she's a *woman*. If she had a husband to oversee her . . . But she doesn't." The older man went silent for a few beats, his gaze turned inward. Then he sighed. "If she were to submit all her writing to me for oversight before she hands it in, then I could make notes to ensure that proper theology is being relayed."

Atley shook his head. "No."

"No?" Uncle Ben shot him a sharp look. "I thought that was incredibly generous. You'd turn down an offer like that? Are you sure she would?"

"Uncle, if you add your notes and your theological discourse, it will no longer be *her* voice, and the people won't read it. Her column would be canceled, and this would be over.

Those Englisher readers don't want to hear you or me; they want *her!*"

The bishop looked at Atley in surprise. "You feel strongly."

"I do." Atley swallowed. "I don't mean to overstep, Uncle, but I feel that God is using her for something, and we cannot stand in the way of the Almighty, or he'll move us Himself."

"If I can't be certain of the validity of the theological stance she takes—" his uncle began.

His uncle was close, but he was still worried, and Atley could understand. The bishop didn't know Maggie like he did. He was concerned for the community, for their reputation, for the young people who might read her words . . . He needed proof, and while Atley knew that Maggie wouldn't easily agree to this course of action, Atley pulled the manila envelope out of his jacket where he'd been carrying it.

"Read for yourself," Atley said. "These are the letters she's answered in her latest batch. They're honest and heartfelt, and nothing she says goes against our theology."

For the next few minutes, Uncle Ben flipped through the letters, reading Maggie's answers in thoughtful silence. He flicked through page after page, chewing the side of his cheek while Atley pensively watched him in the soft golden glow of the kerosene lamp. A horse nickered, and the pages crinkled as the bishop set them carefully aside.

Outside, the sound of horses' hooves crunching through the snow and the laughter of teenagers broke the stillness. Some of the voices were chatting, and a few were singing a line or two of a Christmas carol. Then they were silent for a moment, some murmuring; then they broke into song.

Hark, the herald angels sing, glory to the newborn king . . .

From his position in the stable, he could see out the window and could just make out the backs of a few of the teens. There was a time when he and Maggie were part of a group like that one, going door-to-door on a hay wagon and singing carols for the Amish homes. They'd even stopped for a few Englisher neighbors they knew.

"You're right," Uncle Ben said after a moment. "I can't fault her answers. I might have phrased them differently or put a different emphasis, but—" He tapped the pages together again. "I see your point, Atley."

Atley stared at his uncle. There weren't many people who could claim to change the bishop's mind once it was made up. Had he just succeeded?

"Are you saying . . . " Atley wasn't sure he should even voice it, lest his uncle change his mind.

"I'm saying that I will allow this," the bishop said slowly. "I will personally read every column that comes out, and if she begins to slide into heretical territory, I will stop it. But as it stands . . . "

"You'll let her write the column," Atley concluded.

"Yah. I'll allow it."

Atley couldn't help the grin that broke over his face. "Uncle, you have no idea how happy this will make her. Thank you for this."

"It's Christmas," the bishop said with a small smile. "There are miracles this season."

The door rattled and then pushed open, and Atley turned. Maggie stood in the faint light of the doorway.

"I'm sorry to disturb you, but I brought some baked treats to the house and your wife said that you were out here. I was hoping to speak with Atley—" It was then that her gaze fell on the envelope and the pages in the bishop's hands. Her complexion paled and her scandalized gaze whipped over to Atley in shock.

"Atley?" she breathed.

He knew what she must be thinking—that he'd betrayed her again. "Maggie, it's not what it looks like," he said hurriedly. "My uncle has reconsidered his decision about your column."

Maggie didn't seem to register what he'd said right away, because her hands still trembled and her gaze flashed with anger.

"Maggie—he's reconsidered," Atley repeated.

"He, what?" The anger bled from her face, replaced with a look of shock.

"I have reconsidered," Uncle Ben said with a nod. "You are free to continue writing the column, but only if you remain careful to portray our faith correctly."

"Yes, yes! I have been careful, and I will continue to be. . . . " Maggie's entire face lit up and she put a hand over her mouth as her eyes welled with tears. "I won't let you down. Thank you, Bishop Graber. Thank you. This means more to me than . . . "

"Happy Christmas," the bishop said, patting her shoulder. "Now I'm going to leave this wheelbarrow with my nephew to empty, and I'm going to go inside for some of those baked treats you were speaking of."

"Thank you!" she repeated.

The bishop went out the door, shutting it behind him, and as soon as they were alone, Maggie flung herself into Atley's arms. He wrapped his arms around her, burying his face into her shawl. She smelled warm and sweet and ever so faintly like baking. She felt so good in his arms, and as they stood there, the sound of the carolers echoing through the cold night, he pulled back just enough to look down into her face.

"You are a good man, Atley," she whispered. "I don't know how to thank you."

"There's no need," he said gruffly. "Call it a Christmas gift."

"Horace is going to be thrilled," she said with a soft laugh.

"Yah, I imagine so," Atley agreed.

"This means so much to me," she said; then she stood up on her tiptoes and kissed his cheek. He closed his eyes, memorizing the feeling of her lips brushing against his skin. "What made you do it?"

Atley looked down into her chocolate brown eyes, and he

didn't have it in him to hide what he was feeling. Because while he hadn't been able to see it before, he suddenly knew why he'd done everything up until now . . . every step he'd taken had been for one reason.

"Why I did it?" he asked, shaking his head. "Because I love you, Maggie. I have for years. I never stopped. It gave me wings when we were together, and it hobbled my feet when I broke it off. But I've loved you for years, Maggie. You have to ask?"

She stared up at him, her lips parted and her eyes wide.

"You love me still?" she breathed.

"Yah." He bent his head down and caught her lips with his. He kissed her tenderly, then pulled back. There was nothing else to say. It was the truth.

"I love you, too," she whispered, and tears misted her eyes. "You were the only one I've ever loved."

"I should have given you the rock I used for target practice," he said with a low laugh.

"No. . . . " She dropped her gaze and her chin trembled. "You should have married Miriam."

Atley blinked. "What?"

"She was the kind of woman you wanted, Atley. Whatever you felt for me, it doesn't change who I am. We know we can't work."

"Maybe we're wrong," he said quietly. "Maybe we do have what it takes. I argued your case to my uncle because you needed this. But if you were married . . . " He stopped, swallowing hard. "You don't have to write those columns if you're married, do you? You could put your heart into your bobbilies and your home—"

Even as he said it, it sounded wrong in his ears. He wanted her to be the kind of woman who wanted to take care of him. . . . He wanted her to need him, not the Englishers out there, hanging on her words.

"You think this is just to keep me busy without a family of

my own?" Her voice firmed, and she took a step away from him. He could see it happening, the distance, the misunderstandings, the heartbreak when he asked too much of her and she offered too little to him. He could see how feelings could be wounded and hearts could be cracked, chipped away over time.

"No." He sighed. "I know what that column means to you."

"I'd never be that quiet, sweetly traditional wife, Atley," she said. "That hasn't changed. I am Amish to the core, but there is more to me, and I'm only finding that out now. It's who I am. I say what I think. With the bishop's permission, I can now continue writing my column. People hear me, Atley. They listen. They *understand* me. I know that it shouldn't mean so much to me, but it does. This is *me*."

Beautiful, individual, and determined to go her own way. He loved her with a love so fierce that it could break stone, but it might also break her, if he let it. He wanted a wife devoted to him and their children. She wanted a husband who could let her go free into that unknown territory with the Englishers. It was one thing to argue for a single woman who needed something to fill her days and nights, but his own wife? Would he be so confident in their love to encourage that? He knew his own limitations, too.

Atley thought of Abram sleeping alone in that bed, and he knew for a fact that love was not enough to keep a man and woman happy together. If it were, Abram and Waneta would be celebrating Christmas together with their children instead of separated by miles, waking up to empty arms.

"We'd love each other deeply," he said, his voice catching with emotion. "And we'd break each other's hearts."

Maggie slid her hand into his, and her lips trembled. "Thank you for what you've done for me today, Atley. I will always love you. I promise you that."

She raised his hand to her lips and kissed the tops of his fingers, then she released him, and he stood there frozen as she made her way to the door. She pulled it open and, without looking back, disappeared outside.

The carolers sang, their song winding its way through the stable, and Atley covered his eyes with the heels of his hands, holding the waves of heartbreak inside.

He loved her . . . he always had! And seeing her again hadn't released him from that burden. But there would be no relief for them, either. He'd have to go back to Bountiful and face his life with the knowledge that he'd love her 'til the day he died.

Love wasn't always enough.

Chapter 6

Christmas morning, Maggie got up early to light the stove. Then she pulled her heaviest shawl over her shoulders and marched out into the winter darkness to gather eggs. She hadn't slept much last night. It had been difficult to try to seem cheerful while the rest of the family laughed and played card games around the table. She'd managed to turn her back to the family while she cleaned up; then she'd slipped away to bed while Amos won his third round of Dutch Blitz and everyone groaned.

This morning, she felt tired and her throat was sore from her tears last night. She loved him. . . . Why couldn't she have gotten over this man? He didn't want her—not all of her. He wanted a life that all Amish men wanted and she didn't blame him, but she wouldn't become like Waneta, spent and tired and angry. She wouldn't be that cautionary tale the younger people whispered about—the kind of wife to avoid.

Although she was already a tale told by mothers to daughters—what happened when a woman couldn't keep her peace, stay quiet, know her place.

The moon was low in the sky, wisps of cloud blocking some of the light. She stood in the cold, her heart heavy.

"Maggie?"

It was Daet, and he stood on the steps, pulling on his own gloves for morning chores. Christmas Day or not, the work carried on.

"Yah, hi, Daet," she said, swallowing the lump in her throat.

"Wait, Maggie. I want to speak with you."

She'd been trying to avoid this, but she stood still, waiting as her father's boots crunched through the snow. He stopped at her side and put a hand on her shoulder.

"Happy Christmas," he said with a worried smile.

"Yah, Happy Christmas, Daet."

"You are not my happy daughter," he said. "What has happened to you? Since yesterday evening, you've been a well of sadness. You've always loved Christmas. . . . "

"I'm not a kinner." She sighed.

"No, but you're not an old woman, either," he retorted. "Now, I heard of a widower who is very interested to meet you—"

"No."

"You haven't met him. Some men my age seem much younger, Maggie. I'm no catch, but he might be. I've heard that he's in good shape. He's kind, too."

"I don't want him, Daet!" she said, and the tears spilled down her cheeks. "I don't love him. . . . I don't *know* him!"

"But you do love someone," her father said with a decisive nod. He pulled her into his arms and patted her back like he did when she was a little girl. Maggie sniffled against his coat, then pulled back. "Who is it, my girl?"

"Who it's always been," she whispered. "Atley."

"And he came just in time to ruin your Christmas," Daet said, then sighed. "I'm sorry, Maggie."

"He didn't ruin it," she replied. "He convinced the bishop to let me write my column, and then he told me that he loved me."

Daet froze. "Wait—so you've got a proposal and you're act-ing like someone died?"

"It isn't so simple!" she said. A burst of wind made her pull her shawl closer. "I'm not the same as Naomi, and you know it. She loves to darn socks and plan elaborate meals. When she works on a cross-stitch, she feels relaxed and happy. She's the perfect Amish wife. But me—I don't like those things, Daet, and that is what makes me unmarriageable. The way Naomi feels when she cleans out the cellar is how I feel when I see my column in the paper. I know I shouldn't, and that my priorities are all wrong, but it's how I feel. And I can't pretend other-wise."

"If you had kinner of your own—" Daet began.

"Waneta has kinner of her own," she said. "And I've never seen a more unhappy woman! I can't be Atley's Waneta. I can't do that to him. He deserves a woman who will make him happy."

Daet sighed, then nodded slowly. "There are unhappy mar-riages, that is true, but marriage is a complicated relationship. There is time for Abram and Waneta to find their balance yet."

"If you say so."

"Explain this to me—what is it about those columns that gives you such joy?"

"Daet, I know you won't see it the way I do," she began.

"Humor me." He nudged her toward the barn, and they started walking together in that direction. "Just . . . pull it apart and put the pieces on the table for me. What about those letters you write fills you up with happiness?"

"I'm heard," she said. "I have something to say that I feel strongly about, and instead of having to crush it down inside of me lest I sound like a chattering female, I . . . I say it! And no one judges me for having said it. No one says I should keep my peace and let the men do the talking. No one laughs to them-selves that this is why I'm still single. I say my piece, and people listen. When people look me in the face, they see an old maid. But when they read Miss Amish, they hear my words, my ideas, and they come back for more."

Daet grunted.

"My column is popular," Maggie went on. "My editor's name is Horace, and he says that ever since people found my column, there are Amish communities as far as Pennsylvania who order our paper. For me, Daet! To read my letters!"

"Yah," he said, and his slow march didn't change.

"And I like it," she said at last. He didn't understand. She could tell. No one did, except for Atley, perhaps.

"What about five years from now?" Daet asked. "Ten? Twenty? Will a column be enough? Will it still be popular? Or will it have been enough for a year or two and then faded away?"

"I don't know, Daet. I do know that if I silence myself I become angry and irritable. And I don't like myself that way. Right now, I know my heart is broken over Atley, but at least I'm being honest. I'm feeling what I'm feeling. I'm speaking my own ideas. I'm just being myself, and there is freedom in that."

"Yah, yah. . . . " Daet slowed his steps, then turned toward her again, coming to a stop just as the cloud slipped past the moon and the watery light spilled over his lined features. "So if I understand you right, you are tired of pretending to be quieter than you naturally are, and you long to be heard and understood by this vast audience of strangers. What about your own kin? What about your own community?"

"I've given up there, I suppose," she admitted. "Daet, you didn't hear how Naomi talked about it. She liked my column right up until she knew I was the one who wrote it!"

"Yah, your sister has always been intimidated by you," Daet said with a sigh. "She was the cook, and you were the smart one. And she always did want to be smart like you."

"She's not the only one—" Maggie began.

"Wait," Daet said, chewing the side of his cheek. "Now, just something to think on, my girl. If you could be understood heart and soul by a vast multitude of strangers, or by one person, what would you choose?"

"Daet, I don't think that's a fair question," she said.

"Yah, it's fair. And I mean being really understood. Having someone look into your eyes and see your heart—that kind of understanding. If you could have that with one person, and if you could write your ideas and thoughts into a hundred empty books, and put them away for your grandchildren to read after you are gone . . . If you could be truly understood by only one person, would that be enough?"

Maggie didn't answer, but his question had settled into her heart.

"Your community will never fully understand you, my girl. You have always been different from the other girls—and God forgive me, but I have done my best to dampen your light to make you less terrifying for the men. But if we are honest, you and I, we know that you'll always be different around here, so having your community's full approval and understanding is never going to happen, whether you write your column or not. So, for the sake of this decision, forget them. This is a choice between a multitude of strangers and one man."

Daet gave her a long look, then started trudging toward the barn once more. He didn't turn, but his last words floated the icy wind back to her. "He loves you, Magdalena."

Maggie stood there with the egg bucket in one hand and her heart hammering in her chest. She was terrified of being married to a man she adored, making him miserable, feeling empty and lonely on a soul level. . . . She was terrified of being so close to happiness and yet still not being able to reach it.

Daet got to the barn door, opened it, and disappeared inside.

Today was Christmas, and five years ago, Atley had given her a little strawberry pincushion and his heart all tied up together. If she could talk to him like she used to . . . If she could have a lifetime of Atley's love and understanding, could she sacrifice that larger audience? Could his love be enough?

She might never be a joyful housekeeper, but if she could sit down in the evenings and write out her thoughts in big, empty journals like her daet had suggested . . . if she could lie in bed next to Atley and be truly understood by one man . . . Would it be enough?

This wasn't about whether she could make a life for herself without a husband. Many women had, Aunt Ruth included. This was about whether she could face a lifetime without Atley, and that was where her heart welled with longing. She'd only ever loved one man, and if he could love her as she was, she could wrap herself in the warmth of his heart and let the hearts of the Englisher strangers go. . . .

She stopped, weighing that possibility inside of her. Could she walk away from her column for him? Yes, she realized. Not for any husband, but for one man she could.

But it wouldn't work. The one man to understand her wanted a woman more like Naomi. Atley understood her like no one else, and that meant he knew her weaknesses, too. Even without the column, she was opinionated and too open. She was filled with emotion that she couldn't just press down. Even without that column, she wasn't that meek Amish woman. She couldn't be the Waneta in his home, breaking his heart day after day.

Atley wanted better, and she didn't blame him. She would celebrate Christmas with her family. The column was all she had.

Christmas night, Atley and Abram sat in the sitting room, mugs of hot coffee in hand. Atley took a sip and looked over at his brother.

"Tomorrow there will be more guests," Abram said. "I heard Aunt Sarah say that the Lapps will be here in the morning."

"Yah. . . . "

It would be Second Christmas, the day for visiting and card games, laughter and eating. Atley wasn't sure he had it in him. Tonight, he listened to the soft murmur of the women talking in the kitchen, interspersed with the clatter of cutlery and plates as they did the dishes.

Uncle Ben sat across the room, his Bible in his lap, but his eyes were shut and he breathed deeply.

"I don't know why you're so miserable," Abram said, setting his coffee down on a side table. "You've been moping around all day."

"I'm not moping," Atley said irritably. There was no privacy here to sort out his own thoughts, and right now he needed to find a way to make some peace with all of this. He loved a woman who wasn't right for him, trying to save them both from future heartbreak. But what of the current pain?

He loved her—that was all he knew right now.

"What are you going to do, then?" Atley asked, changing the subject. "About Waneta? You can't go on like this."

"I don't know," Abram said, and he pushed himself to his feet and ambled to the front window. Snow was falling softly, and for a moment both brothers watched it drift down.

"Will you separate?" Atley asked.

"No."

"Then you have to fix this."

Abram heaved a sigh and turned away from the window again. His gaze moved over to his uncle, who was still asleep in that chair.

"I loved her, you know," Abram said softly. "I was besotted. Everything turned around her."

"I remember that," Atley replied.

"But we were too different, and I was too stubborn to see it." Abram scrubbed a hand over his hair.

"If you could do it all over again, would you still marry her?" Atley asked.

Abram was silent for a few beats; then he smiled sadly. "In a heartbeat."

Atley blinked. "What? You would?"

"I loved her. I do love her still. She's . . . frustrating and emotional and insists upon me talking about my feelings. She gets her own feelings hurt far too easily, and she won't accept an apology unless I say the actual words. She wants tenderness when I don't know how to give it, and she wants me to understand those passing emotions of hers as if a man could! She drives me crazy every single day, and yet . . . " Abram's face softened. "I love her."

"Did you tell her?" Atley asked.

Abram sighed. "Yes, I told her, but maybe not enough. I don't know how it went so wrong. I never thought we'd be in this place—me away from them while they celebrate Christmas without me."

"And no doubt, her family hears all about you," Atley said with a small smile.

"Shut up," Abram muttered. "But yes, no doubt. We were arguing like always, and then something changed. A wall went up. Neither of us would back down. . . . I didn't know we were that close to the edge."

"Love wasn't enough, was it?" Atley murmured, but Abram's attention had shifted to the window and he shaded his eyes. Headlights were coming down the drive, and Atley rose to his feet and met his brother at the window.

"An Englisher guest?" Atley said.

The car stopped, and the back door opened. It wasn't an Englisher guest; it was an Amish woman, her kapp gleaming and her shawl pulled tight around her. She turned to the window, her eyes large, her face ashen, and Atley recognized his sister-in-law immediately.

"Waneta . . . " Abram breathed, and he took four long strides to the front door, flung it open, and marched out into the snowy night. Frigid wind whipped into the house, and Atley went to the door, watching his brother plunge through the falling snow toward his wife.

Waneta shut the car door, and the vehicle backed out again. She stood there looking at Abram in the light of those receding headlights. For a long moment there was nothing but tension, and then Abram closed the distance between them and wrapped his arms around her.

Atley shut the door with a solid thunk. This was a private moment. Uncle Ben blinked his eyes open and rubbed a hand over his beard. The Bible slipped closed, and he caught it before it slid from his lap.

A moment later, there were footsteps outside and the door opened again and Abram and Waneta came inside together.

"Waneta!" the bishop exclaimed. "What's happening? Is everything all right?"

"I left the children with my aunt," Waneta said. "And I came to find . . . my husband."

She looked up at Abram hesitantly, tears shining in her eyes. Abram touched her cheek tenderly.

"The children will be fine," Abram said gruffly. "Waneta, let's go upstairs and talk, you and I."

Uncle Ben's gaze moved between Abram and Waneta; then he smiled. "Waneta, we are so glad you came. Please, go on upstairs and take as much time as you need."

The married couple would go home later, and Atley would have that bedroom to himself again. Abram and Waneta disappeared from the sitting room, and there was an eruption of voices in the kitchen when the women saw Waneta had come.

"That's marriage, my boy," Uncle Ben said, stroking his gray beard with a strange little smile on his face. "Those vows bind a couple in a way that you cannot fathom before you're married yourself."

What did Atley know of the internal workings of a marriage? Perhaps his brother was right that he knew nothing about this domain.

"Will they ever be happy?" Atley asked.

"They'll sort it out," the bishop said, placing the Bible onto a table next to the chair. "That's what married couples do— some more gracefully than others, of course. When a man and woman finally realize what they have to lose, that is the moment that they finally bend."

"You think Abram will bend for her?" Atley asked.

"I know it." The bishop smiled ruefully. "And he'll be a better man for it, too."

That wasn't the answer that Atley had expected from his rigid uncle, the bishop.

"Did you . . . bend?" Atley asked uncertainly.

"Oh, yes!" Uncle Ben laughed softly. "Many years ago, and more than once."

Abram and Waneta's footsteps creaked up the stairs, the murmur of their voices filtering through the wall. Abram loved his wife still, Atley knew. He loved her so deeply that even when he was most angry with her, he reached for her in his sleep.

Abram's and Waneta's voices upstairs had gone silent, and the bishop rose to his feet, stifling a yawn.

"Happy Christmas, Atley," his uncle said. "I'm going to bed now. It's too late for an old-timer like me."

"Good night, Uncle."

Atley stood by the window, watching the snow fall. Maggie wanted to write that column, and Heaven knew she'd never be a traditional woman, finding her bliss in the laundry, as she so humorously put it. She'd always be Maggie with the big heart and the even bigger emotions. She'd be funny and frustrating and harder to fill than other women would be. Her happiness wasn't so easily acquired. . . . But if he could call her his—

An idea had sparked inside of him and he knew it was too late to go hitch horses and wake up the Lapp household, but he would see her for Second Christmas.

Maybe, just maybe, she would be willing to take a chance on him. He wouldn't make his brother's mistake and wait until they were six years married before he bent for the woman he loved. Because like his brother, his arms would feel empty until the woman he loved was in them as his wife.

Chapter 7

Maggie sat on her bed, a rock in the palm of her hand. It was small and round, perfect for target practice . . . and she'd kept it all these years.

When Atley gave that rock to Miriam Peachy, she'd smiled her thanks ever so sweetly, touched his arm, batted her lashes, and the minute he turned his back she just tossed it away. Maggie had gone back for it, scouring that part of the road until she found it. Atley had thrown that rock away on a girl who would never appreciate it for its true value. He should have given it to her, she'd told herself.

But this rock had never been about target practice or their time together; it had been a symbol of his affection. Miriam could have learned to be worthy of *that*.

So why, fifteen years later, did it hurt so much to think about another woman in Atley's arms?

Loving him should mean loving him enough to let him have the life he wanted. He deserved a beautiful, sweet wife who would cook up a storm and starch his Sunday shirts with a smile on her face and no desire for anything else.

The family had left for the Grabers' place a few minutes ago, and Maggie had decided to stay behind. She couldn't face him—not like this. She rose to her feet, her heart still feeling sodden and heavy in her chest.

Atley had to return to Bountiful, and once he was gone it would be easier. She had her column, at least, and she had her aunt Ruth to show her how to live this single life with some grace and dignity, because she would not throw herself away on some old widower, either.

Maggie fiddled with the rock as she descended the stairs and headed into the kitchen. There were some Christmas treats that her mother had left on the counter for her, and she picked up one of the shortbread cookies but put it back on the plate.

She wasn't hungry.

Outside she heard boots on the step, and she glanced at the clock on the wall. It was nearly ten in the morning. It could be anyone—friend or extended family coming by to wish them a Happy Christmas. There was a knock and she instinctively put her hands up to check her kapp before she went through the mudroom to open the door.

When she pulled the door open, Atley stood on the step, and he gave her a hesitant smile.

"Atley?" she said, stepping back. "What are you doing here?"

He came inside and swung the door shut behind him. He held a little package in one hand and he lifted his shoulders.

"It's Christmas," he said. "You were trying to avoid me, weren't you?"

"Yes," she said. "I was."

"Any other girl would have tried to spare my feelings," he said.

"I'm a grown woman, and I think we're past that, aren't we?"

A smile spread over Atley's face, and he caught her hand, tugging her close. "I love you, Maggie."

Maggie pulled her hand free and went back into the kitchen. She couldn't do this—not again.

"Maggie?" He followed her, that little package in his hands still.

"Atley, stop it," she said, her voice tight. "It doesn't matter how we feel."

Atley was silent for a moment; then he held out the little package toward her. "Open it—"

She looked down at the rock in her palm, and when she took the package from his fingers she pressed the rock into his palm. It was time to give the rock back.

"What's this?" he asked with a frown.

"It's the rock you gave to Miriam. She tossed it aside when you left, and I went back for it. It was silly of me, and I feel foolish for having kept it. But I should give it back. You deserve a girl like Miriam."

Atley rolled the rock around in his palm, then shook his head. "Who cares what I deserve when I know what I want?" His dark gaze met hers; then he tapped the gift in her hand. "Open it."

She pulled on the string and unwrapped a clothespin doll, this one dressed like an angel with wings made of real feathers. She frowned, looked up at him . . .

"It's pretty," she murmured.

"We always hear the Christmas story and we're told the moral, right?" He licked his lips. "For the girls, they're told that they should be like Mary—sweet, obedient, allowing their husbands to care for them. And the men should be like Joseph, strong and faithful. And those are the only options."

"That's true."

"Well, I was thinking about it last night, about the Christmas story, the stable, a man and a woman starting out their marriage . . . and I realized that you aren't Mary. And I'm not Joseph."

No, they weren't. The lifetime of love and marriage would not be theirs. She nodded, a lump rising in her throat.

"Mary was quiet and demure, or so we're told," Atley went on. "But out in the hills that night, angels exploded into song. Their joy knew no bounds! They weren't quiet or proper . . . Maggie. You're not the meek and mild wife; you're my Christmas angel."

Tears welled in her eyes. "Then who are you?"

"Me? I don't know. . . . Probably just a grateful shepherd." His eyes welled with tears. "Last night Waneta came back to find Abram. And my uncle told me something about marriage. He said that married people realize what they have to lose and it is only then that they choose to bend for each other. I don't want to wait as long as Abram did, Maggie. I want to bend *now,* because I know what I have to lose—"

"What are you saying?" she whispered.

"I'm saying I want to marry you, Maggie," he breathed. "And I know as I say it that you will probably say no. But I do want to marry you, just as you are. I want you to write that column for the Englisher paper, and I want you tell me what you feel about things, and your opinions and your observations. I want you to be yourself, open and funny and kind and . . . I want to be your husband."

She blinked at him; then her fingers fluttered up to her lips. "Atley . . ."

"Marry me, Maggie," he pleaded. "We'll sort it out. And I mean that. I'll bend for you."

Maggie sucked in a breath. "Do you mean that?"

"Yah. From the bottom of my heart."

"Because last night my father asked me if I had to choose between being understood by one man, or by a whole multitude of Englisher strangers, which would I choose? And I chose you. If I had to give up the column, I could if it meant a lifetime of being understood and loved by you. But it wouldn't change who I am . . . not who I am deep down. . . . "

"I don't want to change who you are. Write for the paper," he said, meeting her gaze. "You're too talented to stop. But marry me, too."

Marry him . . . Dare she? But as she looked up into those dark eyes it was impossible to say no. She couldn't watch him leave again.

"Yes," she breathed, and Atley's lips came down over hers. He lifted her off her feet and spun her in a slow circle as he kissed her. When he pulled back, she smiled up at him.

"Now we should go back to my uncle's place," Atley said, grinning down into her face. "Your daet had a good idea of what I was going to ask you, and he said we have his blessing. It's okay. He's keeping it a secret."

"Are you serious?" She shook her head.

"Sometimes your people know you better than you think," he whispered.

Maggie kissed him again, and her heart welled with love. Then she pulled back and reached for her shawl. She had her Christmas miracle—Atley in her arms. And now it was time to share Christmas with the friends and family she loved most. This was why she loved her Amish heritage so much—for better or for worse, this community was hers . . . and now so was Atley Troyer. Her heart was full, and she couldn't wait to marry him.

Epilogue

The wedding was held at the Lapp farm that fall. They were supposed to keep their engagement a secret until spring, but it hadn't worked. With their visits to each other, their letters, and the fact that Maggie's father had known since Second Christmas that they'd be getting married, it hadn't been feasible.

Waiting was difficult for Atley. Maggie would finally be his, and he had ten months before the wedding would happen. He worked hard, saved money, and even crafted a special wedding gift for his bride—a writing desk with a sliding roll top that covered the desk when not in use. He'd made tiny drawers and letter slots for the back of the desk, fitting everything to perfection and carving the front of each drawer with strawberries and leaves. Every time she sat at that desk to write, he wanted her to remember how much he loved her.

The day of the wedding, Atley stood in a bedroom with his brother at his side, carefully adjusting his black suit. His brother tugged at the sleeves, brushing them off with the flat of his hand and tugging them again.

"I'm surprised her parents are willing to have her live in Pennsylvania after the wedding," Abram said.

"Yah, but my work is there, so they've agreed."

In fact, Atley had arranged to rent a small apartment nearby the carpentry shop in Bountiful. The desk was already set up in the sitting area—waiting for him to finally be able to show his bride the gift he'd been laboring over all these months. It went against tradition, but he'd have his wife all to himself right after the honeymoon, and he couldn't wait.

Atley licked his lips and looked toward the window where autumn leaves were blowing in a chilly wind. They'd had frost already, and winter was coming fast. Downstairs, he could hear the chatter of voices—their two families together for the celebration. His daet and mamm were down there, Waneta and the children, too. The smell of cooking food was already wafting up to them.

"I have some advice," Abram said. "Before we go down."

"Yah?"

"I've learned a few hard lessons, as you know. And you could do better than I did. In those early days of marriage, it isn't easy. You think it will be all sweet moments now, but the more you love each other, the angrier you'll get when you disappoint each other. It's just the way of things. So in those early days, be quick to say you're sorry. It won't be easy. It never is, but if you dig in your heels, you'll only regret it in the end."

"Bend for her," Atley said quietly.

"Yah." Abram nodded. "Bend."

Atley looked toward the closed bedroom door, and his brother nodded briskly.

"You'll do fine," Abram said. "A good wife is a gift from God, and it takes a humble man to accept it."

"I hear you, Abram," Atley said, and he shot his brother a grin. "I'm getting married today."

"Yah. About time you grew a beard." Abram returned his smile with a more serious one of his own; then he opened the bedroom door. "Let's go."

As Atley went down the stairs toward the chatter of voices, he sent up a silent prayer of thanks. He was finally marrying the girl he'd loved all along. That Second Christmas had been a second chance, and he wouldn't squander it. He'd bend for her, and this very night he'd have his beautiful wife in his arms.

At long last, his heart could rest.

An Heirloom Christmas

VIRGINIA WISE

To my husband, who has always believed in me

Acknowledgments

Thank you to everyone who made *An Heirloom Christmas* possible—my wonderful, supportive agent, Tamela Hancock Murray, the Steve Laube Agency, my gifted editor, Selena James, and everyone at Kensington Publishing Corp. who contributed their time and talents.

Chapter 1

Lancaster County, Pennsylvania

Joseph Webber blew into his hands as the buggy pulled into the driveway. November air nipped at his fingers and cut across his face. Wheels crunched against gravel as his horse snorted and shook her head. Her breath puffed upward in little white clouds. Joseph tugged at the reins. "All right then, girl. I don't want to be here any more than you do." Joseph pulled the brake, rubbed a calloused hand over his face, and sighed. There was no putting this off any longer.

Well, he could buy himself another five minutes to put his horse in the barn. It was the shortest five minutes of his life. Joseph sighed again and trudged across the lawn toward the whitewashed farmhouse where he could see a yellow glow behind the tall kitchen windows. The sound of laughter filtered through the glass. The warm, familiar smell of baking bread wafted toward him. The homey scene might have felt cozy. It did not.

Just until Christmas, he reminded himself. And then I'm out of here.

It wasn't that he had anything against the Millers. They were a nice family. The mother, Ada, had round pink cheeks, a ready smile, and hands that were always pulling a fresh-baked pie from the oven. The father, Samuel, was slower to smile but had a soft gleam in his eye that communicated unspoken contentment.

The problem wasn't the family. The problem was Rachel.

Joseph stood at the front door with his hand raised and forced himself to knock. He might as well get it over with. He had made a mistake and now he had to pay the price. He just hadn't counted on the price being so *awkward*. He hadn't seen Rachel in years—not since they graduated from the one-room schoolhouse after the eighth grade. Her family had moved into another church district, and even though her new home was a short buggy ride from his, he hadn't thought of her again.

Now he had to work for her. She had been so reserved back then. Perhaps she had just been painfully shy—but Joseph had often thought she simply didn't want to bother with the boys' antics. And Joseph had been the ringleader of those antics.

What would they talk about as they spent hours together? How could he stay cooped up with her silence day after day? Worst of all, he didn't know what to say about her long illness. He wanted to tell her he was sorry for what she'd been through, but was that the right thing to say? What do you say in a situation like this? It can be so hard to know how to be a friend when bad things happen.

Joseph frowned. He was the type who usually opted to say nothing—and then felt guilty for not expressing his sympathy. But what if he said something and it only made Rachel feel worse? Should he remind her that her world fell apart?

The door opened and Ada Miller appeared. She wiped flour-covered hands on her apron and grinned at Joseph. "*Ach*, it's *gut* you're here. You are just what our Rachel needs. *Kumm* in!" She shooed him inside as she repeated, "*Kumm* in!"

The warm, rich aroma of baking bread strengthened as he crossed the threshold. Joseph wiped his boots, took off his straw hat, and turned it in his hands as he paused in the sparse but comfortable kitchen. Rachel was nowhere to be seen.

"Hello, Joseph!" Samuel Miller bounded into the room and slapped Joseph on the back. "Glad you're here. Go on back to the greenhouse." He motioned toward the far side of the room. "It's attached to the kitchen through that door. Rachel's expecting you. Ain't so, Ada?"

Ada cleared her throat and turned back toward the gas-powered stove. "Hmmm. Well. Not exactly."

"You still haven't told her?"

Ada picked up a yellow dish towel, folded it with a quick, uncertain gesture, and set it back down on the counter. She smoothed the crease with her fingers. "Not exactly."

Samuel let out a long breath. "By 'not exactly' you mean . . . "

Ada turned to her husband. "Not at all."

"Oh, Ada."

"I'm sorry, Samuel. But what will she say? You know how she wants her independence."

Samuel's face fell. Suddenly, the middle-aged man looked ten years older. "It's all right." He put a large, work-worn hand on his wife's shoulder. "I'll talk to her."

Ada shook her head. Tears welled in her eyes and Joseph looked away before Ada knew that he had seen them. She dabbed her eyes with the corner of her apron and forced a smile. "I will speak to our Rachel. This was my idea, after all."

"It's all right," Joseph said. "I'll tell her that she's got to put up with me—but just until Christmas."

Ada's smile brightened. "Would you?"

Samuel nodded at Joseph. His eyes looked thankful. "Rachel hasn't been herself lately. You understand. She doesn't want any help. But, what can we do?"

"She thinks I'm too overbearing since—" Ada cut herself off and turned back to the stove. "But she can't do all of the things she used to. How could she?"

"It's all right, Ada." Samuel kept his hand on his wife's shoulder and looked down at her with a soft expression.

Joseph nodded and eased out of the room. He wondered what he had gotten himself into. How could he convince Rachel to accept help—especially from him of all people!

Rachel sat in a wheelchair with an old kerchief covering her auburn hair and a worn apron over her dress. She slid her palms along the large rubber wheels to inch closer to a pot of pink roses. Rays of sunlight streaked across the barren November fields and filtered through the damp glass walls of the greenhouse. The light fell on her lap and sparkled against wet rose petals. The world outside looked cold and bare, but inside felt as warm and humid as a summer's day. Rachel ran a slim finger across a shiny green leaf. She could be happy here, alone with her plants. Almost.

"It is beautiful, ain't so?" Rachel said aloud. Her voice sounded loud in the still, silent room. Through the open door that led to the farmhouse, she could hear the distant muffled clang of pots and pans in the kitchen. The only other noise was the drip of water and the rasp of her breath. Sometimes she wished that her plants talked back to her. Other times she was thankful for the solitude. Either way, she had resigned herself to life with her thoughts and her plants. It would be enough because it had to be.

"*Ya*. It is," a male voice announced from the other side of the greenhouse.

Rachel gasped and spun around in her wheelchair. A tall,

lanky man leaned against the doorframe. Why didn't she hear him come in? And what was he doing *here,* in the only space she could call her own? And why was he looking at her like *that?* "I didn't know you were here."

"But you were talking to me."

Rachel turned back to the heirloom rosebush and ran her finger along a velvet-soft petal. "No. I wasn't."

Out of the corner of her eye she saw the man flash a wide smile. She pretended not to notice. It wouldn't do to encourage interlopers. She needed to be alone.

"Talking to yourself or to the plants?" The man straightened his posture and loped toward her. He carried himself with a confident, casual gait that Rachel admired, even though she had already made up her mind that he had to go.

"Does it matter?"

The man smiled again. "It might. I heard somewhere that plants like that kind of thing."

Rachel dropped her hand from the rose and turned to look up at the man. "Do you believe that or are you making fun of me?"

The man shrugged. "I don't know if I believe it, but I'm not making fun of you. I talk to my horse."

"That's different."

"Is it?"

Rachel smiled. Then she remembered she was irritated with him. It was getting harder not to like him. "You aren't supposed to be here."

"*Ya.*" He ran his hand through his dark brown hair and looked away. "About that."

Rachel narrowed her eyes. "Do I know you?"

"Joseph Webber. We were in school together."

"You're . . . " Rachel flinched. "Are you sure?"

Joseph laughed. "Pretty sure."

"You look . . . different." By "different," Rachel meant way more handsome. And muscular. Not that she was looking. She definitely was not looking.

Joseph flashed a familiar grin. That grin she did recognize. He had smiled like that in school before he committed some silly act to disrupt the class and make the other boys laugh. Some of the girls had thought it was cute and laughed too, but not Rachel. She did not go in for tomfoolery.

"I'm a few inches taller, I guess."

"More than a few." Rachel frowned and looked away. She had to make sure he did not hear the interest in her voice. Well, she refused to be interested, so there wasn't anything to notice, anyway. She had given up on boys. So that was that.

"Anyway. Why are you here?"

Joseph's smile dropped to a frown that matched hers. Rachel realized that her voice must have sounded sharper than she had meant. Oh well, best to make her feelings clear.

"Your mother hired me to help you in the greenhouse."

A flash of emotion tore across Rachel's face. "She what?"

"She . . . hired me." Joseph cleared his throat and looked away. "I didn't mean to disturb you. . . . " He sighed, pinched the bridge of his nose, then dropped his hand and looked her squarely in the eye. "Look, my parents arranged the job and didn't give me a choice in the matter. I don't want to be here any more than you want me here, so let's just make the best of it, okay?"

"So that's how it's going to be."

"Only if you want it that way."

"I do."

"Okay."

"Okay."

Rachel crossed her arms. Joseph crossed his. They both stared at each other for a long, hard moment. "I don't need any help," Rachel said at last.

"I know."

Rachel narrowed her eyes. "Do you? I can't walk very well right now. So you must think that I need help."

Joseph shrugged. "I can see that you can handle yourself just fine."

"*Ach.*" Rachel spun one of the wheels on her chair to turn herself away from Joseph. "I had bone cancer, you know. It's in remission, but it hurt my legs."

"*Ya.* I know. I heard."

Rachel stared out the window at green rolling hills and brown fields covered in stubble from the harvest. "So that's that." Rachel liked to come straight to the point. No sense drawing things out.

"Thank God."

"What?" Rachel's eyes shot up to Joseph's.

"That you're alive." Joseph motioned toward the rows of plants. "And can still do all this. It's amazing in here. Like a rain forest or something."

"*Ach.* If you thought that then you wouldn't be here. But you're wrong. Like I told you, I can manage on my own."

Joseph nodded. "I believe you. But you have to think of your *mamm* and *daed* right now. They're worried about you, ain't so? Let me stay for their sake. I won't touch anything." Joseph shrugged and gave a charming half grin. "I'll just pull up a chair and sit. It'll be the easiest job I ever had."

Rachel frowned. She hadn't thought about how much her parents would worry if she refused to let Joseph stay. "Okay. But only for their sake. I don't need any help."

"*Ya.* You've mentioned that." Joseph walked to the corner of the greenhouse and picked up an old wooden chair. He carried it toward Rachel, plopped it down a few feet behind her, dusted it off, and sank onto the seat. "And I agree that you don't need help. But, whether you need it or not, it's okay to ask for it sometimes." Joseph cracked his knuckles, leaned back in his chair, and closed his eyes. "Of course, it doesn't matter to me either way. But everyone needs help sometimes. I had to ask my *bruder* to help me keep up with my chores at home while I'm here."

"That's not the same thing."

"Isn't it?"

"No."

"Hmmm. I guess everyone's entitled to their opinion. But I don't think you're any different than me, or anyone else for that matter. You just have to figure some things out, that's all."

Rachel flinched. She had never thought of it that way before. But she was not about to let some class clown from grade school barge into her greenhouse and tell her everything was okay. Because it was most definitely not okay. "I don't believe my parents are paying you to give advice." Rachel felt contrite as soon as the words left her mouth, but she could not take them back. She was tired of hearing positive speeches that left her feeling even more distant and alone. Even if Joseph's point *did* make sense . . . Up to now, everyone had focused on her being different. What if Joseph was right and she wasn't so different after all?

Chapter 2

Joseph was not happy about how the day went. Not at all. His older *bruder*, Eli, said something to their *schweschder*, Hannah, about a new calf in the barn, but Joseph barely noticed. He heard the distant thump of a casserole dish and the clang of a serving spoon as he stared at the rough pine walls of his family's farmhouse.

"Joseph. What's got into you, Son?"

"What?" He flinched a little, snapped his attention back to dinner, and took the warm serving bowl from his mother's hand. "Mmmm. Smells great, Mamm." He ladled out a heaping spoonful of mashed potatoes and reached for the gravy boat.

"Work didn't go well?" His mother, Erma, looked at him with her warm, concerned blue eyes. He knew that look all too well.

Joseph opened his mouth to protest, but he knew his *mamm* would see right through him. "No. Not really."

"First days are always the hardest. It'll get better."

Joseph's father, Abraham, gave him a thoughtful look from

across the long wooden table. "And even if it doesn't, you stick it out and do your best, *ya?*"

"*Ya.*" Joseph dropped his gaze and studied his plate. He didn't want to think about the mistake that landed him in this situation. Actually, make that plural. His mistakes kept piling on lately.

"Admitting that you're wrong is the hardest part. It'll get better from here on out."

Joseph pushed a green bean across his plate. He hoped his *daed* was right. But he couldn't shake the guilt he felt over crashing the buggy his *daed* had bought him. What had he been thinking to race his friend Abner like that? What if someone had been hurt? Joseph had a chance to pay his *daed* back for the repairs from the money he would make working for the Millers. But how could his new job end in any way but disaster? "I don't know if I'll make it until Christmas."

"Of course you will, Son." His father looked stern but kind. "You will because you have to."

"Your *daed* promised the Millers you would take this job and we expect you to follow through," his *mamm* said. "Besides, it's the only job we could find close to the farm, so you can still help with the milking each day." She gave him a kind but knowing look. "Perhaps, more important, you may find it's a better fit than you realize."

"What I mean is, I don't know if Rachel will let me stay."

"Why not?" Erma asked. She set down her fork and waited for him to answer.

Joseph didn't respond.

"Surely it can't be that bad. She's always been a nice girl. Quiet, but nice."

"*Ya.* She is. It's just that she really doesn't want me there. She wants to be independent."

"*Ach.* I see." Erma nodded and sighed.

"And I've already made everything worse."

Abraham wiped his mouth on a cloth napkin and shook his head. "You're being too hard on yourself, Son."

"I tried to make her feel better and I ended up upsetting her instead. I didn't know what to say and, of course, I said the wrong thing."

"It isn't easy to know what to say in a situation like this," Erma said. "Try telling her what you would want to hear if the situation were reversed."

Abraham nodded. "Your *mamm*'s right."

"That's what I did. . . . " Joseph shrugged. "I don't think it worked."

"Hmmm." His father paused and looked thoughtful. "Maybe it did work and you don't know it yet."

"I hope you're right. Because I have to go back tomorrow and I don't look forward to spending it sitting in a chair."

"You sat in a chair all afternoon?" His mother looked surprised. Eli and Hannah laughed.

"*Ya.* And I feel bad taking the Millers' money for doing nothing." Joseph raised his hands and dropped them. "But what else can I do? Rachel has a right to run the show. It's her greenhouse."

"Can't argue with that." Abraham tugged on his full gray beard.

"And I don't want to insult her by pushing my way into her life," Joseph added.

"Don't worry, Son." Erma patted his hand. Her fingers felt warm and soft. "*Der Herr* has a way of making these things work out. I am sure that there is a purpose in your being there, even if you can't see it yet."

"More than having to pay Daed back for crashing the new buggy?"

Erma shook her head. "No need to dwell on that. You're working to make it right. It's over now."

Joseph wished his mother were right. But he had nearly two months ahead of him working in a place where he wasn't wanted. It wasn't nearly over yet.

Rachel glanced at the battery-powered clock on the old wooden shelf above the heirloom cucumber plants. Joseph should be there by now. She tightened her lips and looked away. Why on earth was she even thinking about Joseph right now? Why should she care whether he came back or not? It would be reasonable of him not to come back, after the way she treated him. She felt embarrassed at the memory. After all, her problems weren't his fault. It was just so hard to convince everyone that she was ready to move on and live her life. The cancer was gone, but her parents still treated her as if she might break at any moment. She needed them to realize that she was still the same old Rachel as before she got sick and that she was still capable of doing everything she used to do, even if she had to find new ways of doing those things.

Rachel flinched. Wasn't that what Joseph told her yesterday? Could it be possible that he understood her? No. That would be preposterous. Absolutely preposterous. Joseph was a shallow, attention-seeking boy who had gotten carried away with his Rumspringa, raced his buggy, and crashed it. The news was all over Lancaster County. Joseph was wild. If he wasn't careful the bishop would have to get involved.

No, Joseph Webber was not the type to give good advice . . . was he?

The door to the greenhouse creaked open and Rachel looked up expectantly. Joseph loped inside with his hands jammed into his pockets, his expression calm and distant.

"You came back." Rachel's voice sounded flatter than she meant. She hadn't meant to seem accusatory. She was genuinely surprised that he had shown up for more. She had not exactly been good company the day before.

Joseph shrugged and looked sheepish. "*Ya.*"

"I wasn't sure you would."

Joseph shrugged again. His dark hair swung over his brow and his brown eyes flashed. Rachel thought he looked adorable— then pushed the thought away and straightened in her wheelchair. What had gotten into her? Joseph Webber *adorable?* The very idea!

"My parents made me take the job, you know."

"*Ach.* You already mentioned that." Rachel frowned. "And I could have guessed, anyway. I heard about your buggy . . . *incident.*"

Joseph looked away. His eyes traced a row of spindly, weedy plants. "What's that?"

So, he didn't want to talk about the buggy crash. Well, Rachel didn't want to talk to him, so that was fine with her. . . . Although she did find herself wanting to know more about him. She wondered why he would to do something so foolish as race a buggy and if he had stopped all that after his crash. Was he still going too far with his Rumspringa? She pretended not to notice that he was avoiding the subject and answered his question. "That's yarrow."

"It isn't very pretty."

"It is when it blooms. But that doesn't matter. I don't grow plants just because they're pretty. I grow heirloom plants because I like the connection to people who came before us." Rachel pushed the wheels on her chair to inch closer to Joseph and the weedy-looking plant. "Yarrow was a medicine in the past." She swiveled in her chair and pointed across the greenhouse. "Foxglove too, even though it's poisonous. So take care, *ya?*"

"Poisonous? What were people thinking back then?"

Rachel laughed. "It's not so different today, if you think about it. If you didn't have to take care with modern drugs, you wouldn't need a prescription to get them."

Joseph looked down at her and smiled. "I like the way you see things."

"You do?"

"Yeah. It's different. You think about things that I never thought to think about."

Rachel smiled. "I just like plants is all." She gave a satisfied sigh and looked up and down the long rows of damp green leaves and brilliant flowers. "And I like history. Put them together and you get perfection. For me, anyway."

"You said something about heirloom plants, *ya?*"

"*Ya.*"

"That means what? Plants from history?"

Rachel laughed again. She had almost forgotten to be irritated that he was invading her space. "You could say that."

"I've never thought about it much."

"What, plants? Or history?"

Joseph grinned. "Both, I guess." He reached out and traced the edge of a serrated green leaf.

"Don't touch!" Rachel leaned forward and tightened her grip on the armrests of her wheelchair.

Joseph jerked back his hand as if burned. "Is it poisonous?" He wiped his fingers on his black trousers.

Rachel almost laughed again. But she remembered that he had crossed a line and kept her frown. "No. I just don't want you to go around touching my plants."

"Oh." Joseph looked embarrassed. "Sorry."

His expression reminded Rachel of a scolded puppy and she wanted to reach out and touch his face. She looked away instead. "No, I'm sorry. Just please don't go around touching anything, okay?"

"Okay."

Things were going as expected. Terribly. And, to make matters worse, Joseph thought he had started to break through to

Rachel. Until she snapped at him for invading her space. He cracked his knuckles and shifted in the old wooden chair. Rachel glanced at him and then looked away again. She reached for a yellow watering can and Joseph sighed. He wanted to ask her more about the different plants and why they mattered to her, but every time he tried, her expression warned him away. Joseph watched from his seat as Rachel inched her wheelchair across the concrete floor.

"Okay. Enough."

Rachel's head whipped around.

Joseph stood up and stretched. "Sorry, but I can't sit here while your parents pay me. I've got to do something."

Rachel's fingers tightened against the watering can. Then she relaxed her grip and offered a sheepish grin. Joseph liked the way her blue eyes lit up when she smiled. He had never noticed how blue they were before today.

"I guess I've been a little too . . . " Rachel frowned and hesitated.

"Overprotective?"

Rachel nodded. "*Ya*. Overprotective. I just don't want anyone hurting my plants. They're the only thing that—" She cut off the sentence and looked down at the watering can in her hands.

"That you can control? That you have to yourself?"

Rachel's eyes shot up to Joseph's. "*Ya*. How did you know?"

"Because it's obvious."

"Is it really?" Rachel's freckled cheeks began to flush pink. Her fingers picked at the chipped yellow paint on the watering can.

"Maybe not to anyone else. But I get it. You just want something that's yours."

Rachel tilted her head. "*Ya*." She looked as if she were seeing him for the first time. "You know what that's like too, don't you?"

"Yep." Joseph flashed a crooked smile.

Rachel stared at him.

Joseph shrugged. "I've been thinking of leaving home."

"Leaving? What do you mean?" Rachel leaned forward.

Joseph sighed and let his gaze wander across a row of bright blue Forget-Me-Nots. "I don't know if I'm cut out for this life." He waved his hand in an aimless motion. "Maybe I can find what I'm looking for among the English."

Rachel opened her mouth, then closed it. She paused and sank back into her wheelchair. She set her elbows on the armrests, steepled her fingers, and studied Joseph's expression.

He didn't like the intensity of the gaze. It cut through him as if she could read his mind.

"What are you looking for?" Rachel asked finally.

"*Ach,* I don't know." Joseph shrugged. "Something that belongs to me. Independence. Same as you, I guess."

"Have you found it running around with the English?"

Joseph laughed. Then his face fell into seriousness. "No."

"Your *daed*'s dairy farm is doing well?"

Joseph nodded.

"That's the problem, isn't it?"

Joseph's expression shifted to surprise. "*Ya.*"

"You want something different for your life."

"*Ya.*" His face brightened. "I've never told anyone that before. How'd you know?"

Rachel gave a short, sad laugh. "We think alike, I guess."

Joseph stared at her, unsure what to say. No one had ever guessed that he didn't want to follow in his *daed*'s footsteps. He loved his parents and he appreciated their way of life. But handling cows just didn't click with him. He had tried to take up carpentry and woodworking, but he hadn't been very good at it. "I wonder if I would find something I'm good at if I left. Something that makes me feel excited to get up every day."

"Maybe. Maybe not."

Joseph shrugged. "*Ya*. Maybe not." He let out a long breath of air. "You know, I don't really want to leave. I just . . . " He frowned and ran his fingers through his thick, dark hair. "I just want to feel valuable."

Rachel's eyes lit up. Her face softened as she stared at him. "Me too."

Chapter 3

Joseph nodded good morning to his *bruder* from across the long, drafty barn. The cows shifted in their stalls. Hooves scraped against concrete and straw. Fog rose from wet noses and warmed the air. Joseph checked the propane heater. "Getting cold, *ya?*" He didn't like dragging himself out of bed before dawn and stomping through the frost to milk the cows.

Other than that, he didn't mind the cold. Cold brought cozy fires in the hearth, pumpkin spice cookies, and Christmas. Joseph patted the warm, solid side of a cow as his thoughts drifted to Rachel's greenhouse. He liked that it held a tiny sliver of summer all year round. It almost felt magic, like a fairy tale. With a greenhouse, you could have the best of both worlds.

Joseph didn't notice as he attached the diesel-powered milking machine to each cow and emptied the milk into a big tank. He had done it so many times that the action had become automatic. He smelled the familiar, earthy odor of the barn and heard the stomp of his boots as he moved from cow to cow, but his mind was far away. When Joseph reached the end of the row and snapped back to attention, he realized that he had been daydreaming about plants. What a strange thing to escape into. He ought to be daydreaming about the English girl he hung out with in Lancaster on Saturday nights. But instead, he was wondering about yarrow and foxglove and why Rachel cared so much. More than that, he had been thinking about the independent spark in Rachel's eyes and the way her face softened when she realized they both wanted to be valuable.

This was not how things were supposed to go.

He should appreciate life on a dairy farm, just like his *daed* and *bruder* did. And he certainly should not be thinking about a girl who wanted nothing to do with him—no matter how much she intrigued him. He had to remember that, after three days of working together she still seemed annoyed by his very presence! And yet that independent streak was what made him admire her.

Joseph paused. Did he just admit that he admired Rachel Miller? What was he thinking? Sure, she was clever and spirited and unlike any other girl he knew—but she had made it clear that she was not interested. Besides, his heart was already halfway in the English world. The last thing he needed now was a distraction—even if it had sparkling blue eyes and a knowing smile that intrigued him.

Joseph hurried back to the house for a hot cup of black *kaffi* while Eli sanitized the equipment and shoveled out the stalls. Joseph filled a glass with water and poured it on his *mamm*'s peace lily in the windowsill above the sink, then picked up his mug and blew across the top. The warm ceramic felt good against his cold fingers. He shifted the peace lily's pot a few inches to catch the sun. The weak rays of early morning light brightened the waxy green leaves. Joseph leaned against the old butcher-block counter and sighed contentedly, then stopped and frowned. Had he always cared about that peace lily? He thought for a moment. Yes, he had. Every morning he came in from the barn, watered the plant, and made sure it was in the sun. How strange. He had never thought about it before.

"What's the matter, Son?"

Joseph turned to see his *maam* standing behind him with a laundry basket in her hands. Gray hair peeked from the front of her blue work kerchief.

"*Ach*, nothing."

"You look like you're thinking about something . . . or somebody." She raised an eyebrow. "A lucky young woman?"

"No." Joseph laughed and pushed away from the counter. "I was thinking about that peace lily."

Erma smiled. "You always had a green thumb."

"I never thought about it before."

"Your *daed* and I have. Why do you think he found you a job in a greenhouse?"

Joseph opened his mouth, then closed it again. He shook his head. "I thought it was because I failed at that woodworking job I tried last year."

Erma pressed the laundry basket against a hip to free one hand and tousled Joseph's hair. "Carpentry isn't your gift. We thought you might like working with plants better."

"I thought you were trying to punish me."

Erma's forehead crinkled and she tilted her head. "Whyever would you think that?"

"Rachel isn't easy to work with. She doesn't want me there."

Erma waved her hand. "*Ach*, that. Easily solved. Just be yourself." She moved her hand to his shoulder and held it there. "Don't you see that we're trying to help you?"

"After I wrecked the buggy and almost got Abner killed? No, I don't see that. Why would you?"

Her hand tightened on his shoulder. "Because we love you. You need to earn money to pay your *daed* back, but maybe a change of scenery will do you *gut*. Get the restlessness out of your system, *ya?* We know your heart's not been in the dairy farm lately."

"You do?" A flash of panic rocketed up Joseph's spine. "I never said that."

"You didn't have to. Your *daed* and I can see."

"You can?"

"*Ya.*"

"I never wanted Daed to know that. The farm is so important to him."

"He's your father. He knows you well enough to see you're unhappy here."

"No. I'm not unhappy. I'm just . . ." Joseph shrugged and turned away from his mother's gaze. Her understanding attitude made him feel guilty.

"It's just you feel as if you don't belong here."

Joseph's eyes shot back to his mother. "*Ya.*"

"Your *onkel* didn't like dairy farming either. That's why he started Webber Creamery. He found a way to fit what he wanted into the life God gave him. Don't you know that God gave you whatever talents you have? He wants you to use them. And I believe you can find a way to use them right here, with us—otherwise you wouldn't have been born Amish. Take a break; work with plants for a while; try and enjoy yourself. Then maybe you'll be ready to settle down on the farm for good."

"What would you think if I did something else, like Onkel Isaiah did?"

"I don't see how you could. Eli will be wanting to start a family soon." Erma shook her head. "This farm can only support so many people. As the older brother, he knows he'll have to work somewhere else. You're young enough to wait until your *daed* retires to take over."

"I know." Joseph looked away. "It's okay. I don't want to leave." The words stuck in his throat because he knew that was already halfway gone.

Erma gave him a long, hard stare. "Really? Then why do you spend so much time running around with the English? I wonder what you think you'll find with them."

Joseph felt uncomfortable. Had he really been that transparent? He thought he had done a better job of hiding his restlessness. And as far as running around with the English . . . well, he sure thought he had hidden the extent of that from his mother. He wasn't sure whether to feel embarrassed or relieved that she was on to him.

"Everyone knows Eli should take over the farm when Daed retires. He loves the work."

Erma sighed and tucked a loose strand of hair under her kerchief. "I wish it were that simple."

"I better get going. Don't want to be late."

Erma nodded. She didn't say another word, but she watched with concerned eyes as Joseph set his empty *kaffi* mug on the butcher-block counter and strode out the door.

Rachel emptied a bowl of kitchen scraps into the compost bin on the greenhouse floor. As the food decomposed, heat rose to help warm the air and save on propane. She checked the thermostat behind the propane heater and nodded. Everything was running smoothly. Except for her thoughts.

As she puttered through her morning routine, Rachel's focus kept drifting back to eighth grade. Eighth grade of all places! She scowled and picked up a pair of gardening shears. What had gotten into her? As she pruned an heirloom cucumber vine, she remembered Joseph's classroom antics. He had such a big personality. The entire room would roar with laughter when he cracked a joke or teased a girl.

Rachel had disliked him for his teasing. He never said anything mean or hurtful or inappropriate to the other girls; he just pointed out something cute or endearing about them. She had thought him very foolish, even though he always had something clever or funny to say about Anna, Rebekah, or Abigail. He would say it loud enough for everyone to hear, so that everyone would react. Then the girl would get a haughty look on her face, sit up a littler straighter, and giggle in an annoying, overly feminine way.

Rachel had always told herself that she was glad he didn't target her for such attention-seeking nonsense. Why should she care? As the metal blades of the shears whispered against each other, Rachel realized why she had always felt vaguely angry with Joseph Webber. He had left her out. He had never targeted her. He had never even noticed her. She had sat quietly in the corner while he grinned at the other girls and they giggled and blushed.

Ach! What foolishness! Why should she want some silly boy to notice her? And yet—

Rachel snapped the shears shut with too much force and clipped a vine she had meant to save. She sighed and set down the shears with a hard clang. "All right. Fine. I admit it." She knew in her heart that she wanted Joseph Webber to tease her instead of the other girls. She didn't want to be the silent, forgotten one.

And here she was, six years later, still silent, still forgotten. Her friends had drifted away into their own busy lives when she got sick. Months stretched into years, but she had not moved forward when everyone else had. They had enjoyed youth groups and singings, buggy rides and festive after-church dinners. She had been home or in the hospital. Now all she had was her greenhouse and her own thoughts. And her plants, of course. They had become her closest friends.

Until Joseph Webber came crashing in like he owned the place. Of all the people to invade her cozy, safe world—it had to be the boy who had made her feel the most alone!

The door creaked open and slammed shut. Ha! Perfect timing. Just when she realized she wanted Joseph Webber *in* her life almost as much as she wanted him *out* of it. Why did life have to be so complicated?

"Morning."

Rachel swallowed and forced her voice to sound steady. "Good morning. You're early."

"Am I?" He flashed that endearing grin of his. "Just wanted to get on your nerves."

Was he teasing her? Was he really? Rachel frowned and turned away. Of course not. Why would he do that now, when he had ignored her in school? That would mean that he was treating her as if she were just like anyone else . . . and so few people did that now. She cleared her throat, raised her chin a fraction, and spoke in a cold voice. "You're succeeding." *Ach.* What a thing to say!

Joseph sighed and shrugged. "Just till Christmas."

Rachel nodded. Her cheeks burned and she kept her face turned so that he couldn't see. "*Ya.* Just until Christmas. Less than two months to go." She hadn't meant to be rude. But, what else could she say? Joseph had told her he didn't want to be there. There was no point in indulging silly fantasies that he might actually see her as a *person.* He never had before. Why would he start now?

"So, what's the goal here?"

"What?" Rachel felt ruffled and uncertain. She didn't understand this boy at all. He had her completely thrown. If only he weren't quite so handsome or quite so tall and charming. She smelled the musky scent of his aftershave as he stepped closer. Her hands fumbled over the shears and they dropped to the floor. The metal clanged against the concrete. She just couldn't think straight. This was getting ridiculous.

Joseph swooped in and picked up the shears. His eyes met hers as he straightened back up, tossed the shears in the air, caught them by the handles, and handed them to her.

Rachel swallowed. She could not pull herself out of his mischievous brown eyes. "Thank you."

"The goal?"

"What? *Ach.* I don't know. . . . "

"You've got all these plants. Why? What are you going to do with them?"

Rachel shrugged. "I used to put a sign at the end of the driveway for the English tourists to see. They would stop in and buy things sometimes." She shrugged again.

"So, why isn't it up now?"

"I couldn't keep up with my plants when I was sick."

"You're not sick anymore, are you?"

"No."

"Then what's stopping you?"

Rachel gave him an irritated look. "Isn't it obvious?"

"Nope."

Rachel raised her eyebrows and stared at him.

"I tell you what, figure out what you want to sell and how much you want to charge, or whatever. And I'll go put the sign back up. I bet you've still got it around here somewhere."

"Not many people drive by. It's too far off the main road."

"Sounds like you're making excuses. The English like to drive the back roads on the way to Bird-in-Hand, *ya*? I bet plenty come by here. You know how they are—they want the 'authentic Amish experience,' whatever that means."

"*Ya.* But I'd do better selling at the Bird-in-Hand Farmers Market. I was going to, you know."

"Okay. So it's settled."

"What's settled?"

"We reopen Rachel's Greenhouse—or whatever you want to call it—and we get you in the farmers market."

"You think people would buy from me?"

"*Ya.* Of course."

Rachel smiled. She felt a tiny spark of warmth build inside her chest. "I've been daydreaming about it." *Ach!* Why had she told him that? Information about her dreams was personal!

"I'm surprised at you. I figured you'd have it all up and running by now."

Rachel frowned. Why *was* she putting it off? "People are complicated, I guess." She didn't want to admit that she was afraid. What if her parents were right? What if she couldn't cope?

Joseph chuckled. "Yes, they are." He turned and headed in the opposite direction. "I think I see a sign in that pile of junk." He nodded toward a stack of plywood, bags of potting soil, and empty pots in the far corner of the greenhouse.

Rachel watched him but didn't answer.

Joseph stopped and turned to look at her. "Unless you want to give up . . . ?" She noticed the glint in his deep brown eyes. He was goading her into trying and she couldn't help but fall for it. *Ach,* if only he weren't quite so charming!

"No." The word came out as a grunt.

Joseph smiled a satisfied smile. He had her. Rachel watched as he strode across the greenhouse with that confident walk of his. She had the feeling that everything in her life was about to change. And she didn't know whether to be excited or terrified.

Chapter 4

The rest of the week passed in an uneasy truce as Rachel considered how to attract tourists to her little out-of-the-way greenhouse. Every day at 12:00 sharp, her *mamm* knocked on the greenhouse door, cracked it open, and announced that lunch would be ready in five minutes.

"Do you have any ripe tomatoes?" she asked on Saturday, and swept her gaze over the long rows of plants. "Would be wonderful good with the meal."

Rachel beamed. "*Ya*. I do."

Ada nodded and slipped back to the kitchen.

"Over here," Rachel said, and led Joseph to a fuzzy vine tied to a wooden stake. Strange-looking fruit with uneven, bulgy sides hung from the vine.

"What're those?" Joseph asked.

"Tomatoes, of course."

"They don't look like it. They look like squishy little pumpkins."

Rachel laughed. "They're heirloom tomatoes. This is what tomatoes used to look like, before people bred them to look like the ones in the grocery store." She plucked a misshapen oversized orange tomato and handed it to Joseph. It felt heavy and smooth in his hand, just like a regular tomato.

"I guess you think it's ugly," Rachel said.

"No. Just different."

"And different is ugly."

"No. Different is . . . different. Nothing more, nothing less. It isn't bad or good to be different. It just *is*."

"Oh."

"Do these taste better than the ones in the grocery store?" Joseph asked.

"Absolutely." She grinned and grabbed the tomato from his palm. "But you'll have to find out for yourself."

The scent of baking bread met them at the kitchen door. Joseph smiled at the sourdough loaf, the Mason jars of pickled watermelon rind and pickled beets, the plate of cheese, and the platter of cold ham on the red-checked tablecloth. "Looks, great, Ada. Thanks." He slid onto a straight-backed wooden chair as Rachel's *mamm* sliced the heirloom tomato and sprinkled each slice with salt and pepper.

"It's good to have you here," Ada said as she set the plate of sliced tomato on the table. "And you're in for a treat. Rachel's tomatoes will be the best you've ever tasted."

The front door swung open and Samuel barged in with a blast of frigid air. "Cold front's come in," he said as he hung his heavy coat on a peg and then held his palms up to the propane heater. "It's good to be home."

"It's good to have you here," Ada said. "Slow day at the harness shop?"

Samuel grinned. "Slow enough to get away for a home cooked meal." He dropped into a wooden chair at the head of the table as Ada poured him a hot cup of *kaffi*. Steam rose from the mug as they blessed the food.

"Have you heard the *gut* news?" Joseph asked as he reached

for the jar of pickled watermelon rind. Joseph smiled and glanced at Rachel. Her eyes narrowed and she shook her head slightly, just enough for him to see. Joseph hesitated. Had he done something wrong?

"Good news?" Samuel leaned forward. "Let's hear it!"

"*Ya*." Joseph cleared his throat. Why was Rachel giving him that look? "Rachel didn't tell you? She's going to start selling plants again. And not just here. She's going to sell at the Bird-in-Hand Farmers Market too."

"Ah." Samuel's eager expression evaporated. He sat back in his chair and ran his fingers through his long gray beard. "I see."

"Rachel?" Ada's face crumpled.

Rachel frowned. She looked down at her plate. "It's what I want to do."

"You can," her mother said. "Later. But it's so soon. . . . " Her eyes swung to Samuel. "Tell her it's too soon. She can't possibly manage."

"Mamm, I'm right here. You can talk to me about it."

Samuel put a large, calloused hand atop Rachel's and patted gently. "Your *mamm*'s right. You need to take care of yourself. She just wants what's best for you."

"But Daed, I'm twenty years old! I can't live like this forever."

Samuel looked very tired. "No, of course not. But just a little while longer. Until you're stronger."

"You've been saying that for a long time, Daed."

Samuel rubbed his forehead. He shook his head. "Your mother is so worried about you, Rachel."

Joseph worked very hard to concentrate on the slice of ham on his plate. He cut it up into small pieces as the Miller family argued around him. What had he started? He only wanted to help but had made things worse instead.

"Can't you let us take care of you?" Ada asked in a small, pleading voice. "Can't you see we worry so?"

"*Ya*. But I need to live again. Can't *you* see *that?*"

Ada didn't answer. She stared at Rachel with tight lips and frightened eyes.

"I'm not going to break," Rachel said, and speared a pickled beet with her fork. "The worst has happened. It has to get better from here."

"She's right, Ada," Samuel said in a weary voice. "She has to figure out how to live the life she's been given."

Ada didn't answer. She opened her mouth, closed it again, and pushed her chair back from the table. She stumbled out of her chair and hurried to the propane-powered refrigerator. "I'll get us some milk. I forgot the milk."

"Ada," Samuel said gently. "We don't need milk."

The room was very quiet. Ada stood still for a moment without opening the refrigerator door, then turned back around. Her eyes looked red. "I'm sorry, Rachel. It is so hard to believe that you'll be okay—that everything can be okay now."

"Joseph will look out for her. He'll make sure she can handle things. Right, Joseph?"

"*Ya*. Of course."

"Give it a try. On a trial basis. If it's too much, you quit. Understand, Rachel?"

"*Ya*."

Samuel nodded and dropped his napkin into his lap. "Let's eat. All this good food is going to waste. *Kumm* sit, Ada. It's decided."

Ada let out a long, shaky breath and returned Samuel's nod. "On a trial basis."

"*Ya*." Samuel slathered fresh butter onto a slice of sourdough bread and took a big bite. "Have some, Ada. It's delicious."

Ada sighed and slid back into her chair. The conversation

shifted to the weather and business at the harness shop. But Joseph noticed that Rachel hardly ate throughout the meal, despite her mother's encouraging smiles.

Rachel didn't want to talk to Joseph when he came back to work on Monday. She let him move bags of potting soil and fix a leak in the irrigation system, but she slipped away whenever he came near. "I'm sorry I made things difficult for you with your parents," Joseph said at last.

Rachel didn't turn to look at him. She kept her attention on a potted plant and shrugged. "It's all right. It was bound to happen sooner or later."

"They mean well."

"*Ya,* I know. That's the trouble." She let out a long breath of air and sank deeper into her chair. "I don't want to stress them out after everything they've been through, but they have to realize that I need to move on with life."

"They'll get it."

"You know what I really hate about it? Everything was going so well. I finally made a plan to get back on track. And we—" Rachel cut the sentence short and shook her head. She had been about to say "and we finally clicked." Goodness! Had she been that close to disaster? What if she had said such a thing out loud? It wouldn't do to let a popular, handsome boy know she enjoyed his company. He could never, ever be interested in her! Rachel frowned and reached for a trowel. He was just being nice, that was all. She had to remember that.

"We still have a plan to get back on track." Joseph's dark eyes glinted with encouragement. He looked like he might actually be looking forward to their new goal.

"But it always seems like that, *ya?* Something good starts to happen, then bam!" Rachel slammed a fist into her palm. "Something bad happens."

Joseph's expression turned thoughtful. "You know that isn't how it works."

"Maybe not. But it sure feels that way."

"Don't be afraid for good things to happen. Just because something bad happened to you in the past doesn't mean bad things will keep happening. You can't live life waiting for the next disaster."

"Humph."

Joseph laughed. Rachel liked the way his eyes sparkled when he laughed. "That's all you have to say? Humph?"

"*Ya.*"

"You're not really trying."

"I'm tired of trying. It's not fair that I have to keep trying. All I ever do is try."

"I get it. But that's life. And fair or not, you can't ever quit."

"Okay, fine. I'll think about it."

"Okay, good."

"Okay, good." Rachel crossed her arms and Joseph crossed his. He looked irritated for a moment but broke into a smile.

"What?"

"I can't help it. Look at you."

"What about me?"

"I can't take you seriously like that."

"Like what?" Rachel scowled.

"When you scowl like that."

"I'm not scowling."

Joseph's smile widened. "*Ya*, you are. And it's not intimidating. It's . . . kind of cute."

"*Ach,* for goodness' sakes."

Joseph shrugged. He had a playful expression that Rachel liked and didn't like at the same time.

"Are you making fun of me?"

"No."

"Yes you are."

"Okay, maybe a little bit. But I can't help it. You look too cute not to." He shrugged and heaved a bag of potting soil onto his shoulder. "I'll leave you alone if that's what you want."

Rachel watched Joseph lope across the greenhouse and drop the bag on the wooden potting table. He whistled an upbeat tune as if he hadn't a care in the world. Her heart felt light and fuzzy in her chest. Had he just teased her like he used to tease the girls at school? He had! He really had!

And she liked it. Heaven help her, she liked it very much.

Joseph wondered if he had crossed a line. This was a job—not a social call. Besides, he had an English girl, Chrissy, to think about. He had been seeing a lot more of her over the past few weeks. He couldn't start thinking of Rachel in *that way*. He had plans to see the world and find himself. It would be cruel to lead Rachel on. The problem was, he liked her company. He liked teasing her. He liked . . . *her*.

Joseph stopped whistling. This would change everything. He snuck a glance at Rachel from over his shoulder. She sat with grave concentration as she examined the leaves of an heirloom rose. An adorable furrow ran through her forehead as she focused on the task. Her eyes moved to his, caught him staring at her, and shot back to the rose. She shifted in her chair and straightened her spine. Her face flushed red as she tried to force a disinterested expression onto her face.

Joseph had seen that look before. It meant that things just got complicated. Way too complicated.

Chapter 5

Rachel met Joseph at the door of the greenhouse the next morning. "I talked to my *aenti* Ruby about our plan. She said I can use her booth at the Bird-in-Hand Farmers Market the Saturday before Christmas. It's one of their busiest days of the year, so we have to be ready by then. But it doesn't give us much time to grow anything." She glanced at the wall calendar. "We have six weeks to prove I can do this."

Joseph gave a quick nod. "All right. Let's prove it, then."

Rachel smiled. "So you're with me?"

"I'm with you."

"Wonderful good!" Rachel's smile exploded into a grin before she realized she might seem a little too eager. She had better clarify. "As business partners, I mean."

"Right." Joseph stepped aside to check the propane level in the heater, but Rachel thought she caught an impish glint in his eye before he turned away. She wished she could decipher him. Because that sure did seem like a friendly sort of glint—the kind of glint a boy might give a girl who caught his fancy.

Rachel frowned. She had to stop these silly notions. She sighed and studied Joseph's tall, muscular frame as he lifted a container of yarrow and moved it to the potting table.

"This one's looking kind of bad. You might want to take a look."

"What?" Rachel cleared her throat. She had been staring at the curve of his biceps beneath the rolled-up sleeves of his blue button-down shirt. The very idea! What had gotten into her? "Right. The yarrow." She eased closer and made a show of focusing on the plant's brown-tipped leaves. "*Ya*. Something's not right."

Joseph rested a hip against the potting table and looked down at her with an indulgent smile. Rachel worked harder to focus all attention on the yarrow. She had a sneaking suspicion that he was on to her.

Rachel worked very, very hard not to look at Joseph for the rest of the day. It was not easy. Especially when he asked about her feelings. She wanted to shout, "Really? You're *that* good-looking *and* thoughtful too?" It just wasn't fair. Who could resist a man like that?

When Joseph asked how she felt about the pushback from her parents, he was considerate enough to add, "It's okay if you don't want to talk about it."

"No, it's all right." Rachel tried to get her thoughts together, but the sparkle in his brown eyes and the concern in his voice distracted her. "I don't mind talking about it. I feel like no matter what I do it will never be enough to prove to Mamm and Daed that I can make it on my own."

Joseph nodded. "Let's see how the next few weeks go. I bet they'll come around."

Rachel let out a long, tired breath. "Maybe."

Joseph grinned. "Why don't you tell me about this plant. Yarrow, right?"

"*Ya.*" Rachel ran her fingers over the feathery leaves. They tickled in a soft, reassuring way. "You can make it into tea to bring down a fever. That's what they say, anyway."

Joseph broke off a leaf, rubbed it between his thumb and fingers, and smelled the crushed leaf. "Smells bitter. I bet it tastes terrible." He glanced at Rachel. "You've never tried it?"

"No." She laughed. "Aspirin works better."

"*Ya.*" His mouth curled into a knowing half smile. "But aspirin comes from the bark of a tree, doesn't it?"

"Willow." Rachel's brows knit together. "How'd you know that? I thought . . . "

"That I didn't know anything about plants?" He winked at her. "You should have asked."

Rachel stared at him with a surprised look, then pointed to a nearby plant. "Okay, Mr. Smarty-Pants, what about Evening Primrose? What's it good for?"

Joseph chuckled. "I didn't say I knew everything about plants."

"So you still have something to learn?" It was Rachel's turn to smile.

"*Ya.*" Joseph shrugged and kept that endearing look on his face. "I guess you'll have to teach me."

Rachel's face felt hot. She dropped her gaze to the yarrow and wondered if Joseph was trying to distract her from her troubles. If so, it was working. It was working too well!

Joseph scanned the greenhouse. "I know about this one." He walked to a pot of redroot on the next shelf and smelled the clusters of tiny white flowers. "My *grossmammi* used to grow it and make tea with it. I haven't had it since she died, but I remember it tasted like wintergreen gum."

"I can't believe you know about redroot." Rachel flashed a competitive grin. "I bet you don't know its other name."

"You'll have to try harder than that," Joseph said as he returned the grin. "New Jersey Tea. My *grossmammi* said our family used to drink it when they ran out of tea and coffee. They came over from Germany really early, back when you couldn't get that kind of stuff."

Rachel straightened in her chair. "Mine came over on the *Charming Nancy*."

"Huh. That's pretty cool." He grinned at Rachel. "I guess we both go way back. Grossmammi traced our family all the way back to a little settlement way out in the middle of nowhere. Well, not anymore. It's probably full of strip malls and big-box stores now." He shrugged. "It's kind of sad when you think about it. Anyway, I think it was the first place the Amish went when they came to America."

"Wait a minute. My ancestors lived there too. Was it at the base of the Blue Mountain—the place where most of the *Charming Nancy* passengers ended up?"

"Yeah."

"Wow." Rachel shook her head. "Our ancestors were neighbors three hundred years ago?"

Joseph raised his eyebrows. "Small world."

"I know most people around here have some kind of connection. We all came from the same place, pretty much. But still. This is pretty amazing." She leaned forward and began to talk faster. "My family can trace all the way back to a man named Jacob Miller, who married a woman named Greta Scholtz."

"Yeah? We go back to some guy named Eli Webber. He married a woman named Catrina, but we don't know what her last name was before she married him."

Rachel stared at Joseph as if seeing him for the first time. "I'm surprised you know this stuff. You never liked history in school."

Joseph laughed. "I remember you were the best in the class." He picked up the pot of redroot and studied the teardrop-shaped leaves. "I don't care about history if I can't relate to it. I like history that reminds me who I am."

"Exactly!"

Joseph set down the pot and smiled down at Rachel. "I think we're going to make a good team, *ya?*"

Joseph noticed that he was whistling as he switched off the milking machine and picked up the battery-operated Coleman lantern. He planned to hang out in Lancaster with Chrissy after he finished his chores, so he told himself that was why he was in a good mood. She had left three messages for him in the phone shanty that week, so he knew that she was looking forward to the evening too.

He thought about Chrissy as he trudged across the backyard and up the old wooden staircase to his bedroom. He needed to pack his English clothes before Abner arrived. As he stuffed a pair of jeans and a flannel shirt into a duffel bag, his mind drifted to Chrissy's dyed-blond hair, gold earrings, and manicured fingernails. Her fancy styles had seemed so sophisticated and exotic when they met. But now—

Joseph realized that he wasn't whistling anymore. Abner and the other guys were jealous—Chrissy was a perfect ten, they said. So why did Joseph feel a heaviness about the whole thing? Joseph frowned and tightened the drawstring on his bag. He looked around his plain bedroom and wondered what he was doing with his life. Everything here looked familiar and safe: the bare, whitewashed walls, the colorful quilt his *grossmammi* had sewed, the unadorned handmade chest of drawers, the black trousers and collared shirts that hung from a row of pegs. Chrissy would say that his room looked empty. But, for some reason, Joseph thought it felt very full.

Joseph sighed as he picked up the bag and hurried down the flight of wooden steps that led to the front door. They creaked under his weight the way they always did. The banister felt smooth and cool beneath his palm. As he passed through the entryway he heard the rattle of pots in the kitchen and his father's deep laugh. The scent of rosemary and roast chicken followed Joseph out the door and onto the spacious porch. His footsteps echoed across the floorboards as he dashed toward Abner's buggy.

"You're late!" Abner shouted, and grinned.

"*Ya.*" Tonight would be fun. Most of his friends would be there, and Chrissy would hang on his arm and giggle at everything he said. So why did he feel a tug coming from the farmhouse behind him? He glanced back before he hauled himself into the buggy. He imagined the warmth of the woodstove and the whisper of paper as his father turned the pages of *The Budget* after dinner. He imagined the click of his mother's knitting needles and the silence. It was that silence that he wanted to get away from, wasn't it? Hadn't he always wanted something louder? Something more exciting? Something . . . unexpected?

A disturbing thought ricocheted up Joseph's spine. What was he really looking for? What would he find that he didn't already have at home? He settled into the seat beside Amos and felt the buggy sink under his weight.

"What's the matter?" Amos asked as he flicked the reins. The horse snorted and lunged forward. The buggy swayed and jerked down the driveway. The movement felt as familiar as breathing. So did the hard, rhythmic clomp of hooves against pavement.

"Nothing."

"Still torn up about the accident? I told you not to worry about that. I didn't have to race you, ain't so?"

"*Ya.* Thanks." Joseph ran his fingers through his hair. "But that's not it. I was thinking."

"About what?"

"I don't know. It's hard to explain."

"Try me."

Joseph sighed and looked out over the countryside. The setting sun sent long, bright rays across the rolling hills, painting the grass yellow and making the world glow. The fields and pasturelands stretched to the horizon in colorful squares like the pattern on his *grossmammi*'s quilt. "I wonder if I would like it better here if I had been born English."

"What do you mean?"

"I think it's easy to dismiss the familiar. What's that expression the English have?"

" . . .'The grass is always greener on the other side'?"

"*Ya*. That one."

Abner laughed. "When did you get so serious? You sound like my *daed*."

Joseph grinned sheepishly and shook his head. "*Ach*, forget it. I don't know what's got into me." But his grin dropped as soon as Abner looked away. Joseph knew exactly what had gotten to him. And it didn't make sense at all.

Chapter 6

Rachel listened for the clop of hooves on the driveway. She tried not to strain to hear the familiar sound but gave up. Her gaze shot to the battery powered clock. Joseph was late. *Ach,* why did she care? She tapped her finger on the potting table and glanced out the window. Less than two weeks ago she had been irritated that he dared set foot in her greenhouse. Now the thought of him sent a shiver of hope up her spine. It was easier to be irritated than hopeful. Having hope felt so dangerous.

The steady beat of hooves cut into the stillness of the greenhouse. Rachel grinned and spun to face the door. Her heart hammered when Joseph loped in with his hands in his pockets. He looked embarrassed, but his expression shifted when he saw the expectant look on her face. "Sorry I'm late. I overslept a little." He gave a playful half smile. "Better dock my pay."

"Don't tempt me, Joseph Webber. I've been waiting all morning to talk to you."

He raised an eyebrow. "Have you, now?"

Rachel's face reddened. "*Ach,* that's not what I meant and you know it."

"A fella can hope, can't he?"

"Joseph, stop teasing me!"

Joseph shrugged but kept the grin on his face. He grabbed the old wooden chair from the corner, carried it down the aisle, and set it down beside her. The chair legs clacked against the concrete floor. He sat down with a satisfied sigh. "All right. Tell me."

"We need to sell something special for Christmas. I want to make an impression, *ya?* I've been wondering what the English would like and I want to know what you think."

"You want to know what I think, do you?" He leaned back in the chair and cracked his knuckles with mock self-importance.

"Joseph, I'm being serious."

"Then why are you smiling?"

"Because you drive me crazy."

"That's a marked improvement from your initial opinion of me."

"You've always driven me crazy."

"Yes, but now you enjoy that I drive you crazy." He winked. "Just a little bit. Admit it."

Rachel laughed. "Joseph, be serious."

"*Ya.* I'm always serious."

"Right." Rachel rolled her eyes, but she felt warm inside. She didn't really want him to stop. "Okay, here's what I'm thinking. Poinsettias are the most popular Christmas flower, so they'd probably sell well."

"*Ya.* But I don't see any here."

"No. I've never grown them before."

"Then it doesn't make sense to start now. You should focus on something you know—something you're good at and want to do."

"*Ya,* but what if nobody wants an heirloom plant?"

"Don't be afraid to be different. People can buy poinsettias anywhere. I think you should stand out from the crowd." Rachel swept her eyes across the greenhouse as she considered Joseph's words. "Okay. That sounds like pretty good advice."

"Of course it does."

"I'd think you were prideful if I didn't know any better."

"But you do know better, because you know I'm joking."

"Always the troublemaker."

Joseph smiled. "Yep."

"You know I'm going to blame you if this doesn't work. The first time someone comes to our booth and asks for a poinsettia I'm going to remind you that it was your brilliant, foolproof idea not to sell them."

"Good thing I gave the right advice, then."

Rachel laughed and shook her head. "I can't win with you."

"Nope. You really ought to just give up."

"Never." Rachel smiled shyly as her eyes met Joseph's. Their gaze lingered for a moment, until he dropped his eyes. The connection that Rachel felt transformed to embarrassment. Had she really just gazed into his eyes like that? Was she flirting with him? Heaven help her, she was! He couldn't possibly be interested in her—not seriously. She shouldn't fool herself into thinking a catch like Joseph Webber would like her. He could have any woman in Lancaster County.

Rachel cleared her throat and hardened her expression. She needed to get back to business. "I've got an idea."

"*Ya?*"

"I've got an heirloom variety of rosemary that I've been growing for years. What if we transplanted it all into little pots and trimmed the branches to look like miniature Christmas trees?"

Joseph slapped the potting table. "I think that's a great idea, Rachel. Practical *and* decorative—sounds like a big seller to me."

"I can't wait to get started!"

Joseph stood up and pushed the chair aside. "Nothing's stopping us."

Rachel felt warm and steady inside. "No," she said. "Nothing is."

Joseph did not feel like himself after his date with Chrissy. Sure, it had been fun getting out, but he had enjoyed spending time with Abner and the other guys more than he had enjoyed his time with Chrissy that night. Had she always had that loud, attention-seeking laugh? Had she always worn such flashy jewelry? He supposed she had. It just hadn't seemed so . . . shallow before.

He tried not to think about it too much. He was going out with a perfect ten English girl and he would be crazy to complain—that's what all his friends kept saying, anyway.

Soon, Joseph forgot to worry about it; he had too much to do. The days ran together as he and Rachel worked side by side. Outside the greenhouse, December swept into Lancaster County to leave a trail of twinkling lights and decorated storefronts. Inside, some of the rosemary topiaries were already beginning to resemble tiny Christmas trees.

Late on a Saturday afternoon, Joseph returned a half-empty bag of potting soil to the corner and stretched his back. "I guess that's it for the day."

Rachel let out a happy sigh. "*Ya*. I can't wait until Monday so we can get back to work."

"Does your youth group meet tomorrow?"

"I'm not in a youth group." Rachel shook her head as she brushed soil from her apron. "I'll just stay here." She looked down. Joseph thought she was about to say "as usual," but her mouth clamped shut. He studied her pale face and large blue eyes. Those eyes, along with her dark lashes and open expression, reminded him of a lost doe. How many days did she spend alone in her greenhouse or sitting on the front porch, watching the world slip past?

"My youth group is having a singing tomorrow night. You should come. I'll pick you up." Joseph had a habit of speaking before he thought. Sometimes it led to unexpected joy. Other times it landed him in a heap of trouble.

Rachel's attention shot to him. He couldn't read her expression. She swallowed and stared at his face. Joseph took off his straw hat and ran his fingers through his dark brown hair. He knew that she wanted to go. He also knew she might need a little convincing. Good thing he was a pro at that.

Rachel looked down again and studied the smudge of dirt on her work apron. "No, that's okay."

"I think you want to go."

"What? No."

"*Ach,* come on. You always say you need to do more."

"*Ya,* but I meant with my greenhouse." Her freckled cheeks began to flush red. Joseph felt a thrill of excitement—she wanted to go with him. That's why she was blushing. He clamped down on the excitement as soon as he recognized the feeling. He shouldn't get her hopes up. Sure, he wanted to spend time with her—she was intriguing and intelligent and fun. But he couldn't promise her a future. Not when he was so uncertain about the path his life would take. Plus, there was Chrissy to consider. They had never agreed to be exclusive, so he wasn't doing anything wrong. Besides, he wasn't asking Rachel on a date. Not exactly, anyway. Still, he should have thought before he spoke. But it was too late to go back on the invitation now. "I think you meant more than your greenhouse."

Rachel frowned and scratched at the stain on her apron. The

red on her cheeks turned even brighter. "Okay. But only because you won't take no for an answer."

"Okay. Good. Because you're right. I won't. And I don't know about you, but I'm getting hungry." He stretched his arms and stifled a yawn. "No point in delaying supper. You may as well admit defeat and let us get on with it."

"Joseph, you're incorrigible."

"Pick you up at seven tomorrow."

Rachel glanced up, smiled, and looked down again. "Okay."

Joseph whistled the entire way home. Why did he feel so good when he had just thrown himself into a complicated situation?

Rachel's heart beat like a hammer. Everything in her wanted to shout and laugh and sing. Maybe she *could* have what the other girls had! Her business was back on track—and Joseph had asked her out! It almost felt too good to be true.

Reality hit as she thought about that. Her joy popped like a bubble of dish soap. Of course it was too good to be true. She shouldn't get so carried away. Joseph had only asked her to a singing and here she was, acting as if it were a marriage proposal! *Ach,* she could be so foolish!

At dinner that night, Rachel worried what her parents would say. Would they try to stop her from going out with Joseph? If they said no, would she be relieved or devastated?

Ada and Samuel looked concerned as Rachel pushed her food around her plate. "What's the matter?" Ada asked as she passed her daughter the chipped blue bowl of brown buttered cabbage. Rachel sighed, scooped out a serving, and stuffed a smoky, earthy bite into her mouth. Ada raised her eyebrows as she waited for an answer. Rachel took a big swig of iced tea and reached for more brown buttered cabbage.

"Rachel, I asked you a question."

"Nothing's the matter."

Ada shook her head and glanced at Samuel as he cut into the chicken potpie. Steam rose from the broken pastry crust and filled the kitchen with the warm, rich scent of chicken gravy. "She's overdone it," Ada said. "I knew all that work would be too much for her." Ada's eyes darted back to Rachel. "You have to take it easy."

Samuel tucked his napkin into his shirt collar. "Let's hear what she has to say."

"She isn't saying anything!"

"*Ach*, Mamm. It's okay. I can explain."

"*Ya?*" Ada leaned forward. Her face looked pinched.

"Joseph asked me to go to a singing tomorrow night."

Ada looked startled. Her gaze shifted to Samuel, then back to Rachel. "I don't know what to say."

Rachel laughed, but it sounded dry and humorless. "I don't either." She wanted to ask her parents if they thought Joseph might be interested in her as more than a friend, but she didn't. She felt too embarrassed.

Samuel held up a large, work-hardened hand. "Say yes. This doesn't have to be so complicated."

"I did."

Samuel nodded. "*Gut*. You'll go to the singing, have a nice time, and that will be that. No need to get worked up about it."

"But, Samuel—"

"Ada, she'll be fine."

Ada clamped her mouth into a tight line and nodded. "*Ya*. You're right, of course. She hasn't been to a singing in ages." Ada put a hand on Rachel's arm. "Just don't stay out too late. Don't overdo it." Her grip tightened before she dropped her hand. "I'm sorry. I just can't help worrying about you."

"I know, Mamm. But I'm not sick anymore, remember? And my legs are getting stronger every day. I can take my crutches instead of the wheelchair. That'll be easier, *ya?* I promise I'll be okay."

Ada nodded. "You can do anything you set your mind to, Rachel."

Rachel gave her *mamm* a strange look. "Then why do you keep telling me that I can't?"

Ada's expression changed to confusion and she pushed back from the table in a fast, sudden motion. "I baked shoofly pie for dessert. Who's ready for a slice?"

Rachel sighed. "Sure, Mamm." Her voice sounded tired. "Shoofly pie sounds great." Would her mother ever be ready to let go of the past and move forward with life?

Rachel was ready thirty minutes early. She wore a crisp, freshly starched prayer *kapp* and a plain purple dress that smelled of sunshine and grass from the outdoor clothesline. She had spent extra time parting her auburn hair, twisting the sides, and pulling it all back into a low, tight bun. She moved her head from side to side in front of the mirror. Her hair looked neat and smooth beneath the translucent heart-shaped *kapp*. The part was straight and even as an arrow.

Rachel sighed and dropped her gaze from the mirror. There was nothing to do but wait. She checked her white apron for wrinkles, then reminded herself that this was not a big deal. Joseph had asked her as a friend. He didn't care how straight her part looked or whether her prayer *kapp* was well starched. He didn't care about her looks at all. She had never been the center of attention. Why on earth would she think she would be now? Joseph was nice to include her—but only out of consideration as a friend.

"Have a snack before you go," Ada called from the kitchen. "I made apple cinnamon doughnuts. You don't want to go hungry."

Rachel couldn't possibly eat. "No thanks, Mamm. They'll have food there, ain't so?"

"*Ya.*"

There was a long silence. "Well, they'll be here if you want them."

"Okay, Mamm." Rachel's stomach churned. She felt as if she had swallowed a stone. An apple cinnamon doughnut was the last thing she wanted to think about. She tried to read a Christian romance novel, but she kept looking at the same line over and over again without ever noticing what it said. Rachel frowned and tossed the book onto the coffee table. This was getting ridiculous.

Rachel heard a faint clip-clop against pavement and sucked in her breath. The pulse of her heart matched the fast, hard beat of the horse's hooves. As the hoofbeats pounded louder, so did her chest. She heard the crunch of buggy wheels on gravel and a high-pitched whinny. Joseph had turned off the road and onto the driveway. She took a deep breath and let it out slowly. Relax. Just relax and act normal. Everything *is* normal, remember?

Rachel felt a thrill of excitement when she saw that Joseph had borrowed an open buggy—the kind that boys used to court girls, for propriety's sake. Closed buggies gave a couple too much privacy. She reminded herself that Joseph was merely being a respectful friend.

But it was hard to feel like friends when the stars twinkled above them and Joseph looked even more handsome than she remembered. As Rachel rode beside him she hoped that he couldn't see her heart pound beneath the fabric of her dress or hear how loud it beat. She tried to make conversation but could not think of anything to say. Not one thing! *Ach,* this was going from bad to worse. When Joseph stopped at a four-way stop sign and smiled at her, Rachel thought she would melt. When he tucked the quilt tighter around her and asked if she was warm enough, Rachel thought she might pass out from happiness. Only a woman with a suitor should feel that way. And Joseph definitely wasn't a suitor . . . was he?

Rachel tried to focus on the red barns and white clapboard farmhouses that dotted the roadside. But all she could think about was Joseph's smile and the fact that, no matter how much she denied it, he had become more than a friend to her.

Chapter 7

Rachel seemed quiet as everyone filed into the Lapps' barn. Gas lanterns cast a warm glow on the crowd. Dust motes drifted down from the hayloft and gleamed in the yellow light. Horses snorted and stomped inside their stalls as the boys joked and the girls laughed. But Rachel did not speak or smile as the handful of adults took seats against the wall and the youth group crowded onto benches in the middle of the barn. Joseph handed her a songbook and frowned. He wondered if he had made a mistake to invite her. She looked like she wanted to go home. He knew that she had always been shy. Maybe he should have suggested a quieter evening together. But that would have been so much more intimate. And he wasn't supposed to be interested in her. He reminded himself that his interest lay with a pretty English girl.

Joseph cleared his throat and opened his songbook. He really ought to straighten out his thoughts. A quiet evening alone with Rachel! Ha! That would be crossing a line. Joseph's frown deepened. If he did cross that line, it could keep him Amish forever. Because something told him that if he let himself fall for Rachel Miller he would never let her go.

Rachel glanced at Joseph and began to open her songbook, but her fingers fumbled across the cover and she dropped it to the floor. Joseph smiled, picked it up, dusted off a piece of straw, and handed it back to her. Their eyes locked and she shyly returned his smile. She looked angelic in the soft yellow lantern light. No one had ever looked so beautiful, Joseph thought, then looked away. He reminded himself that life was complicated enough right now without falling in love.

Love? Had he just thought the word "love"? Now that was going too far.

Joseph glanced back at Rachel. Her cheeks had flushed pink. She seemed so nervous and unsure of herself. He had assumed it was because she felt shy and out of place in a crowd of strangers. But what if—

A rich baritone voice broke the silence as a man sang the first few notes of a song. The rest of the group joined in, until the entire barn filled with the happy, carefree sound. Joseph tried to keep his attention on the words in the songbook, but his eyes kept moving to the side. Rachel caught him watching her and her face turned an even deeper shade of red. She swallowed, forced her eyes back to the songbook, and put her index finger on the page to mark her place as she read. Joseph noticed that her breath rose and fell too quickly.

Maybe she was out of breath from the singing. But Joseph didn't think so. She had seemed fine until she caught him watching her. The thought made Joseph feel an unexpected warmth inside. He shifted on the bench so that he could move a fraction closer to her without seeming too obvious. Her shoulder brushed his arm and she glanced back up at him with a quick, happy look. He pretended not to notice. She kept her shoulder pressed against his arm for the rest of the singing. Joseph couldn't remember a time that he felt happier.

The singing wound down after a couple hours and everyone drifted to the refreshment table. A few people recognized Rachel and stopped to chat. She looked surprised, and a little overwhelmed that so many people wanted to catch up. But her eyes glowed and Joseph knew that she felt excited. He remembered the timid wallflower who sat in the back of the classroom all those years ago and refused to join in the fun. It was time that she came out of her shell. After all, she had so much to offer the world.

"I'll get us something to eat, *ya?*"

Rachel glanced at him and nodded, then turned her attention back to Abby Lapp, who was in the middle of a story about a lost goat that wandered into the public library last Wednesday.

Joseph piled two plates with sweet gherkin pickles, homemade soft pretzels, and pumpkin whoopie pies. He nibbled on the rich nutmeg- and cinnamon-flavored icing as he walked back to Rachel. Abner saw him and cut across the room. He caught up as Joseph reached Rachel and handed her a plate. Rachel looked up at Joseph and beamed. "Pumpkin whoopie pie! My favorite!"

Joseph nodded. His mouth was too full of icing to respond.

"Hey there!" Abner cut between Rachel and Joseph and slapped his friend on the back. "Since when did you start coming back to singings? You're never around anymore."

Joseph could sense the disaster coming but could not stop it. He wanted to shout at Abner not to say another word. He tried to force down the bite of whoopie pie without chewing. His mouth opened, but it was too late.

"How come you're here and not out with Chrissy?"

Rachel flinched. The color drained from her face. "Chrissy?" She said the word without emotion but Joseph could see the alarm in her eyes and the quick rise and fall of her chest.

"*Ach*, nobody."

"Nobody?" Abner laughed and shook his head. "That girl's a perfect ten."

"Chrissy?" Rachel repeated in a small voice.

"She's nobody," Joseph repeated.

"You sure spend a lot of time with nobody then."

Joseph swallowed. He didn't mean that *she* was nobody. He meant that she was nobody to *him*. He had not realized that before. And now it was too late. Rachel would never believe him now. "She's an English girl. We hang out sometimes."

Abner laughed. "You're acting so weird." He turned to Rachel. "Chrissy's his girlfriend."

Joseph frowned and set his plate down. He didn't feel like eating anymore. "I wouldn't say that. Yeah, we've gone out, but . . . " Joseph didn't know what to say. He should have told Rachel that he had been seeing an English girl.

"Gone out?" Abner rolled his eyes. "You've been talking about running off with her."

"No. I've been talking about running off, but not with her. Or maybe with her—but that's not the point. I haven't been thinking like that in a while. Not since . . . " He wanted to say "not since I've been working with Rachel," but he didn't. It was too hard to explain.

Abner clapped his hand on Joseph's shoulder. "Okay, okay. Calm down. Just telling what I know."

"*Ya.* Sorry. It's just . . . " Joseph's voice drifted away. He took off his straw hat and ran his fingers through his hair. What *was* he trying to say? Everything felt so wrong. Especially when everything had felt so right just a few minutes ago!

"Hey, look over there." Abner nodded his chin toward a teenage girl in an emerald green dress. She stood alone as she poured a glass of lemonade. "I've been trying to get a chance to talk to her all night. See you later."

Joseph let out a long, hard breath. What was he going to say to Rachel now?

Rachel refused to look at him. She stared at the plate in her lap as if nothing else existed. "I'm sorry, Rachel. I should have said something earlier—"

Rachel's eyes shot up to Joseph. He could sense the anger and hurt hiding beneath the steady gaze. "Why? It's none of my business. We just work together, remember?"

Joseph sighed and ran his fingers through his hair. "Right."

Rachel looked back down at her plate. She picked up the pumpkin whoopie pie and set it down again. "I'm ready to go home."

"Okay." Joseph wanted to sink into the dusty wooden floorboards. But he couldn't tell Rachel that he had begun to see her as more than a friend—it wouldn't be fair to her. He had to figure out his own future before he could drag someone else into it.

The night had been one of the best, most exciting of Rachel's life. Until she learned about Chrissy. Of course Joseph wasn't interested in her! How foolish she had been! How could she have entertained such a ridiculous notion? Rachel had never felt so humiliated in her life. This was far worse than those lonely days spent in the corner of the one-room schoolhouse. Back then she knew she didn't fit in. But since Joseph had come into her life again, she had dared to dream. Ha! That was a mistake she wouldn't make again.

The ride home passed in a haze of hurt and humiliation. The horse's hooves beat the pavement in a hard, steady rhythm as they trotted down the winding, country lane. Wispy white clouds passed over the moon and sank the fields into darkness. Rachel shivered and pulled the quilt up to her chin.

"You okay? Too cold?" Joseph asked in a gentle voice. His eyes looked concerned. Concerned for a friend, Rachel thought—which only makes it worse. Why couldn't he be the loud, an-

noying schoolboy she remembered? That would make everything so much easier!

"I'm fine."

That was the only conversation they had the entire ride
home.

Rachel held back her tears until the front door shut behind
her. Ada saw her daughter's face and flew out of her chair with
her knitting needles still in one hand and a gray mitten in the
other. "Rachel! What's wrong? What happened? Are you
okay?" Ada turned toward Samuel, who sat in a rocking chair
with *The Budget* in his lap. "I told you she shouldn't go out
like this! She isn't ready!"

Samuel sighed, set *The Budget* on the coffee table, and stood
up. "Rachel? What has happened?"

"Nothing." She shook her head. "It's all right."

"Clearly, it's not," Ada said.

Samuel pulled at his long gray beard and motioned for Rachel
to come into the living room. "You best tell us all about it."

"It's too embarrassing."

"Nonsense. We'll understand."

Rachel hesitated, but her *daed*'s calm expression won her
over. "*Ach*, okay. But only because you asked."

Samuel's eyes twinkled. "Only because I asked."

Ada sank back into her chair, set the knitting needles and
mitten on the coffee table, and clasped her hands together.
"Go on."

"It's nothing," Rachel said, and looked away.

Samuel reached over and put a hand on Rachel's shoulder. "I
bet it doesn't feel like nothing. I bet it feels like everything."

"*Ya*. That's exactly how it feels. How did you know?"

Samuel smiled. "Because I was young and in love once too."

"In love!" Rachel and Ada said at the same time. They both
looked at each other, then at Samuel.

"*Daed!* What makes you think . . . ?" Rachel's voice faded

away. She didn't know what to say. Samuel raised his shoulders a fraction. "Because I've seen the way you look at him. And I've heard the way he talks about you. When he went on about your plans to sell at the farmers market I knew that boy was smitten."

"No, Daed, that's just it. He's not."

Ada kept looking from Samuel to Rachel with a confused look on her face. "Joseph and Rachel . . . ?"

"There's nothing between us, Mamm."

"You sure about that, Rachel?" Samuel's face looked kind and thoughtful.

"After tonight, *ya*."

"Ah. And now we get to it. What happened?"

"Joseph has been going out with some *English* girl."

Samuel nodded and ran his fingers through his beard. "*Ya*. I've heard he's been running around a lot. And there was that buggy crash too."

"*Ya*." Rachel pressed her hands over her face and shook her head. "But I didn't know about a girlfriend."

"This is why I said she shouldn't go out, Samuel. Look what's happened. She's beside herself. I told you she wasn't ready for this."

"You said she shouldn't go out because she wasn't strong enough. This is something completely different."

Ada raised her eyebrows and stared at Samuel with a hard expression. "Is it?"

"Ada, this is what you want to happen to our Rachel."

"It is not!"

"You want her to be well enough to live life, don't you?" He lifted his hands and dropped them. "Well, this is what living looks like." Samuel took his wife's hand and met her gaze. "She's living, Ada. Really living for the first time in years. Falling in love, getting her heart broken—that's all part of living. It might not feel good right now, but I thank *der Herr* that she's finally living life like everyone else. And that means we have to take the bad with the good, *ya?*"

A single tear eased out of Ada's eye and slid down her cheek. She wiped it away in a quick, jerky motion and shook her head. "*Ach,* Samuel. I don't know what to say. I never thought of it that way."

Samuel squeezed her hand. "Time to let her go, Ada. She's a grown woman with a life of her own."

Ada let out a long breath and closed her eyes. "I can't make any promises, but I'll try."

Samuel smiled. "That's all anyone can ask." He turned his attention back to Rachel. "Tell me about this girlfriend."

"I don't know anything about her."

"He's never mentioned her before?"

"No. But we're not together, so there's no reason he would."

"Hmmmm. We'll see."

"*Daed!* He has a girlfriend."

"I never heard you say they're serious. How old is Joseph? Same age as you, right?"

"*Ya.*"

Samuel nodded. "Boys that age don't know what they want yet. He's restless. He doesn't know what to do. He'll figure it out. You know, his *daed* mentioned that he's settled down a lot since that buggy accident. He could have been killed or killed someone else. I think that shook some sense into him."

"But what's that got to do with me?" Rachel looked down. She was tired of this conversation. She wanted to sink into her bed and bury herself under the quilt.

Samuel shrugged and reached for *The Budget.* "Maybe nothing. Or maybe . . . " He shrugged again and turned the first page. "Time will tell." He flipped to the next page and glanced at Rachel over the top of the newspaper. "It depends if Joseph decides to take advantage of a second chance or if he decides to keep heading down the wrong path."

"I think it has to do with a girl named Chrissy," Rachel said.

"I think it has very little to do with her."

"It has everything to do with her!"

Samuel sighed. "Get some sleep. You'll feel better tomorrow."

"I have to see Joseph tomorrow! That's not going to make me feel better."

"We can tell him the job's over," Ada said. "I'll go down to the Webber place early in the morning before he leaves."

"No, Ada. Let the girl live her life." Samuel held up a hand. "She's got to resolve this herself."

Ada hesitated. She opened her mouth to speak, then closed it again.

"Good night, Mamm." Rachel started toward her room.

"I'll fix your favorite breakfast tomorrow, okay?" Ada called after her.

"Okay."

Rachel sighed. Not even biscuits and gravy with maple-cured bacon could make this better. Nothing could.

Chapter 8

Joseph flew across a snowy field. Moonlight sparkled over frosted branches and frozen ponds. He knew he should be cold, but he felt comfortably warm and snug as he zipped faster and faster through the air, until a strange beeping sound rose over the horizon and swept in with the snow. It pounded inside his head until he fell out of the dream and into his bedroom.

He slammed his palm onto his bedside table as he searched for the alarm clock. BEEP BEEP BEEP. His hand made contact with a plastic button and the room returned to silence. He sighed and buried his head under his down pillow. The house felt cold and dark. The sun wouldn't be up for another couple of hours.

"Joseph!" Mamm's voice drifted up the stairs. "Those cows won't milk themselves, Son."

Joseph grunted and forced himself out of bed. He shivered as he threw off the quilt and his bare feet landed on the cool wooden floorboards. I can't do this for the rest of my life, he thought as he pulled on a pair of work trousers and shrugged into a heavy coat. His *daed* and *bruder* loved the farm. They called each cow by name and lingered beside each stall to pet a warm, firm shoulder or scratch behind a velvet-soft ear. He wished he felt the same way.

It wasn't that Joseph disliked cows. He just wanted something different for his life—something that made him want to get up in the morning. Once again, his thoughts turned to the English world. He could live in the English world forever and never milk another cow.

But what would he do there instead?

He sighed and pushed the thought away. At least he had something to look forward to today—after he milked the cows. He was eager to see if the rosemary he transplanted last week had done well. Maybe he should take Rachel to Bird-in-Hand for supplies. They needed more potting soil and some ribbon to decorate the pots.

Joseph flinched. Rachel wouldn't want to go anywhere with him today. She wouldn't want to see him at all. And he couldn't blame her.

Frosted blades of grass crunched beneath Joseph's boots as he loped across the yard. Lantern light glowed through the cracks in the barn. He braced himself for his *daed*'s lecture about being late to the milking. Joseph hesitated at the door, took a deep breath, and slipped inside. The hinges creaked as the familiar, earthy scent of farm animals and hay welcomed him.

Joseph smiled when he saw Eli standing beneath the yellow glow of a propane lantern. His brother, not his father, had beaten him to the barn. "Eli. I thought you were Daed."

Eli patted the warm, solid side of a cow and grinned. "You got lucky this time."

"*Ya.*" Joseph started for the milking machine. He wanted to hurry and get the job done so that he could head over to Rachel's.

Eli ran his hand up the cow's neck and scratched behind her ear. She lowered her head and shifted closer to him. "That's a good girl." Eli glanced at Joseph. "I think Betsy's gaining weight. She must be feeling better, *ya?*" Eli had been worried for weeks over Betsy's pneumonia. He had even slept in the barn during the worst of it.

"*Ya.*"

Eli sighed and traced a red spot on Betsy's coat with his index finger. "I'm getting a job with Onkel."

"You're what?" Joseph spun around and stared at Eli.

"I'm leaving."

Joseph shook his head. "You can't do that."

Eli let out a sad little laugh. "Well, I have to find a way to support a family, Joseph. I'm twenty-seven years old and I'm tired of being alone. It's time I get settled."

"But you're the dairy farmer, not me."

Eli kept his eyes on Betsy. "You know that our profits have been going down for years. This place can't support all of us forever—especially once I have a wife and *kinder.*"

"Eli, be sensible. You're not even engaged."

"Joseph, I am being sensible." Eli's voice sounded soft but firm. "If I want to be engaged I have to start making plans now."

"But you love it here."

Eli patted Betsy's neck. "*Ya.* I do."

Joseph's stomach burned. This was all wrong. "You should stay here. I'll go."

Eli turned to face Joseph. He looked very tired. "If you leave you might never come back. I know you won't be content working for Onkel. I've seen how restless and independent you are. I know you hope to find what you're looking for among the English. But you won't. The best thing for you is to settle down here and accept your lot in life."

Joseph opened his mouth, but Eli cut him off. "Besides, you know it's traditional for the youngest brother to inherit the farm. I can't wait for Daed to retire like you can. I'm already pushing thirty."

"Eli." Joseph ran his fingers through his hair. "Are you leaving because of me?"

Eli gave a sad but genuine smile. "Not *because* of you. *For* you."

"Please don't."

"You'll be thankful someday." Eli pushed away from the metal bars of Betsy's stall. "Let's get the milking done. We shouldn't make them wait."

"What if I promise that I'll work for Onkel?"

Eli squeezed his eyes shut and rubbed them with his thumb and forefinger. "Don't make promises you can't keep."

"Eli, I'm serious."

Eli stopped. His expression hardened. "I can't stand to see Mamm so sad all the time. Maybe if I leave you'll straighten up and realize your place is here. Do you realize how worried she is that you'll leave us for the English?"

"Please don't bring Mamm into this."

"I didn't." Eli shook his head. "*You* did."

Joseph flinched. He realized what was happening. "You're trying to force me to stay. If I'm the only one left to take over the farm I won't be able to leave. You want to trap me here."

"What else can I do?" Eli stared at him for a few beats before he turned away. His eyes looked sad and distant.

Rachel stared at the house across the field as an *Englisher* strung Christmas lights along the porch. Morning fog hovered over the bare ground. In the distance, a tractor roared to life. The neighbors were starting their day. Rachel sighed and turned back to the biscuit and gravy on her plate.

Rachel's *mamm* bustled into the kitchen and sailed past the table with a basket of eggs. She stopped when she saw Rachel. "You're not in your greenhouse yet?"

"No."

"That isn't like you."

Rachel sighed and set down her fork.

"You've barely eaten."

Rachel didn't answer. She turned her face to the window again, but the woman had gone inside, so Rachel studied a flock of blackbirds instead. They swooped over the rolling hills, skirted the neighbors' silo, and settled on the roof of a red barn.

"You were right about those chickens."

"What?" Rachel turned back to her *mamm*.

Ada held a brown spotted egg in her hand. "Heritage breeds do give better eggs. I love these."

Rachel managed a half smile. "So you agree that we should get a heritage breed pig? They're better too."

Her *mamm* laughed and set the basket down on the counter. "No. But nice try. We'll leave the farming to the neighbors who rent our land. Your *daed*'s got plenty to do down at the harness shop."

"As a pet. Not a farm animal."

"*Ach*, Rachel."

"Chickens are farm animals, you know."

"That's different. Chickens are practical. People in cities keep them nowadays." Ada opened the pantry and pulled out a canister of flour. "We've been over this a hundred times."

Rachel sighed. "You don't know what you're missing."

Her *mamm* laughed again. "Oh, I'm pretty sure I know." She scanned the pantry, stood on her tiptoes, and pulled a sack of sugar from the top shelf. "I'm making gingerbread. Want to help?"

"No. I've got work in the greenhouse."

"Maybe you should take a break today. You look tired."

Rachel sighed again. "It's not that."

Ada wiped her hands on her work apron. "He's not the boy for you, Rachel. He's a good worker, but he's not a good suitor." She shook her head. "Not with those worldly notions of his."

Rachel pushed her plate away. She wished she agreed with her *mamm*.

Rachel tried to act busy when she heard buggy wheels crunch against the gravel driveway. She hunched over the rosemary and forced herself to focus. She wouldn't let Joseph see how distracted she felt. She wouldn't let him know that she cared about Chrissy. It was ridiculous anyway. Why should she care?

Joseph's presence filled the greenhouse as soon as he strode through the door. Rachel's stomach jumped as he flashed his signature grin. That was why she cared. That grin, that carefree laugh, that gentle voice. *Ach!* What a mess she was in!

"You look like you haven't slept all night."

Rachel frowned and tried to keep her attention on the rosemary.

Joseph leaned against the potting table and gazed down at her with a glint in his eyes. "Couldn't stop thinking about me?"

Rachel's frown deepened. "I'm not in the mood for your jokes, Joseph. We've got a lot to do before Christmas."

Joseph held up his hands and backed away. "All right, all right. Let's get to work."

"I am working. You're the one who's not working." Rachel forced her eyes to stay on the rosemary topiary. She wished that she had been nicer. But if she apologized she would have to admit why she was upset—better to just go on and pretend everything was okay.

By Wednesday afternoon, Rachel realized that she couldn't just pretend everything was okay. Every time Joseph spoke to her—or even looked at her—her heart leapt into her throat and then her stomach fell at the memory of Abner's words about Chrissy. *That girl's a perfect ten.*

By the end of the week, Rachel felt as if steam might come out of her ears. Her exasperation and hurt had been building for days. To make matters worse, Joseph wasn't himself either. He seemed upset and distracted. When he tried to trim one of the rosemary topiaries on Friday morning, he cut a gap in the foliage so that it looked more like an umbrella than a Christmas tree. Then he dropped a pot and it cracked open on the concrete floor.

Joseph frowned as he swept black, moist soil and shards of pottery. Rachel stole a glance at his face and her heart jumped again. Then her stomach clenched up and she sighed. He hadn't cracked a joke since she had rebuffed him Monday morning. He really did seem contrite. Rachel froze as a thought flashed through her mind. What if *he* was upset that *she* was upset about Chrissy? Even better, what if he was upset because he liked her more than Chrissy but didn't know what to do!

Rachel tried to push the thought away. It was ridiculous.

"Go ahead and say something," Joseph said as he shook the dustpan over a plastic bin.

"Next time, break a pot before we put in the soil. It would make the cleanup easier."

"Great. I'll remember that." He walked to the spigot, turned the metal handle, and watched as a plastic bucket filled with water.

"I was joking."

Joseph's eyes shot to hers. "Were you?"

"*Ya.*" She turned back to the rosemary in front of her. "I was."

Joseph didn't answer. Rachel heard water slosh into the bucket, then the rusty grind of the spigot turning off. She forced herself not to look at him again. She had already crossed a line that she hadn't meant to cross. She had promised herself that she wouldn't joke with him anymore. Joking was only a hair away from flirting and flirting with Joseph Webber would be ridiculous, now. Preposterous.

"I guess that pot wasn't all it was cracked up to be." Had she just said that out loud? It wasn't even a good joke! Why couldn't she keep her mouth shut?

"Funny." Joseph smiled, but it didn't reach his eyes.

Rachel kept her face down. She could feel her cheeks flame red. No wonder Joseph wanted to run around with some perfect ten named Chrissy! *She* probably didn't make corny jokes.

They ignored each other for the rest of the day.

Chapter 9

Monday morning didn't go much better. Joseph still seemed distracted and upset. Rachel dared to hope that maybe, just maybe, he was having second thoughts about Chrissy. They barely spoke until Joseph shook the last bit of potting soil from the last bag. "We'll have to get more," she said as she cut a tiny branch of rosemary. She picked up the broken end and inhaled deeply. She loved the sharp, piney scent and hoped the English tourists would too.

Joseph folded the empty bag and dropped it in the trash bin. "We can go after lunch. I'll run over to the phone shanty and call my driver."

Rachel stiffened. We? What had she gotten herself into? He assumed that they would go *together*? She liked the idea, of course. It strengthened her hope. But hope could be a dangerous thing.

Rachel leaned against the car window as the countryside zipped by. The day felt heavy with gray, low-lying clouds and many of the English houses had already turned on their Christmas lights. The red, white, and green cut into the somber weather and cast a cheerful glow. Rachel loved the way Christmas lights transformed a dreary day into a magical one.

The driver took them to Ken's Gardens in Smoketown first. Rachel loved the smell of damp earth and fresh, green plants that filled the store. She decided to take her wheelchair, rather than crutches, so she could wander the aisles in a distracted haze, smelling flowers and running her fingers over shiny, feathery leaves.

"Rachel. We're not even in the right section."

Rachel startled and laughed. "I love it here; don't you? They've got everything."

Joseph looked irritated for a moment; then he smiled and shrugged. "I like it too, I guess. If I stop and take the time to appreciate it." He bent to smell a yellow flower. "I never thought about doing that before."

Rachel smelled the flower after he lifted his face from it. "You should."

Joseph gave an indulgent smile. "All right. Let's time our time."

Rachel beamed. She liked being here, at her favorite store with her favorite friend. Her smile evaporated as she reminded herself that *she* wasn't *Joseph*'s favorite friend. He had Chrissy. *Ach*, well. Rachel should take her own advice and enjoy the outing anyway.

And that's exactly what she did.

After lingering far too long among the merchandise, they rushed back to the car with shopping bags stuffed full of potting soil, fertilizer, and miniature clay pots. Rachel balanced the bags in her lap and screeched with laughter as Joseph zipped her across the parking lot. She felt as if she were flying as the chair soared over the pavement and the December air stung her cheeks and lungs.

"Sorry we took so long," Joseph said to the driver after they shuddered to a quick stop. The driver shrugged and adjusted the cuff of his red flannel shirt. "I'm getting paid for my time, so you won't hear any complaints from me." Joseph transferred their loot and the wheelchair into the trunk, then climbed into the back seat beside Rachel. She caught his eye and grinned. They had been a bit irresponsible to linger so long in the store— but it had been so much fun!

The car felt snug and secure as the heater blasted warm air against the biting wind. Rachel leaned against Joseph while the driver backed out of the parking space and clicked on his blinker. She didn't want this day to end. She felt like Cinderella at the ball, knowing that at midnight the clock would strike and she would be alone again, while her prince returned to the arms of a perfect ten *Englisher*.

The next stop was the Quilt and Fabric Shack in Bird-in-Hand, the closest town to her house. Rachel loved going into Bird-in-Hand. The shops that lined Old Philadelphia Pike looked like a scene from a postcard. Everything felt neat and tidy and cozy—red clapboard buildings, white picket fences, white shutters, and handmade quilts and crafts hanging in the store windows. Going with Joseph made it even more perfect.

They picked out several yards of red and green plaid ribbon at the fabric store. On the way out, Joseph stopped beside a craft kit with a picture of a reindeer hat on the box. He picked up the display hat and shoved it onto his head. Rachel laughed out loud.

"How do I look?" he asked with a dead-serious expression.

He looked so ridiculous and adorable that Rachel wanted to hug him. She didn't, of course. But oh, she wanted to!

Rachel didn't want their outing to end. Her heart sank when Joseph helped her into the car and slammed the door shut. She looked out the window and stared at the Christmas tree that glittered and shimmered through the window of the shop across the street. A life with Joseph felt distant and unreachable, just like the twinkling warmth of that tree, trapped behind glass.

"It's so cold today," Joseph said, and blew into his cupped hands. "What do you say we stop into the Bird-in-Hand Bake Shop for some hot chocolate before we head back? It's on the way."

Rachel's face lit up and she straightened in her seat. "*Ya!* That'd be great."

Joseph smiled and asked the driver to take them there. The driver flicked on the radio and the car filled with music as a deep, rich voice sang "O Come All Ye Faithful." Rachel felt so warm and cozy inside that she thought she might burst.

The car breezed past the quaint little boutiques that lined Old Philadelphia Pike. Evergreen boughs, wreaths, and vintage Christmas decorations lined the display windows and wooden porches. When the Bird-in-Hand Farmers Market came into view, Rachel felt a thrill of excitement. She thought about the ribbons and supplies in the trunk of the car and hoped that the tourists would like what she sold. The parking lot looked filled to capacity as *Englishers* with bright scarves and heavy coats walked toward the glass doors of the indoor market.

"They'll be coming for your stuff soon," Joseph said. Rachel watched a little girl in white knee socks, a red wool coat, and matching red mittens skip across the parking lot with a faceless Amish doll in her hands. The girl adjusted the doll's black bonnet and kissed the top of its head. "I hope so," Rachel said. But a stab of doubt cut into her. Could she compete with all the crafts and goodies for sale?

The driver flicked his signal and pulled into a parking lot across the street from the farmers market. "I'll be back in about thirty minutes to pick you up. Is that okay?"

"*Ya,*" Joseph said. "That sounds about right. With all the tourists here today, it'll probably take half that time just to get through the line."

The driver chuckled. "Probably. Everyone wants to come to Amish Country at Christmastime. There's nothing quite like it this time of year." He shrugged and chuckled again. "But I guess you know that."

Joseph nodded but didn't smile. He looked thoughtful and Rachel wondered if he *did* know that. Or was he still chasing something bigger and brighter among the English? As Joseph helped her out of the car, she studied the picturesque redbrick building and knew that she didn't want anything more. Everything she wanted was there in Lancaster County, among the rolling hills, cornfields, and Christmas warmth. Why couldn't Joseph see what he had here, right in front of him?

As he helped her inside, Rachel wondered if Joseph was beginning to see how good home could be. It had been a lovely outing and the concern that lined his face earlier that day had disappeared. He had even suggested they stop for hot chocolate. It almost felt like a date! She stopped the thought and took a deep breath. She had already been stung once by his kindness. She shouldn't mistake friendship for romance again. And yet . . . here he was smiling and joking and asking her what she wanted so he could order for her. Maybe he was rethinking his relationship with Chrissy. Maybe he had been distracted and worried because he knew he had to break up with her! Oh, the thought felt too good to be true! Her mother was fond of the saying "If it seems too good to be true, then it probably is." Rachel hated that saying.

"I'm going to try the peppermint hot chocolate," Joseph said as he navigated them through the jumble of chattering tourists. "Me too!" Rachel said. "Or maybe the eggnog latte. It's hard to decide." The bakeshop smelled of cinnamon, nutmeg, and evergreen. A variety of seasonal pies and cakes, along with Christmas ornaments, lined the display shelves. Rachel picked up a snow globe and shook it. White glitter drifted over a miniature red barn and buggy. She smiled and set it back.

"You've got time to decide," Joseph said as they staked out a place in the back of the line.

"That's what you think. I can never make up my mind about things like this."

"So you're one of those people who get to the cash register after waiting for fifteen minutes and hold up the line because you still haven't made up your mind."

"Yep." Rachel flashed a grin.

"Deciding what to eat is a harder decision, *ya?*" Joseph scanned the glass case. "The pecan sticky buns look really good."

"I want one of the frosted sugar cookies." She pointed to a snowflake-shaped cookie decorated with blue and silver icing. "That one."

"That one it is," Joseph said, and smiled.

They chatted as they waited, and Rachel felt surprised when they reached the front of the line. The wait had flown by and she still hadn't decided whether to get the peppermint hot chocolate with whipped cream or the eggnog latte with whipped cream. At least she had the whipped cream part figured out.

"Two of those snowflake sugar cookies," Joseph said to a middle-aged woman behind the counter.

"You got the same thing I did," Rachel said.

"You convinced me." His eyes moved to the drink menu on the wall. "And to drink?" Joseph saw her hesitate, smiled, and shook his head. "Two peppermint hot chocolates and a small eggnog latte."

Rachel looked up at him in surprise. "You got me both?" She felt warm and fuzzy inside. How could such a small gesture make her feel so special?

Joseph shrugged and looked sheepish. "I guess it's a little excessive. But I thought you deserved a treat."

"Thanks. I like the way you think."

He gave a half smile. "I know."

They found a round table for two and settled in with their

hot drinks and iced sugar cookies. Christmas carols drifted across the seating area from a hidden speaker. *Englishers* bustled past with shopping bags and trays of desserts.

Rachel studied Joseph's expression as she removed the plastic lid from her cardboard cup and blew across the top of her hot chocolate. The minty scent wafted upward and bathed her face in sweet-smelling steam. Rachel felt so happy to see that Joseph looked happy. He didn't seem worried or distracted anymore. Maybe he really was enjoying his time with her. Maybe he was happy because they were together. Well, it wouldn't hurt to ask—in a roundabout way, of course.

"Joseph."

"*Ya?*" He leveled his warm brown eyes at her.

His steady gaze sent tingles down her spine. She cleared her throat and tried to keep her mind on task. "I've noticed that you've been down all week, until we went out. Are you okay?"

Joseph's expression tightened. He looked down at the cookie on his paper plate. "Not really."

"*Ach*, what's wrong?" Rachel leaned forward. Please let it be Chrissy. Please let it be Chrissy. Please let it be Chrissy.

He hesitated. "I don't want to burden you with my problems."

"Go ahead. It's no burden." If Chrissy is the problem, that is!

"Okay." He took a sip of hot chocolate, swallowed, and set down the cardboard cup. "My *bruder* is going to go work with my *onkel*. He buys some of our milk and makes ice cream. I guess you know he owns the creamery down in Strasburg?"

"*Ya.*" Rachel frowned. When would Chrissy come into this scenario?

"My *bruder* knows that I've been thinking about leaving the Amish and he's trying to trap me here. He knows I can't leave if I'm the only son left to run the dairy farm."

The frown stayed on Rachel's face. "Is that all?"

Joseph flinched. "*Ya.*" He looked away and took another sip of his hot chocolate. His eyebrows knit together in an angry line. "Isn't that enough?"

"*Ach.* I didn't mean . . . " Rachel shook her head. Her hope deflated as her stomach dropped to the floor. This wasn't about Chrissy. She had been foolish again. He only saw her as a friend. He was doing the wallflower a favor by spending time with her. No, it was worse than that. Her parents were paying him to spend time with her. Oh, the indignity of it all. The indignity!

And, to make matters even worse, she had just acted uninterested in Joseph's problems. What a mess she had made.

Joseph pushed his chair back. "It's time to get going."

"But we just sat down." Her chest tightened as Joseph stood up. Everything had been going so well. And now it had all crashed down around her again.

Chapter 10

As the car roared down Old Philadelphia Pike, Joseph realized that he hadn't thought about Chrissy the entire time he had been out with Rachel. He had a wonderful good time. It didn't make any sense—Chrissy was what his English friends told him he should want. Rachel was, well, Rachel. She didn't sparkle with glamour and mystery the way Chrissy did.

So why was Rachel more fun?

Oh well, it didn't matter anyway. Rachel had pushed him away for the last time. She had made it clear from day one that she didn't want him invading her space. Today she reiterated that when she dismissed his problems. He had been foolish to think she cared about him or that she was attracted to him. He should have remembered that their relationship wasn't real—he was a paid employee, not a friend or a suitor.

Rachel didn't speak or look at him even though she sat beside him in the back seat. She kept her face turned away and when he glanced over he could only see the curve of her jaw and her white prayer *kapp*. Joseph sighed and craned his neck so that he could see Bird-in-Hand disappear behind them. He watched the Christmas lights from the shops shimmer and fade into the distance.

Joseph realized his confusion went beyond Chrissy. That familiar restlessness had disappeared for the afternoon. He wondered if the warm, settled feeling that stayed with him during the outing had been contentment. He wasn't sure because he had never felt that way before.

Joseph swiveled back around and stared at the long, winding road ahead. He wondered what direction his life should take.

Joseph was supposed to meet Chrissy that weekend, but he didn't feel up to it. He pulled on his winter coat, stepped into his boots, and pushed open the back door. Frigid air rushed into the kitchen.

"Don't let the cold in!" his mother shouted from beside the stove, where she stood in her old apron and slippers stirring a pot of caramel. The rich candy scent followed him into the cold and empty December air. He slammed the door shut behind him and the warmth and coziness of the house disappeared.

Joseph pulled his hat lower, crossed his arms, and told himself it was too cold to see Chrissy tonight. He knew that was an excuse. The truth was, every time he thought of Chrissy he saw Rachel's face instead. When he tried to remember Chrissy's girlish, flirtatious laugh, he heard Rachel's hearty, genuine chuckle. Why couldn't he get that girl out of his mind? He jammed his hands into his pockets and tried to push both Chrissy and Rachel out of his head as he trudged to the phone shanty.

Thankfully, Chrissy's phone went straight to voicemail. Joseph stumbled through a weak excuse, apologized, and hung up. She was a perfect ten—all his friends agreed—so why didn't he feel disappointed to back out of their date? It couldn't be because of Rachel. She was a wallflower who had never been any fun. Back in school, she had always sat in the corner and watched everyone else have fun.

Except she *had* been a lot of fun since he started working with her. Maybe she was one of those people who come out of their shell among one or two good friends but close themselves off to large groups of people. Of course, that would mean that he was a good friend of hers. Which he definitely was not. If he were, she would have cared about his problem with his *bruder*, and his future, instead of dismissing the entire situation.

Joseph felt irritable the rest of the night. He didn't talk during supper and retreated to the living room as soon as he could. He snapped at his *schweschder* when she bumped his chair as she arranged pine branches in the windowsill behind him. Joseph sighed and apologized.

"Help me decorate and maybe you'll snap out of your pouty mood," Hannah said.

"I'm not pouting."

Hannah laughed and handed him a white candle in a simple wooden holder. "Put this in the middle of the windowsill. And add one of those holly branches with the red berries." She pointed her chin toward a basket of greenery on the floor.

"All right, you win."

Hannah laughed again. "You'll thank me when the house smells like a pine forest."

"I'm not pouting, you know."

Hannah raised her eyebrows. "Whatever you say. But you've been stomping around the house for days. What's gotten into you?"

Joseph glanced toward the kitchen. He didn't want to upset his mother. "Have you heard about Eli's plan?"

"To work for Onkel?"

Joseph nodded.

"*Ya.*"

"And you're okay with it? Don't you see what he's trying to do to me?"

"Keep you from ruining your life?"

"He's trying to trap me here!"

His sister's gaze shot toward the kitchen. "Keep your voice down. Do you want to upset Mamm?"

"I am keeping my voice down."

Hannah raised her eyebrows and leaned against the white-washed living room wall. "He's trying to help you."

"I never asked him to."

"No. But you've had one foot out the door for months now. And you could have been killed in that buggy crash. We feel like you're living on borrowed time if you don't settle down. What do you think that does to us?" She tightened her grip on the pine bough in her hand. "We just want you to stay with us. You're not going to find what you're looking for among the English."

"We? You're in on this?"

"Shhhh."

"Hannah! Don't you see what a bad plan this is? You're going to push me away from here."

Hannah shook her head. "Desperate measures."

Joseph looked around the room. "Everything about the English world feels so much more exciting than this." He swept his hand in a big circle.

Hannah sighed. "Have you ever heard that English saying 'Not all that glitters is gold'?"

"*Ya.*"

"Think about it."

"You don't know what it's like to need more."

"How do you know?"

"You're happy with what you have here."

"Not always. But when I really think about it . . . " Hannah shrugged. "I feel like anything else would be empty, no matter how full it seems. Does that make sense?"

"I don't know. Maybe." Joseph picked up a pine branch and ran his fingers through the soft, whispery needles. "I've been noticing how nice home feels lately." His eyes shot to his sister's. "But I still don't want to milk cows for the rest of my life."

"*Ach*, Joseph. You'll settle into it. Trust me."

Joseph turned away from his sister to set the pine branch on a windowsill. He wished that he felt as confident as she did. He wondered which would be worse—leaving the Amish and wishing he had stayed or staying and wishing he had left. He imagined waking up in twenty years to this same house, same barn, same cows. The thought sent a surge of panic down his spine. His life could slip away from him, even while he lived it.

Rachel knew she should apologize to Joseph. She kept telling herself to say something, but she was afraid all her emotions would come rushing out. What if she burst into tears right there in front of him while she apologized?

So she kept her mouth set in a tight line as they worked side by side. The hours crawled by in an agonizing trickle. Rachel realized how much she missed Joseph's jokes and quick laughter. They barely spoke the entire day.

When her mother called them into the kitchen for gingerbread and *kaffi*, Rachel let out a long sigh of relief. Joseph would leave for the day soon and her *mamm* could fill in the cold, hard silence until then. "You baked another batch today?" Rachel asked as she breathed in the rich, spicy air that filled the kitchen.

"*Ya.* Your *daed* made quick work of the last batch." She poured a mug of *kaffi* and pulled a carton of half-and-half from the propane-powered refrigerator. "Cream and sugar?"

"*Ya,*" Joseph answered. "*Danki.*"

Rachel began to relax a little. She loved when her mother started the Christmas baking. The kitchen felt so safe and snug. Happy memories flooded her as she bit into a square of ginger-bread still warm from the oven. Joseph added a log to the woodstove before he sat down with his *kaffi.* Rachel glanced at him. Maybe everything would be okay after all.

Ada slipped into a chair across from Joseph and smiled over the steam that curled from her mug. "How have you been, Joseph?"

"Okay."

Ada frowned. "You look like you haven't slept all night."

"I'm okay." Joseph stared into his *kaffi.*

Ada kept her eyes on him. "I hear that your *bruder* is taking a job with your *onkel.*" She waited a few beats, but when Joseph didn't respond she pressed on. "I guess that means you'll be taking over the dairy farm for good, *ya?*"

Joseph opened his mouth, then closed it again. His expression darkened.

"You probably can't keep working here. Not with your *bruder* gone."

"I can keep my commitment." Joseph's jaw set into a tight line. "We never agreed to anything past Christmas."

Ada took a long, slow sip of *kaffi,* while keeping her eyes on Joseph. He never looked up. "It's okay if you need to quit sooner."

"*Mamm!*" Rachel's eyes narrowed. She couldn't understand why her *mamm* would suggest that. "We have a plan, remember? It's only two weeks until Christmas and there's so much left to do."

Ada nodded and placed a cool, smooth hand on Rachel's. "I know. But Joseph might need out."

"No." Joseph shook his head. "A deal's a deal."

Ada frowned. "All right."

"My *bruder* isn't planning on leaving the farm until the New Year." Joseph sighed and fidgeted in his seat. "So nothing changes until then."

Ada smiled. "You'll have to put everything into that farm once he leaves."

Joseph's fingers tightened around his mug until the skin over his knuckles turned white. "I'm not going to do that."

Ada flinched. "What?"

Rachel's eyebrows knit together as she leaned forward. What did Joseph mean?

Joseph cleared his throat and looked up for the first time in the conversation. "I have to leave after Christmas."

"Leave?" Rachel shook her head. "What do you mean, leave? Leave where?"

Joseph's face set like a flint. "I'm leaving home to go live with the English."

Rachel froze. This couldn't be happening. Her chest tightened like a cold, metal vise.

"Ah. I see." Ada leaned back in her chair and took another sip of *kaffi*.

"What about the farm?" Rachel blurted out. "You're going to abandon it?"

"No." Joseph gave a soft, weary smile. "My *bruder* will stay if I leave. He loves that farm."

"Sounds like you have it all figured out." Ada took another sip of *kaffi* but kept her gaze on Joseph.

"How can you say that, Mamm?"

"Let Joseph live his life, Rachel. He can always come back and be baptized if he changes his mind."

"No. This isn't right." Rachel turned to Joseph with pleading eyes. "Why are you doing this?"

Joseph took a moment before he spoke. "Because I can't stay trapped in this life."

"But what about your family? What about—" Rachel wanted to shout the word "me," but she clamped her mouth shut instead.

Joseph let out a long, heavy breath of air. "Eli wants the farm. This is better for him. And Hannah will leave when she marries. It's best for everyone this way." His gaze moved to the window and he stared out over the bare trees and rolling hills. "I don't know what else to do."

The words poured out of Rachel as soon as Joseph shut the door behind him. "This can't be happening! What am I going to do?"

Ada's face softened and she put a hand on Rachel's shoulder. "It was only until Christmas, anyway."

"No. You don't understand." So many emotions churned through Rachel that she couldn't get her words out straight. She wasn't even sure what she was feeling.

"Things will go back to normal."

Rachel shook her head. "I don't want things to go back to normal. I thought we could keep working together after Christmas. If we do well at the farmers market, we could make it into a real job."

"You don't have to do that. Your *daed* makes enough from the harness shop and from leasing our land to the English farmers. Anyway, there's plenty for you to do around here. There's always baking to be done."

"I don't like to bake. I like to eat."

"*Ach*, Rachel. There's always sewing. Quilting would be good for you."

"No. Working in my greenhouse would be good for me. Selling plants with Joseph would be good for me."

Ada closed her eyes and rubbed her temples. "You were the one who didn't want help, remember?"

"That was before I realized we could try and make a go of this. What if we made it into a full-time job? It doesn't feel like just a hobby anymore."

"If it means that much to you we can hire someone else after Christmas. A nice teenage girl who needs something part-time."

"No." Rachel shook her head too hard. "I don't want some teenage girl. I want Joseph."

"Now, Rachel."

"Please don't 'now, Rachel' me, Mamm." She hesitated, then plunged ahead. "He means a lot to me, Mamm. I like him." She looked down at her half-eaten plate of gingerbread and lowered her voice to a whisper. "I really like him."

Ada swallowed hard. "That's what I was afraid of."

Rachel's eyes shot up to her mother. "What's there to be afraid of?"

"Just look at you. You've been upset for days over him. It's not good for you."

"You can't protect me from everything."

Ada's chin raised a fraction. "I can try."

Rachel's stomach felt heavy and tight, as if it were slowly sinking toward her feet. "That's why you encouraged him to quit."

Ada looked away. "*Ya.*"

"How could you do that to me?"

"Because I love you and know what's best for you. He's no good for you. You heard him—he's leaving." She shook her head. "That boy's too wild for you."

"No, Mamm. He's not like that."

"Then why doesn't he settle down on the farm like he ought to? What's the matter with him?"

Rachel didn't answer. She didn't know how to explain it to her *mamm*, but she thought she understood why.

The question was what to do about it.

Chapter 11

Joseph couldn't believe he had said it out loud. And to Ada Miller of all people! He shook his head and stared at the stars scattered across the sky. White Christmas tree lights on the farmhouse across the road mirrored the stars. His breath came out in soft white puffs that disappeared into the cold dark. He shifted in the porch swing and listened to the whine of rusted metal as it moved. He could hear the murmur of voices from inside the house. The clang of metal pots drifted through the clapboard wall, followed by a shout and laughter.

Joseph tried not to hear. He wanted to be alone. He hadn't told his family yet. But now that Ada knew, word was sure to get out. Word had already spread that he was taking over Eli's place at the farm. Joseph shivered and tightened the scarf around his neck. He had almost been locked in. Now he could go anywhere and do anything.

He didn't know which option made him more afraid.

Joseph checked the messages in the phone shanty before bed. Chrissy's soft, feminine voice played through the speaker.

She sounded hurt and frustrated. He picked up the phone to call her back. She would be his only family soon. He couldn't strike out on his own completely. He would need her help.

But he couldn't think of what to say to her. She would be overjoyed when he announced he was leaving the Amish. She had been trying to convince him to do that for months. They would probably end up getting married. What else would he do? Life would never be boring. She would always drag him somewhere new. They would meet new people and go new places, listen to music he'd never heard, eat foods he'd never eaten. She would giggle and cling to him and exclaim that he just had to try this or that.

Joseph frowned and held the smooth, black receiver in his hand. A long minute passed before he hung the receiver up and walked out of the phone shanty. He would call her tomorrow, after he'd had a good night's sleep. A good night's sleep made everything easier.

He thought about a life where everything was new and nothing was familiar. It would be a grand adventure. And that was what he wanted, wasn't it? Joseph kept his head down as the wind bit into his skin. He decided to keep his decision to himself that night and the next morning. He would have to tell his family sometime, but he couldn't bring himself to do it yet. A man could only take so much, and facing Rachel the next day would be hard enough.

Rachel wouldn't let this happen. She just wouldn't. Life had spun out of her control in the past. She didn't have a choice about getting cancer. But she could control the choices she made now that she was well. And she would not let Joseph go. She closed her eyes and tried to gather her courage.

Joseph stood over her with a smile. "You'll make a wreck of it."

"*Ach.*" Rachel set the clippers down on the potting table. "I wasn't going to keep my eyes closed."

Joseph looked like he wanted to crack another joke, but his face closed off and he wandered away. Rachel couldn't bear to live like this until Christmas. She swallowed and closed her eyes again. Help me not to embarrass myself too much. Rachel had spent the night lying in bed, staring at the ceiling, and listening to the rain patter against the tin roof. She had to think of a plan. She *would* think of a plan. Of course, there was the obvious one. It was glaringly obvious. But she would be foolish to suggest it! And she had been foolish enough already.

Rachel let out a long breath of air and cut her eyes to Joseph. His eyes looked sad and lost. He didn't want to leave. She knew what he wanted—what he needed—but she didn't know if she was brave enough to offer it to him.

Well, she would have to try.

"Joseph."

"*Ya?*"

"What will you do when you leave?"

He frowned and ran his fingers through the feathery leaves on one of the rosemary topiaries. "I don't know. I'll probably try and get a job landscaping. At least then I'll be working with plants. Kind of." He sighed. "Maybe Ken's Gardens will take me on."

Rachel nodded. She knew what she had to do—what she wanted to do. She would ask Joseph to work at her greenhouse permanently if they did well enough at the farmers market. He would always have a job here, if he wanted it. That way his *bruder* could stay on the dairy farm and Joseph would still have a job. He wouldn't have to leave home. She licked her lips and opened her mouth to speak. He might reject her offer, but she had to be brave enough to speak up.

The crunch of gravel beneath tires interrupted her. It had to be a car, because there weren't any hoofbeats.

"Did you call a driver?" Rachel asked.

"No." Joseph beamed. "Must be your first customer."

"They must have seen that old sign you put out!" Rachel pressed her hands to her cheeks. "Do you think everything looks good enough? Do you think we have what they want?"

Joseph gave an indulgent smile and headed for the door. "*Ya.* I think everything is perfect here."

The smell of perfume and hairspray drifted into the greenhouse as soon as the door flung open. Joseph froze in place. Rachel watched his face fall and inched closer to him. Who could it be?

"Chrissy?" Joseph's voice sounded flat.

A tall, curvy blonde slid past Joseph and into the greenhouse. White-hot indignation burned through Rachel. What was that girl doing in *her* greenhouse? Had Joseph invited her here?

Joseph stumbled backward as Chrissy breezed in. "What are you doing here?"

Chrissy laughed. "You told me where you work, remember?"

Joseph swallowed and nodded. He glanced at Rachel.

She plastered a neutral expression on her face. She refused to show her hurt. "Feel free to look around. Almost everything's for sale." Her voice cracked and she cleared her throat.

"Aww, how cute!" Chrissy said as she picked up a miniature succulent. "But I didn't come to buy anything." She set the tiny pot back down. "I came to find out why my boyfriend hasn't been around." She leaned into Joseph and slid her arm through his. "You okay?"

Joseph cleared his throat. He glanced at Rachel, but Rachel wouldn't meet his gaze. She studied Chrissy's tight jeans and heavy gold earrings for a moment, then turned away. She couldn't compete with that. Chrissy was everything she could never be.

Joseph rubbed the back of his neck with his free hand, then slowly slipped his arm out of Chrissy's. "You sure? There's lots of stuff to choose from. Maybe a Christmas present for your mom?"

Chrissy shook her head. "No thanks. I do most of my Christmas shopping online. It's cheaper than family-run places." She flinched and glanced at Rachel. "Sorry. It's just . . . well, you know how it is."

Rachel did not know how it was, but she nodded anyway. Joseph sighed. Chrissy bent down and rubbed a spot of mud on her red shoe. "You got a paper towel or something? It's dirty out there."

"You look fine."

Chrissy straightened back up, shrugged, and smiled. "Thanks." Joseph stared at her without speaking.

"Look, I'm sorry for bothering you at work. But you haven't been around and . . . " Chrissy frowned and shuffled through her red leather shoulder bag. "We've got something going tonight. Bet you've never been clubbing before, right? We're driving over to a place outside of Philly. You should come." She pulled a red-and-white-striped travel-size plastic bottle from her bag and squeezed a dollop of peppermint-scented lotion into her palm. "It's supposed to smell like candy canes." She flicked the lid of the bottle shut, dropped it in her bag, and rubbed the lotion into her hands. "Cute, right?" She smelled her hands. "I love Christmas; don't you?"

Joseph didn't answer. The peppermint smell made Rachel's nose itch. It must be made of chemicals. She had always been sensitive to that kind of thing.

"So, what about tonight? You coming?" Chrissy leaned closer to Joseph and flashed a gorgeous smile. "Don't say no."

Joseph frowned. Chrissy returned the frown, but hers looked pouty instead of troubled. "It'll be fun."

Joseph glanced at Rachel, then back at Chrissy. "Come on, I'll walk you to your car. We can talk outside."

Rachel watched them leave. When the door shut the room felt empty and still. Had she ever enjoyed being in here alone all day? She let out a long, hard sigh. The rasp of her breath sounded too loud in the silence.

"Sorry about that," Joseph said when he returned ten minutes later. His face looked tired and his hand kept rubbing the back of his neck.

"You okay?"

"*Ya*. No problem."

Rachel listened as the car engine roared to life and gravel crunched in the driveway. "I've never met anyone like her before."

Joseph laughed, but his eyes stayed serious. "No. I wouldn't think so."

"I can see why you like her."

Joseph looked surprised. "You can?"

Rachel nodded. "Like I said, she's not like anyone around here."

Joseph looked thoughtful. "Mmmm."

"So are you going clubbing tonight?"

He shook his head and picked up a pair of shears. "No."

"Why not?"

Joseph looked uncomfortable. "We've got an early day tomorrow. There's still a lot to do before Christmas."

Rachel looked away. What had she hoped that he would say? That he had broken up with that flashy *Englisher* right there in her driveway? "I guess we'd better get to it then."

Joseph nodded. He didn't mention Chrissy for the rest of the day.

* * *

"I'd like to talk to you about Chrissy," Joseph told Rachel the next morning. Rachel felt her stomach drop. She couldn't bear to hear what he had to say. She couldn't bear to hear him announce that he wanted to be with Chrissy. To think she had almost invited him to stay on at the greenhouse! He would have said no and she would have been humiliated. Of course he'd rather live in the fancy English world with his fancy English girl.

Rachel shook her head. "No. Let's not talk about that." She fumbled for an excuse. "Our big day is almost here and we have to be ready." She pointed to the wall calendar. The Saturday before Christmas, when Aenti Ruby would share her booth at the farmers market with them, was marked with a big red X. "There's a lot left to do. We should focus on that."

"Oh." Joseph looked surprised, then confused. Rachel turned away. "Look how this one turned out." She picked up a rosemary topiary. The conical shape looked just like a tiny Christmas tree. "Nice work, *ya*?"

Joseph stared at her for a moment. Rachel pretended she didn't feel his eyes on her. After a moment he sighed and forced a smile. "*Ya*. You're going to sell a lot of those. Everyone's going to love them."

"I hope so. If I do, then maybe . . . " Rachel set the pot down. She wanted to tell Joseph that she could hire him permanently if her business proved a success. But she remembered Chrissy and didn't finish the sentence.

Things almost went back to normal. They daydreamed about how many plants they'd sell. They chatted and joked as they hunched over the potting table. Joseph teased Rachel and Rachel tried not to laugh. At the end of each day, Joseph marked the wall calendar with another big red X. Christmas was coming fast.

"What do you want for Christmas?" Joseph asked one afternoon. The December sun had already begun to set and it cast long shadows over rows of plants.

"To get all of this ready on time. We only have two days left until Saturday."

Joseph laughed. "Other than that."

"*Ach*, I don't know. A new scarf, I guess."

"What if you could have anything you wanted?"

"Anything?" Rachel smiled. "There *is* something I've always wanted."

"What?"

"A pig."

"A pig?" Joseph laughed. "That's a surprise."

"Not just any pig. A heritage breed like the ones the first Amish settlers brought over from Germany. I want it for a pet. You can housebreak pigs, you know."

"A historical pig." Joseph looked at her with warm eyes. "You never disappoint, Rachel."

"You're making fun of me."

"Only a little."

Rachel smiled and looked down.

"Why not a heritage breed dog or cat? Don't they have those?"

Rachel bit her lip.

"Go on and tell me."

"How did you know I wanted to tell you something?"

"You've got that glint in your eyes."

Rachel laughed. "Okay. There's a story in our family about Jacob and Greta. Do you remember who they are?"

"The ancestors you told me about, *ya*?"

Rachel nodded. "According to the story, they fell in love after he threw her into a pigpen."

"Why'd he do that?"

"He was trying to help her. Nobody knows the whole story. Details get lost over the centuries. It might not even be a true story."

Joseph smiled. "I like to think it is. It's a good story."

"*Ya.* It is. What a way to fall in love." Rachel looked down. She hoped Joseph didn't hear the catch in her voice when she talked about love. She tried to laugh so that he didn't sense her discomfort. "I'm here because of a pig, if you think about it."

"Will your *mamm* and *daed* buy you one?"

"There's a farm on the other side of Lancaster that sells them, but Mamm and Daed are afraid it would be too much on me. They still worry about me, you know."

Joseph nodded and slipped his hand over hers. "I know."

Rachel didn't know what to think. Did friends touch like that? Did friends feel the rush of emotions she felt over a touch like that?

Joseph looked down at his hand. It covered Rachel's perfectly. Her skin felt smooth and warm beneath his. This was the time to tell her he had broken up with Chrissy the day she came by the greenhouse. That's why he had taken ten minutes to say good-bye in the driveway. He was saying good-bye to her for good.

"Rachel, I really need to talk to you about Chrissy. I tried earlier, but—"

Rachel pulled her hand away and shook her head. Joseph frowned. Maybe he should wait. He still didn't know what to do about his future. He wanted Rachel to be a part of it, but how could he work that out? If only he could stay and work with her here, in the greenhouse. It had become a second home to him. He loved the long rows of plants, the view of the cornfields through the hazy glass walls, the smell of earth and moisture. He even loved the squeaky spigot and the rusted metal shelves.

But the greenhouse wasn't the only thing he loved. Joseph turned to look at Rachel. She looked beautiful in the yellow evening light. He wanted to tell her that he loved her. He felt certain that she loved him too. He had seen it in her eyes for weeks. He had tried to convince himself that it wasn't true after their day in Bird-in-Hand, but he knew that was only because he was afraid. He was afraid to believe that she loved him.

He was afraid because, once they admitted their love, there would be no going back. His future would be locked in, forever. Was he ready for that?

Her *mamm* wrote Christmas cards at the kitchen table that night while Rachel sat in front of the woodstove, closed her eyes, and let the heat radiate against her face. She couldn't bear that Christmas was almost here. Soon, her time with Joseph would be over. Ada watched her with tight lips. She offered strawberry eggnog pie, pumpkin pie, and molasses cookies, but Rachel just shook her head.

Ada threw up her hands. "You can't let Joseph get to you like this." She pulled her daughter close. "You'll forget about him."

"*Ach*, Mamm." Rachel shook her head. "You don't understand. I don't want to forget about him." She leaned back to look her *mamm* in the eyes. "He made me feel alive for the first time in years. I felt like I had a life again."

Ada knit her brows together and studied Rachel. "No one's forcing him to leave."

"You wanted him to leave! You tried to convince him to quit early."

"*Ya*." Ada reached out and straightened the work kerchief that covered Rachel's hair.

Rachel sighed and readjusted the kerchief. "Thanks, but I've got it."

"I know."

"No you don't." Rachel's voice tightened. "You promised you would try to let me go, but you haven't."

Ada stepped away from her daughter and sank into a chair. She didn't speak for a long, quiet moment. Then she nodded her head. "*Ya.* I know." She swallowed and looked down. "But when I saw how hurt you were over Joseph having a girlfriend, I wanted to protect you."

"You can't protect me from life, Mamm."

A deep voice spoke from the doorway. "She's right, Ada. We've been over this."

Ada nodded. "I know. I know." She twisted her hands in her lap. "And I've learned my lesson. I see how much she cares for him. I'm sorry I tried to interfere."

"What do you mean?" Samuel leaned against the doorjamb with a serious expression on his face.

Ada sighed. "I wanted Joseph to quit early. I thought it was better for Rachel. She's been so upset lately."

"*Ach*, Ada." Samuel shook his head.

"I know, I know." Ada's gaze stayed on her lap. "But he didn't leave early. So that's something, ain't so?"

Samuel nodded, then turned his attention to Rachel. "He still has a girlfriend?"

"*Ya.* And she came by here the other day."

"Ah. I see." Samuel walked across the room, bent down, and kissed Rachel on the top of the head. "I'm sorry."

"Me too."

Samuel frowned. "You know, I was sure he was sweet on you."

"I don't know what to think anymore," Rachel said.

"I think he's afraid to commit," Ada said. "He's afraid of making the wrong choice for his life." She shook her head. "He's running around trying to find something and he doesn't realize it's right here under his nose."

Samuel chuckled. "Sounds about right."

Ada's eyes glinted and she opened her mouth, then closed it again.

"Mamm, what is it? You look like you have an idea."

Ada gave a shy smile and shook her head. "I just thought of how I can make up for trying to push Joseph away."

Chapter 12

Joseph worked alone the next afternoon while Rachel went to her physical therapy appointment. "I'm getting better on crutches, *ya*?" she had asked before hurrying out the door. The greenhouse felt empty without her. He was glad when he had to go outside to empty the trash. He needed a break from the silence.

He thought he heard the greenhouse door open and close as he emptied the bins, but when he walked back inside no one was there. Was he hearing things? Did he miss Rachel that much?

Joseph sighed and began to clean up for the day. As he reached for a trowel, he noticed something catch the light on a metal table beside the door. He was sure that table had been empty before. He frowned, set the trowel back down, and walked to the table. He found a yellowed sheet of paper in a plastic sleeve.

Joseph glanced around, then looked back down at the paper. The plastic sheet felt cool and slick beneath his fingers. He squinted at the faded cursive until he realized it was an old letter. Joseph scanned the date at the top of the page. "Seventeen Thirty-Seven?" That was almost three hundred years ago.

Joseph tried to make out the text, but only a few lines were legible. *My dearest Greta . . . it should never have taken this long to . . . I should have known that I would find what I wanted right here, at home. . . . She could never compete with you, my darling. When I look on you, I see all that is good and Godly. Hers is the distraction of that which is worldly—that which wilts as a . . . Nothing in this great world can compete. . . . You, my darling, and the joy of a plain life together.* Joseph shifted the paper to move the glare from the plastic. *With great love and admiration, yours always, Jacob Miller.*

Joseph stared at the letter for another moment before he set it back on the table.

A car door slammed and Joseph jumped. When Rachel breezed in he felt embarrassed, as if he had been caught doing something he shouldn't.

"What's the matter?"

Joseph looked down at the letter and Rachel followed his gaze. Her breath caught in her throat. "What's that doing here?"

"I don't know."

"Did you read it?"

"*Ya.*"

"It's over three hundred years old. It shouldn't be in here with all this moisture."

"No, probably not." Joseph liked the way Rachel blushed when she was embarrassed. It made him want to hug her. "I'm glad you left it here."

"I didn't—" Rachel pressed her hands to her face and groaned. "I know who left it here."

"Who?"

Rachel looked embarrassed. "Mamm. She means well. She's trying to . . . fix a mistake. Never mind. Just forget it."

Joseph wanted to smile, but he didn't want Rachel to know he caught on. Ada had tried to shoo him away. And if Ada felt bad for meddling, she would try to meddle again to fix it. That was Ada, for you. He couldn't help but like her. Rachel was right; she meant well. And he had to admit he couldn't get that line out of his head. *I should have known that I would find what I wanted right here, at home.*

"Tell me the story behind it."

"All right," Rachel said. "You know I love to talk about history. Daed's family has kept that love letter all these years. We don't know much more about Jacob Miller beyond what's in this letter. We've found his name on a passenger list with a few other German Anabaptists, but that's about it."

"You know he fell in love with Greta in a pigpen."

Rachel laughed. "*Ya.*" She ran a finger down the plastic sheet. Her face turned serious and her voice softened. "And we know that he must have been tempted by something else before he married her. Something fancy, *ya*?"

Joseph looked at her and their eyes met. "Something fancy, *ya.*" They stared at each other for a long, silent moment before Joseph dropped his gaze. "Do you think he ever wondered if he made the right choice?"

"No." Rachel's voice sounded steady and strong.

Joseph raised his eyes back to meet hers. He didn't know what to say. But he knew he couldn't fight his heart much longer.

The weekend before Christmas came at last and the Bird-in-Hand Farmers Market bustled with holiday preparations. The fragrance of nutmeg, clove, and cinnamon hung in the air as the bakery booth unloaded fresh-baked cookies and pies. Evergreen wreaths lined the counter across the aisle from Aenti Ruby's booth and the scent of fresh pine mingled with Rachel's rosemary. The butcher in the adjacent booth nodded to Rachel as he dusted a big red sign advertising Christmas turkeys. Vendors chatted and hummed as familiar Christmas carols played in the background.

This was the day that would decide Rachel's future. Would her business be a success? And if it were, would she have the courage to ask Joseph to stay on as her business partner? If he did, could that partnership blossom into something more? So many questions. So much pressure!

Rachel arranged and rearranged the rosemary topiaries along a wooden counter at the front of her *aenti* Ruby's booth. She turned a pot around so that the bow on the green and red plaid ribbon faced the aisle. Ruby shook her head. "You've been at it for twenty minutes. They're going to either sell or not sell. Fiddling around with them won't make a difference."

"Aenti Ruby, I'm just so nervous! What if no one buys anything?"

Joseph leaned his hip against the counter and gave a reassuring smile. "You did your best. That's all that matters. No matter what happens, you can feel good about that."

"I wish it were that easy." Rachel glanced at the clock. "The doors open in five minutes."

Ruby put her hands on her hips. "Joseph's right. Don't judge yourself on how much you sell. Judge yourself on the effort you put in." She scanned the row of handmade Amish dolls, quilted potholders, and crocheted Christmas ornaments on the shelves behind the counter. "My stuff doesn't always sell. But I always manage in the end." Ruby had a creative knack for making ends meet since her husband died.

"You're good at everything, Aenti Ruby. Gardening is the one thing I'm good at, and I really want to be successful with it. . . . " Rachel felt a catch in her throat and she glanced over at Joseph. There was another thing that she wanted to work out even more than her business.

Ruby straightened a box of crocheted snowflakes she had made to hang on the *Englishers'* Christmas trees. "You two have had fun working together, ain't so?"

Rachel nodded and glanced at Joseph again. He winked. "*Ya*," they said in unison, and laughed.

"I'm glad you found each other." She wiped a spot from the counter with her sleeve and nodded. "It's *gut, ya*?"

Rachel and Joseph broke eye contact. Joseph fidgeted and Rachel cleared her throat. "Joseph and I aren't together."

Ruby's green eyes flicked to Rachel. Her brows drew together. "I thought . . . " She studied Rachel for a moment, then shook her head. "Sorry. You two just seem so natural together. Honest mistake, *ya*?"

Rachel didn't answer. What could she say to that?

Cold air blew down the aisle and the sound of eager voices filled the long, rectangular room. "They're here!" Rachel shouted. She was so relieved to change the subject that the words came out louder than she meant.

An elderly woman with a candy cane pin and matching candy cane earrings made a beeline for the rosemary. She closed her eyes and inhaled deeply. "Mmmm. So lovely. They call it the herb of remembrance, don't they?"

"*Ya*." Rachel grinned. Things were off to a good start.

The old woman straightened her back, leaned on her cane, and smiled a soft, wistful smile. Her face looked as pale and delicate as crumpled tissue paper. "It always brings back memories, doesn't it?" She ran a finger over the tiny, needle-like leaves. "My mother's garden, the meals I cooked my late husband, so many things . . . " She sighed but kept smiling. "How nice it is to be young." She motioned to Rachel and Joseph with a soft, shaky hand. "You two are still making your memories, not just reliving them."

Rachel cut her eyes to Joseph. How she wished she and

Joseph could make memories after today! He met her gaze and raised his eyebrows. Rachel wondered what he was thinking.

"I'll take five," the elderly woman said as she pulled twenty-dollar bills from her wallet. "One for each of my grandchildren. They're grown now and you never know what to get them." She picked up one of the pots and inhaled again. "This will be perfect."

A group of young women stopped at the booth as Rachel zipped the twenties into her money pouch. They asked a few questions about the Amish, gushed over the rosemary topiaries, and bought one apiece. Joseph sank onto a stool, laced his fingers behind his head, and leaned back. "They sell themselves."

Joseph was right. The rosemary flew off the shelves and it sold out before lunch.

"I can't believe it!" Rachel said as she watched a man in a red sweater walk away with the last potted plant. "I never dreamed we'd do this well!"

Ruby smiled. "You did a lot better than I did today. You ought to make a go of it."

"They loved your crocheted snowflakes," Rachel said as she pointed to the half-empty box.

"*Ya*, but they loved your rosemary better. They stopped to look at your stuff, then bought a snowflake while they were here." Ruby watched another shopper stroll by with one of Rachel's potted plants in his hands. She hesitated a moment, then nodded. "I tell you what, let's make this a regular thing. I want you to sell your plants here year-round. It's good business for both of us. You brought a lot of new people to my booth today."

"Really, Aenti Ruby?"

"Really."

Joseph jumped to Rachel and wrapped her in a big, enthusiastic hug. "You did it!"

Rachel leaned her face into his warm, solid chest and smiled. "No, *we* did it." She felt as if she might melt from happiness. Everything was perfect. She had proven that she could be independent—with the help of the man she loved. Loved? Had she really thought those words?

Yes. Yes, she had. Love. That was the way she felt about Joseph. It wasn't a crush or a passing fancy. This was the man she wanted to spend the rest of her life with. He understood her. He loved what she loved. He made her laugh when no one else could. He made her realize that she could have a second chance at life. Rachel breathed in the smell of him and tightened her arms around his neck.

"I don't want this to be good-bye," she whispered. Rachel hoped he hadn't heard.

Joseph pulled away and looked her in the eye. "Let me explain about Chrissy."

He had heard her! Rachel cringed. "No. Not today. Today is a perfect day. Let it stay perfect."

"You don't understand."

Rachel shook her head. "Please."

Joseph looked frustrated but didn't argue. "There's nothing left for me to do in the greenhouse, now that we've sold all the topiaries. But I'll come by on second Christmas for a visit, *ya*?"

"You will?" Rachel's face lit up. She couldn't hide her joy. Even if it would be the last time they would be together.

Chapter 13

Joseph hurried home on Christmas Eve. He had not seen Rachel since Saturday, but her whispered words still echoed in his mind. She had said she didn't want to say good-bye. Joseph checked for oncoming traffic and flicked the reins. He had been thinking a lot over the last few days and he finally had a clear vision for his future. He felt sure of himself for the first time in years. He knew what he wanted and what he needed to do. The realization had been building and building inside his heart until it reached a crescendo. *I should have known that I would find what I wanted right here, at home.*

After their success at the farmers market, the last piece had fallen into place. He could have love and the future he wanted. Why had he been so afraid of this decision? Joseph smiled and glanced at the box on the seat beside him. He had picked up Rachel's present in time to have Christmas Eve dinner with his family and announce his plan.

That announcement would be the best present he could give Eli—and the best present he could give himself.

* * *

After a good, hearty meal, Rachel and her parents gathered around the woodstove and listened to Samuel read the Christmas story in German from the family Bible. The fire crackled and popped behind the stove's black iron grate as her father recited the familiar story in his deep, gentle voice.

Rachel picked up the Bible after her father set it down. She slid her hands down the soft, cool leather and opened to the faded names recorded in the front. She wondered about the lives and marriages of the men and women who had come before her. Had Jacob and Greta sat beside a fire on a dark, cold night and longed for each other? Had they ever felt alone among other people? Had they ever wished with all their hearts for a future they feared would never come to pass?

Christmas morning dawned clear and cold. The day passed in quiet simplicity and Rachel felt a peace she did not understand. Even though her heart felt heavy with longing, she appreciated the solemnity of the holiday as they spent the day in prayer and contemplation. In the evening, as the sun sank below the cornfields, they sang Christmas hymns by lantern light.

Second Christmas was a day for celebrating with friends and family. Rachel awoke before dawn. Her heart leapt into her throat as she threw back the quilt and took a deep breath of frigid winter air. The shock of the early morning chill made her feel alive. In the kitchen, the woodstove would be crackling merrily and her mother would be preparing the last-minute dishes for the daylong feast.

Rachel's thoughts stayed on Joseph all morning. She couldn't wait for him to arrive. If it was their last day together, she would make it the best day they'd ever had. She wouldn't think of what might come tomorrow—only of the joy she felt in the moment.

"You need a distraction," Samuel announced as the clock crept toward noon. "Let's open presents."

Rachel beamed. She couldn't wait to give her parents the rosemary topiaries she made them. "That's a great idea."

"Joseph will *kumm* today," Ada said as her eyes shifted to the window. "I know he will."

"Mamm, I know you tried to help."

"What?" Ada looked sheepish.

"The letter." Rachel shook her head at her *mamm*, but she had a smile on her face.

"Ada, did you meddle again?" Samuel asked as he carried a stack of brown paper packages to the coffee table.

Ada cleared her throat. "For the right reasons this time."

Samuel and Rachel laughed. Ada held out a moment before she shook her head and joined the laughter.

Rachel scooted one of the packages on the coffee table toward her parents. "This one's from me."

Ada ripped the paper, pulled open the cardboard flaps on the box and grinned. "I was hoping I'd get one."

"This is *wunderbaar!*" Samuel said as he picked up one of the rosemary topiaries and turned it in his hands. "I still can't figure out how you get them to look like little Christmas trees."

Rachel beamed. "I can't tell all my secrets."

Samuel laughed and kissed the top of her head. "You can do anything you want to do, ain't so?"

Ada's eyes misted as she held the rosemary to her face and inhaled the scent. She shook her head. "Your *daed*'s right, Rachel. I'm sorry I didn't see that earlier." She pressed the topiary to her chest. "You did it, Rachel. You showed everyone that nothing will ever hold you back."

Rachel didn't know what to say. She had waited years to

hear her mother speak those words. Could there ever be a better Christmas gift than her mother's belief in her?

The moment stayed with Rachel for a long time. After a warm silence, Ada set down her rosemary topiary, patted her eyes with the corner of her apron, and gave Rachel her gift. Rachel tore open the brown paper wrapping to uncover a new woolen scarf. She pressed the cloth to her face and closed her eyes. "It's so soft. Like wearing a cloud."

Samuel laughed and stood up. "Time to eat again, *ya*?"

It was almost lunchtime, and still Joseph hadn't appeared. Ada noticed Rachel's expression and patted her shoulder. "Eating will make the wait easier. There's still plenty of time for him to show up."

Her *mamm* was right. The turkey and dressing, schnitzel, apple Jell-O salad, brown buttered noodles, yeast rolls, and homemade cinnamon applesauce did make everything feel better. Rachel began to butter her third roll when she heard a knock at the door. She froze. "When are Aenti Ruby and the cousins coming over?" Her heart jumped into her throat.

"Not until suppertime," Ada said as she stood up.

Rachel's heart jumped even higher. "Are we expecting anyone else?"

Ada hurried for the door. "Not until mid-afternoon."

Rachel set down the roll and the butter knife. She tried to appear calm. She could not. When the door swung open and Joseph strode inside with a big cardboard box in his arms, Rachel burst with joy. Her face lit the entire kitchen. "You came!"

"Of course I did."

"*Kumm* and sit, Joseph," Ada said as she shooed him toward the kitchen table.

Joseph grinned and shook his head. "Not until I give Rachel her present. I can't wait another minute."

"My present? What is it? Is it in that box?" Rachel straightened in her chair.

Joseph brought the box to Rachel and gently lowered it onto her lap. "Careful, now." The box shifted against her legs and she gasped. Her fingers fumbled as they tore open the cardboard flaps.

An adorable black piglet stared up at her with huge, wet eyes. He shook his tiny curly tail and snuffled his glistening pink snout. "Joseph! He's the cutest thing I've ever seen!" She reached into the box and pulled out the warm, wriggling piglet. He nuzzled against the curve of her neck and snorted. Rachel laughed. "He's a heritage breed, isn't he?"

Joseph smiled, bent down, and scratched the piglet behind the ears. "Of course he is. I got him from that farm you mentioned. It wasn't hard to find."

"It's what I've always wanted!"

"I know."

Rachel looked up and their eyes met. She saw her joy reflected back at her in his eyes. "Thank you! Thank you so much!"

Samuel and Ada did not look happy. They exchanged their own looks—and there was no reflected joy. Samuel cleared his throat. He looked reluctant but determined. "Joseph, we appreciate your thoughtfulness. Truly, we do. But that tiny piglet will grow into a huge hog. How will Rachel handle it? She's shown us that she is capable of a lot, but a hog is taking things a bit far, *ya*? She's got her greenhouse to think about."

Joseph nodded. His smile faded and he looked very solemn as he locked eyes with Samuel. "*Ya*. That's true. Except she won't have to handle it alone. I'll be here to help her."

Rachel gasped. "You will?"

Joseph turned his attention to Rachel. "I want to stay here and work with you. You'll need help making your greenhouse into a full-time business."

"For how long?" Rachel held her breath.

"Forever. I want to marry you, Rachel Miller."

"You want to—" The words froze in Rachel's mouth. She couldn't speak. This was too *gut*. This was more than she had ever hoped for. She wanted to shout and sing and leap into Joseph's arms.

"Is that a yes?" Joseph asked with a wry smile on his face.

"Yes! It's a yes!"

"*Wunderbaar*," her *mamm* whispered. "*Wunderbaar*."

Her *daed* nodded. His eyes glistened. "This is *gut*. Very *gut* for Rachel."

Joseph pulled Rachel to him and held her tight, with the tiny piglet tucked between them. She thought she would melt with joy. Nothing had ever felt so right or so good. Then the piglet squealed and everyone laughed. Joseph eased away, patted the piglet on the head, and slipped into the chair beside Rachel. He wrapped an arm around her and pulled her close to him. She rested her head on his shoulder and let out a sigh of perfect contentment.

"My only concern is for your *daed*," Samuel said after the laughter died down. "What will happen to your family's farm if you and Rachel stay here to make a living from her greenhouse?"

Joseph moved his hand to Rachel's and held it beneath his warm, calloused palm. "I talked to my family on Christmas Eve and told them I wanted to marry Rachel and go into business with her. They think it is wonderful good. You see, my *bruder* was going to leave the farm to force me to stay. He wanted to stop me from running away to the English and he knew I would never leave if Daed depended on me. Now he can stay and take it over when Daed retires. Even though he's the older *bruder*, he is the one who should inherit it. He loves it there."

Samuel shook his head and leaned back in his chair. "What a *gut* turn of events. I'm happy for you—and your *bruder*."

Joseph smiled and squeezed Rachel's hand.

Everything had turned out perfectly. Until an uncomfortable thought zipped through Rachel's mind. There was still a loose end. "What about Chrissy?"

Joseph shook his head. "*Ach*, Rachel. I broke up with her the day she came to the greenhouse."

"But you didn't tell me!"

"I tried. You wouldn't let me."

"I thought you were going to tell me something I didn't want to hear."

Joseph laughed. "It all worked out in the end. That's what matters."

Rachel smiled and stared into Joseph's eyes. The piglet snuggled against her chest. "Are you happy with the choice you made?"

"*Ya*, I am." Snow began to fall outside the kitchen window. Everything felt bright and beautiful and full of promise. "And I know I will be happy with my choice for the rest of my life." Perhaps one day, three hundred years from now, their descendants would talk about Joseph and Rachel and the great love they shared—a love that goes on and on, forever, beyond the bounds of history.

You'll find more warm-hearted, joyous Amish Christmas romance in *The Amish Christmas Letters*, available now!

'Tis the season for sharing . . .

THE AMISH CHRISTMAS LETTERS

Patricia Davids
Sarah Price
Jennifer Beckstrand

With Christmas around the corner, it's time for Amish families to include holiday greetings in their circle letters, each writer adding to a growing collection as it travels on to the next. In this delightful trio of stories, three cousins scattered across the country share their blessings—and reveal news of romantic surprises. . . .

To win a friendly annual competition, matchmaker Marybeth Martin must bring one more couple together by Christmas. Her only prospect is a man more interested in a nanny than a wife—until his little girl shows him the light. . . . Struggling farmer's daughter Katie Mae Kauffman discovers that she and a local widower and father of four can harvest more crops—and profits—together than separately. But she'll have to put pride aside to make room for unexpected love. . . . Corralling an unruly brood of seven is not babysitter Carolyn Yutzy's first choice for celebrating the season—but the sparks between her and their unsentimental yet irresistible uncle may be a gift neither was counting on. . . .

Now, one by one, each resourceful young woman will have a holiday to remember—and to write home about. . . .

Connect with U(s)

Visit us online at
KensingtonBooks.com
to read more from your favorite authors, see books
by series, view reading group guides, and more.

for sneak peeks, chances to win books and prize packs,
and to share your thoughts with other readers.

facebook.com/kensingtonpublishing
twitter.com/kensingtonbooks

Tell us what you think!

To share your thoughts, submit a review,
or sign up for our eNewsletters, please visit:
KensingtonBooks.com/TellUs.